T0353091

Jeremiah Bourne in Time

BY THE SAME AUTHOR

Neil's Book of the Dead (with Terence Blacker)
I, An Actor: Nicholas Craig (with Christopher Douglas)
A Good Enough Dad
Let's Get Divorced (with Terence Blacker)
Therapy and How to Avoid It (with Robert Llewellyn)
Unlike the Buddha
The Right Man
Faking It

JEREMIAH BOURNE IN TIME

Book I in The Time Shard Chronicles

Nigel Planer

First published in 2023

Unbound
c/o TC Group, 6th Floor Kings House, 9–10 Haymarket, London,
United Kingdom, SW1Y 4BP
www.unbound.com

Text design by PDQ

A CIP record for this book is available from the British Library

ISBN 978-1-80018-248-6 (hardback)
ISBN 978-1-80018-249-3 (ebook)
Printed in Great Britain by Clays Ltd, Elcograf S.p.A

1 3 5 7 9 8 6 4 2

To Roberta, without whom…

ONE

So, imagine if the apocalypse, when it does happen, comes about not through some lack of effort by the human race to bring down carbon emissions, not because of alien invasion, nor from one of the several pandemics, but from the side-effects of a different, and new, catastrophe. Well, two actually. DigiMelt 1 and DigiMelt 2. Known as digital meltdowns, but in fact more like digital vanishing acts.

All information is out there, all our data, swimming around in the virtual world, literally in a cloud. The Cloud. Our Cloud. Or a balloon, perhaps; a helium balloon filled with our data. And one day the string is cut, or we let go of it. Deliberately or by mistake. Like a little child with a birthday balloon who, just for a second, releases her grip on the string, and off floats the bubble. 'Bye bye, balloon,' says the daddy, 'never mind.' But the little girl does mind. Her face puckers up to cry. 'Never mind,' says Daddy, beginning to panic a little now, 'Daddy'll get you another one.' But she doesn't want another one, she wants that one. That one is everything, it has everything in it; all our information, the entire database of the human race is in that birthday balloon, now a small jolly green dot somewhere in the wide sky. So small now, their eyes prick trying to see it still. That was the only balloon that mattered.

Jeffrey Pritchard bears no relevance to this story other than his final click. Sometime around the middle of the twenty-first century, he sits down at a table outside a bar in Bermondsey, in south-east London. It's a very hot day, even for September – 44 to 46 degrees Celsius – and on his mobile device he begins to go through the usual portals to order a beer – security settings, ID verifications, credit check, targeted advertising, system updates and menu choices – until he reaches the final purchase confirmation click. One pint of beer, please – yes. Neither he nor anyone else is aware at the time that Jeffrey's final click is The Final Click. The moment that the Internet of Things, or IoT, becomes the Internet of Nothing. Zilch. Nada. Jeffrey's is The Final Click that overloads the system and tips it into oblivion.

By the time of Jeffrey's last click, every single human activity has become digitised. From the entire contents of the British Library to world banking, transport, brushing your teeth, how to open your front door, feed your baby, find your way to the corner shop. So after that Final Click, or Post-Pritchard if you like, some large behavioural adjustments have to be made. Not many people who use a computer would know how to build one, nor do many drivers know how to make a car, but after so much digitisation, who knows how to sew on a button? Or produce paper from wood pulp?

The Butterfly Effect states that the tiniest of changes in the initial state of things – a butterfly spreading its wings in India in 1862, for instance – can result in large differences in a later state of things, such as space travel or the Second World War. Jeffrey Pritchard's final click is like that butterfly. And that's the last you, or anyone, will ever hear of Jeffrey. I promise.

Of course, in this particular, non-digital London future, there's furniture still, and houses and cooking. Recipes have to be remembered, something which is tricky to do when you haven't used your memories for almost a hundred years. Old-style technologies emerge, stuff that works by mechanics: pumps, pulleys, steam. Those who can make things with their hands are popular again. So is chemistry. Organics. Growth. Chemical reactions. Vitrification; a process by which a solution is solidified and preserved in glass. Or rather, embedded in a glassy matrix, which can preserve it, rapid-cool it, before ice crystals form. So no need for fridges, nor ice, and no need for massive storage depots for toxic waste. A cryogenic future, sitting in its glassy, pollution-lite world.

Toto Chairman's gnarled hand grabbed the arm of the chair. Her arthritic knuckles almost looked as if they were part of the carving. The chair was old – perhaps eighteenth-century – so, four hundred years old. Toto Chairman was old too. She was tired of chairing this meeting. The one thousand and whateverth meeting of the Blackfriars Road Residents' Association sub-committee for Recall and Maintenance.

A middle-aged, balding committee member in a blue collarless tunic was droning on. 'Can I draw the committee's attention to the fact that the steam door system needs fixing? And can we please, please, this time, get someone professional in to fix it?' The other members were sitting as if hypnotised, their minds awash with sub-clauses and procedural regulations. One member, Artemesia Plutarch, who, younger than most of the others, brought the average age of the committee down to about sixty-two, was gazing out of the floor-to-ceiling windows at the leaf canopy of London plane trees outside. It was September. She was wondering why the trees were called 'London planes', as opposed to plain 'planes'. Her chair was also old, but without the carved arms. It must once have been part of a set with Toto Chairman's; the only really old pieces of furniture in the room. Toto Chairman filled her pen with ink and made a note.

'The steam doors are not actually the next item on the agenda,' said another committee member, an elderly man with a white beard and a bony face, sporting huge round glasses. 'I think we should proceed in the correct order, otherwise it will be *total, utter, unadulterated MAYHEM*—' He spoke with emphases, several of them.

A third member interrupted him. 'Look, it's just steam doors, OK? Fix? Or not fix? Can we just make a decision, any decision, this time?' pleaded a wide-faced woman whose large earrings made a tinkling noise as her head moved.

Artemesia Plutarch shifted in her chair and yawned, which she tried to hide by clenching her teeth. She wondered how many other bottoms had sat on this chair. What dalliances had it witnessed? What deaths? All of the people who had sat in this chair before her, over the last four hundred years, were dead. And yet the chair still lived on. She almost resented the chair. Resenting furniture just for surviving must be a sign of getting old. But she was still a way off forty. There was a silence while all eight faces of the committee turned to Toto Chairman for her decision on fixing the steam doors.

'All right,' she said, 'let's get a preliminary report drawn up to find out where we are and then, perhaps, move forward to an assessment of the possible parameters for a full report,' and they moved on to other pressing matters: pest infestation, water ingress on the third floor, the glass ceiling. No, not the glass ceiling that matters so much to us all at this point in time, but an actual ceiling of glass containing argon gas by which the house was heated. And it still was what you and I would describe as a house. It had the original bricks and foundations – steps up to a front door – but this was more by way of a façade. Inside, it was an atrium of glass compartments, some transparent, some not. A world without digital tech does not have to be a world without tech. People just have to write more things down, or better still, retain more in their memories. And some people are better at that than others. Because human memory is not like a balloon that's gone forever, and providing there are no medical issues, it's something that can be retrained, put into rehab, and grown, like a sample in a petri dish.

It is thought that the use of electronic calculators, Google and easy information access had reduced human memory capacity by two thirds by the time of the first digital meltdown – DigiMelt 1 – in the middle of the twenty-first century. Before the digital age, people were used to remembering huge reams of stuff; phone and bank account numbers, passwords and poems, whole Shakespeare plays. Take, for example, the original London black taxi driver; if you wanted to be the driver of an official London black taxi, back in the twentieth and early twenty-first centuries, you had to do an exam called 'The Knowledge' which entailed remembering the name of every single street in London and also the quickest way of getting from one place to another, say, from Oldhill Street in Stoke Newington to Glendarvon Street in Putney. It used to take trainees years of going round the streets on a moped with a clipboard on the handlebars, before they were ready to take the Knowledge exam. That's how it was in the days before satnav and Uber and things like that, which of course died out completely after DigiMelt 2.

There were tests done as far back as the late twentieth century that found some London taxi drivers had brains which had physically grown over the years. Grown as in actually having larger hippocampi. Rather like the super-recognisers who help the police identify criminals after one glance, there are those with super-memories that can be developed beyond normal capacity. These people had become higher status after DM2 and, of course, more highly paid.

There was a society of super-memorisers and an institute, Super-Recall, where there had been experiments to try to locate genetic memory; a sort of collective recall that they hoped might be inheritable. Remembering things that hadn't happened to you, but to people before you. Birds know how to fly south, after all.

'Any other issues?' said Toto Chairman, hoping there wouldn't be. Her memory was average and diminishing. She had been running these meetings for too long; her knees hurt. When younger, she could have remembered the entire agenda and all of the costing estimates; now she had to rely on the handwritten sheet in front of her. The only one in the room still using paper.

An enthusiastic young man called Beatlejohn Basho piped up, keen to prove himself. 'Yes!' he said. 'Item two hundred and ten, b.' He had no notes. He was the only member younger than Artemesia Plutarch, who let out an involuntary sigh. The committee turned their minds to item 210 (b): 'the continuing disposal of plastic waste from seventy-five years ago'. There was no rustle of paper nor pinging nor swiping of screens, just a mild panic as each of them looked into the blank space just below them to the left – the place we all tend to look when trying to recall (and our brains tend to prefer looking above and to the right for new information or searching for a new idea, by the way) – and scrolled through their mid-range memories for item 210 (b). Artemesia concentrated on the little frayed section of the sleeve on her tunic.

'So, what's the problem?' Toto Chairman asked.

Beatlejohn Basho sat up straight and spoke too loud, little bits of saliva gathering at the corners of his mouth. 'Our dissolve rates are down. And if we were to take on, for example, Lambeth Road as well, we could increase negation yield by...'

There was another sigh, this time a collective one. Not this again. Not going back there. Someone else's problem.

'Anybody want to pick this up?' asked Toto Chairman.

There was another silence. People wanted to get back to their apartment pods and lunch. 'I think there's a general feeling of... not much,' said Artemesia, taking it on herself to sum up the general mood of the room.

'Well, let's put it on the agenda for the next meeting, hmm?' said Toto Chairman, making herself popular. There was an instant flurry of activity as people scraped back their various chairs and headed for the glass door. Basho accepted defeat. Toto Chairman was up swiftly and moving towards the door, despite her arthritis.

A tall man stood in the doorway, in matching beige shirt, tie and trousers, like a pale brown question mark, blocking Toto Chairman on her way out. Other committee members were stuck behind her.

'Just a quick word with you, Toto Chairman-ji,' the man said, smiling apologetically at her.

'Yes?' said Toto Chairman, looking up at him without cracking a smile back.

'Yes, I'd like to have a word with, well, with all of you, about Enid? We had a visit from Super-Recall about Enid.'

Artemesia Plutarch was a small woman, androgynous and delicately featured. She managed to become even smaller behind Beatlejohn Basho.

Conrad, the man in beige, continued, 'They know she lived here. Before I joined, of course, but you people knew her, did you not?' His attempt at calm nonchalance was unsettling.

'Well, only vaguely…' said Toto Chairman, edging nearer the doorway.

Conrad stood, gently, in her path and said nothing, waiting for her to carry on speaking. She didn't. She waited too. So he went on.

'Nobody remember anything about her? Was she close to anyone in particular?' He waited again, looking at each of them in turn. Then, peering over Beatlejohn Basho's shoulder, he homed in on Artemesia Plutarch. 'Artemesia, isn't it? Artemesia Plutarch?' he said. 'I would have thought you knew her well?'

Beatlejohn Basho stood to one side, allowing Conrad to make direct eye contact with his prey.

'No?' said Artemesia, with a tiny croak in her voice.

'No? Really?' asked Conrad, in mock surprise. 'Surely you must have.'

'Well, there is quite an age difference between us, so… not that well, actually.'

'She is your sister, isn't she? So she must have mentioned something of her plans to you?' said Conrad. If he'd needed paper, he would have been stacking it menacingly now, to assert his authority.

There was a general stir as everyone turned to look at Artemesia. Whispered remarks showed their surprise: 'Ooh, I didn't know Archie was Enid's sister…' and 'Well, they kept that quiet!'

Conrad shushed them. 'Well?' he said.

Artemesia paused, shaking her head. She tossed a lock of her curly hair from her forehead. 'Sorry, but…' she said, with a look of what she hoped was concern on her face, 'don't recall a thing. I'm not great at remembering stuff like that, you know, family relationships…'

Conrad's eyes narrowed. He wasn't getting the whole story: he sensed it, he felt it in his sphincter. But no, he couldn't be sure. Because no matter how super your memory might be, and however many Super-Recall medals you might possess, you still could not know for certain when someone was lying.

'You know they've been trying to find her,' he said, studying Artemesia's face.

'Have they? Oh. I didn't know.'

'Yes, they think they may know where she is…'

'Oh. Where?'

'2019.'

TWO

Wire wool is better than sandpaper. It's gentler on the blemishes in the wood if the piece is really old. And this little semi-upholstered armchair was at least two hundred years old. Wire wool is also less abrasive on your hands, which is a consideration when you have several items to restore. Jeremiah Bourne stood back to view the work so far. He blew off the grubby residue and admired the elegant curve of the arms. The rich smell of Danish oil hung in the air like incense in a temple.

How many bums had sat on that seat? he thought. What scenes had this small piece of furniture witnessed? Been a part of, even? All those people long dead now, no doubt, but the curved armchair was still here, its deflated cushion pad evidence of generations of use.

Jeremiah reached for his mug without looking for it. The coffee was cold. Never mind. He had that sensation again. That he had already restored this armchair, in this workshop, with this cold coffee. Perhaps more than once. A déjà vu. The feeling that you've already been somewhere, already seen what you're looking at, already done what it is you're doing. Looking at this two-hundred-year-old piece of furniture, it seemed to Jeremiah that not only had he done this before, but he'd had a déjà vu the previous time as well. A déjà vu in the middle of his déjà vu.

But he was probably going a little crazy after five weeks inside the house without going out. The last time he'd been outside, he had managed to get ten yards down the street before the trembling started again. And the difficulty breathing. He wasn't under house arrest, or lockdown, or quarantine; the Covid pandemic was still a year away. No, the problem must be in his mind, somehow. Anxiety, panic attack, trembling, breathlessness. He reached in his pocket for his inhaler and took a puff, putting it back down beside the cold coffee cup.

'Havink fun, Doctorr?' A loud foreign accent suddenly broke his reverie. 'Velcome to my experriment! Aha ha ha ha!' The tinny sound of a mobile phone ring tone. His stepsister Ruby must be in the vicinity.

'D'you like your new ring tone, Jem?' she said. How long had she been in the basement, watching him?

'Is that my phone? Did you change my ring tone?'

Ruby was always messing with his stuff. 'Don't you like it?' she pouted.

'It's a kids' one.'

'I thought you liked *Doctor Who*.'

'That was ages ago. I was never that into it. And I stopped collecting the merch and stuff, like, years ago. When I was twelve or something. Can you *not* mess with my phone, please?'

Jeremiah took his phone off her. She'd put all sorts of things on there. She could be annoying. 'Little stepsisters are meant to be annoying,' she would say, 'that's what they're there for.' Squidgy Face? What did he want Squidgy Face for? He deleted it.

'It's free,' she said.

'That's not a good enough reason to put it on my phone. And what the hell's this?'

Family Ancestry Net. Find out where you came from. 'All

you have to do is put some saliva on a cotton bud, or send in a piece of hair, and they can tell your whole DNA.'

'It cost thirty-nine pounds ninety-nine pee. Ruby? How did you get my password? This is my account!'

'They use it in murders, and things like paternity cases... in case you don't know who your mum and dad are,' she said, throwing herself into an old armchair which was sprouting horsehair from its seat pad.

Oh, that again. Although she was six years younger than him, she could sometimes be quite a bully. 'We know who my mum is. She just went away, that's all,' he said.

'Ruby!' Stepdad Pete's voice from the hall. 'Ruby! Let Jem get on with his work. You've got the whole weekend with us. You'll have plenty of time with him later.'

Ruby lived with her mum over in Whitton. About half an hour by train from Waterloo and then a ten-minute walk. By a strange set of circumstances, Jeremiah had ended up living with his stepdad, Pete Pappadalos, in the house in Blackfriars Road. Mum had gone, leaving a note for him, on a card, when Jem was nine. Eight motherless years had passed, but he had strong and clear individual memories of her. The sound of her voice, a London voice with a rasp from shouting over her shoulder in her taxi. Her hair, dark and curly with greying strands. Her eyes and the roughness of her hands. Her smell, clean but with a hint of diesel. But somehow, all of these details did not make up a whole person, one coherent memory. Mum: a disassembled puppet whose parts needed hooking together. But she had promised she would return, and Jeremiah believed her.

'You come upstairs with me, Ruby.' Pete was trying to keep the peace between them, as usual. 'I need some help with the colour charts. Need to work out what colours they'd have used on these walls in 1910.' Pete was an obsessive. For him, restoration wasn't just a question of bringing things back from the past, they had to bring the past with them. 'The past is never dead. It's not even past. As someone or other said. I think it was William Faulkner,' Pete would repeat often, 'whoever he was.'[1]

'I'll pay you back, Jem,' said Ruby, reluctantly sliding off the armchair and following Pete upstairs.

'Now, now,' said Pete, 'no grudges in this house.'

'No, she meant the thirty-nine pounds and ninety-nine pee she used from my account,' Jeremiah shouted after them, but they were clomping up the stairs and into the front hall by now.

Jeremiah's mum had moved into this basement flat with Jeremiah when he was two. The whole building had been flats then. Pete had the top two floors. When old Mr Varma had died, Pete had managed to buy the middle flat with a loan that the bank shouldn't really have let him have, and, after he and Jeremiah's mum got together, the house became one unit again, as it had been when it was built in the early nineteenth century. Four storeys, with tall, square windows, set back from the road by six steps going up to the front door. In terms of money, Pete, or rather his bank, was sitting on quite a large slice of prime London property.

Having Jeremiah stuck at home, unable, or unwilling, to go out, was an opportunity, as far as Pete was concerned.

---

1 Stepdad Pete had never read anything by William Faulkner, and neither have I. But it's lucky for me and my editor that Stepdad Pete actually got the quote right. The Faulkner estate once sued Woody Allen for misquoting it with: 'The past is not dead, actually it's not even past.' Which sounds similar enough to me. But it is evidently one of the most quoted, or misquoted, aphorisms in America, and like most quotable aphorisms, it is sometimes attributed to others and could possibly be interpreted as twaddle. Its existence is more about our need to have little flags ahead of us, like the numbered posts in a golf course showing where the holes are, because from where we stand, most of what lies ahead looks very much like a scraggy, pointless field.

He preferred to call Jeremiah's bout of agoraphobia an 'apprenticeship', which was partly true. Exam results had not been good and he was picking up furniture-restoration skills.

'Dado rails, that's what we need, Jem, all round here, and up the staircase. Dado rails.' Pete was back down in the basement, talking Jeremiah through his plans. Ruby was upstairs in her bedroom, playing Brain Farm. Pete had pulled out several old boxes from a cavity that must once have been a fireplace. 'And what's in all these? Keep a record, Jem. Every stage of the process, write it down. Or photos on your phone. We don't all have a photographic memory like you.' Pete's ambition was to open the house to the public, make a book, or a brochure, or a TV programme. In his dreams he wrote the speeches he might have to make one day, on authenticity and community memories.

Jeremiah's memory was good, but it was not so much photographic as sequential. As a London taxi driver, his mum had taken the Knowledge in record time and she'd taught Jem how to remember almost anything by starting at one and letting that one lead to another in a sequence, like going on a walk. One thing recalled two, and each of those things recalled a further two, and so on. It was a pity for Jeremiah that this memory system fell apart under the pressure of schoolwork. It hadn't done him much good in his GCSEs. When it came to anything competitive, panic trumped memory every time. People think that memory is like a filing system in your brain; that all your memories are just sitting there in little drawers, waiting for you to open them. Then they seize up, thinking that they've lost the key. But memory is more like a muscle: a muscle which needs regular exercise.

'And what's this? Ancient Roman biscuit tin? Heh, heh.' Among the boxes in the cavity was a grimy old

Victorian-looking tin, about six inches square, the lid jammed shut. Pete pulled it out and then wiped his fingers on the seat of his corduroy trousers. He gave the tin a shake. Something rattled around inside.

In theory, if you train it up, give it regular exercise, memory can do extraordinary things. Recall experiences from a past we all share. We're all made of the same stuff that's been here all along, after all – the same atoms. We're all recycled goods. So it's not impossible that we might have inherited traces wired into our hard drives. In other words, those birds fly south because other birds flew south before them and they remember how to do it: morphic resonance.

'I found lovely old stripy wallpaper underneath the beige wallpaper upstairs. Amazing, isn't it! You take off wallpaper, and underneath—'

'More wallpaper,' said Jeremiah, flatly. Sometimes he found it hard to match his stepfather's levels of enthusiasm.

'So, when you're done down here, come upstairs and we'll get some pizzas in,' said Pete on his way out, 'maybe watch some telly in the box room.' Pete had relegated television and other evidence of the twenty-first century to the kitchen and a small box room at the back of the house on the ground floor. It meant that the rest of the ground floor was impressive, but not exactly adjusted for modern living.

THREE

Jeremiah picked up the grimy old tin. It was dark blue and covered in a patina of dirt, as if it had been kept above a cooker for decades. He gave it a shake. Sounded like cards or perhaps some other, smaller boxes in there. To open it, he had to wriggle his nails under the lip of the lid. The edge was sharp and it needed some coaxing, pulling first from one side and then the other, until eventually it came away with what almost sounded like a fizz. The air that had been trapped in there for perhaps a hundred years wafted out and hit Jeremiah full in the face.

Have you ever had that sensation when you're looking for something and you just can't find it – a cup on a table perhaps, a pair of glasses, or your phone – and then you see that it has been right there in front of you all along? On that table, unseen, until, at the third or fourth search there it is, fully materialised. Somehow, you had just blanked it. Well, the past is like that. It's been there all along and then, suddenly, you just notice it for the first time. That's how it felt when Jeremiah opened that biscuit tin.

There were a couple of old photographs in there, faded and brown. One was of a tall, stiff-looking woman with long hair. She felt familiar to Jeremiah, and not in a pleasant way. He couldn't place exactly why, but he knew he didn't like her. Had he seen a picture of her before? Was she famous for doing something? Probably something bad, like a politician or something. The other, a larger photo, on card, was of what appeared to be this room. This basement, lit by candles, with a circle of old women sitting around a big table, wearing robes with symbols embroidered on them. There was a low hissing sound, as if the air was still being released from the tin.

'Is anyone there? Are you there?' A high, wavering voice seemed to come from behind the photo card. Jeremiah couldn't work out whether the sounds were outside or inside his head. In fact, his head felt swollen, insulated from the surrounding atmosphere. As if he had a high fever.

'I see him! Speak to us!' A second voice; female, old. The hissing noise grew louder until it became an unignorable ringing.

'I see him too! What is your name, oh spirit?' A third voice, also female. The hissing was now a thundering torrent.

Jeremiah tried to speak. 'What?' he mumbled. 'What just happened?' As soon as he spoke, the roar stopped. As if the sound of his own voice inside his skull had swallowed it up.

'He speaks!' said the first voice, which had the accent and precision of a BBC children's presenter from the early days of television. 'Speak to us, if you are there! What is your name?'

'Jeremiah Bourne,' said Jeremiah, hearing his own voice now inside his head, like wearing noise-cancelling headphones. 'Who the hell are you?'

'Language, please, young man!' said the first voice, from within the room now. 'You may be dead, but that is no reason not to mind your Ps and Qs.'

Dead? Jeremiah looked at his hand. It didn't look like a zombie's hand. No dripping flesh there. He looked around him. The light had changed. He was still in the basement, but, with increasing clarity, he could see the robed women from the second photograph, sitting around their table. They were holding hands. There was a candelabra on the table with five candles burning, which gave the room an eerie, flickering ambience. The women were all staring at Jeremiah with total focus. They could see him. They were definitely talking to him. He could see them. They could hear him, he could hear them.

'Oh my God! That is so freaky!' he said. 'Where am I?'

'You are in the Blackfriars Road. London.' The second voice belonged to an old lady with her hair pinned up behind her neck. She had several layers of necklace drooping across her chest, and lace sleeves, visible at her wrists. The robe she was wearing over her dress, like all of the other women's, was a pale blue silk with silver moons and stars sewn onto it. It was more like a loose poncho, slung over her shoulders. 'And where are you from?'

'I'm from here. I mean, Blackfriars Road. In fact, this is my house. I think. Is this some kind of prank? You're joking me, right?'

The first woman spoke – the one who'd told him to mind his language. 'None of us are laughing, are we, ladies? So perhaps you can explain your appearance among us.'

'Are you from the after-life?' asked the third woman to speak. She was smaller and rounder than the others, with a large undercarriage to her chin, like a pelican.

'What did she say?' a fourth elderly woman joined in. She was the oldest of them, dressed entirely in black – apart from her blue silk poncho. She broke their circle of hand-holding to pick up an ear trumpet and hold it to her ear.

'She asked him if he was from the after-life, dear,' number two shouted into the trumpet.

'What can you tell us of the after-life, young man?' asked the first woman, who seemed to be in charge, or at least chairing the meeting.

'I just opened an old biscuit tin – there were a couple of photos in it – and then, whoosh! Suddenly I'm here. I'm not from the after-life. Definitely. This is really, really weird.'

'Is my husband there in the here-after? His name was Ebeneezer. Ebeneezer Tandy. Do you know him?'

'And mine? Mr Stimples. Tell him I've not forgiven him.'

'And my dear brother, Algernon Stevens – is he there? He was such a lovely boy—'

'Look, I'm not dead, all right? At least I don't think I am,' Jeremiah butted in, beginning to doubt it himself. I wonder if I've been killed by a biscuit tin? he thought.

'What did he say?' said the one in black with the ear trumpet.

'He said he doesn't think that he is dead, Mrs Morepath.'

'Ladies, please! One at a time,' said the first woman. She was perhaps a little younger than the others, and her dress was plainer – no jewellery, no lace, no satin. 'Well, Jeremiah Bourne, thank you for visiting us. We were expecting one Petroc Grimstead, a fisherman from seventeenth-century Cornwall. That was who was summoned, but you will have to do. How did you get here? Magic trick, was it? Are you with the circus?'

'No,' said Jeremiah, 'I don't really like circuses. The clowns aren't funny.'

'I beg your pardon!' said the second woman, indignantly. 'What could be funnier than a man in a pointy hat falling over his too-big shoes?'

'Just about anything?' said Jeremiah.

There was a general murmur of agreement from all except number two.

'So, if not from the circus, from which century do you hail, oh spirit?' said the woman with the chin.

'I hail from the twenty-first century, of course,' said Jeremiah. 'Where do you lot think you are?'

This seemed to perplex them.

'How is that possible?' They all looked to number one for a lead on this. 'Mrs Stokes?'

'What did he say?' asked the ear-trumpet woman.

'He says he is not dead. He says he is from the future.'

'Oh. So are *we* all dead, then?'

The one called Mrs Stokes decided to step in and take control. 'No, dear, you are not dead, yet. Although, with any more surprises like this, the time could be soon. This young man, it would seem, is not a spirit, but flesh and blood.'

'He don't look real to me. Nice-looking boy, but not very real. His clothes are strange.'

'Disgusting, if you ask me,' said number four. Jeremiah was wearing a T-shirt, trainers and jeans. They were a bit disgusting, actually, from the wire-wool residue.

'He looks real enough to me. I like 'em with a bit of flesh on 'em,' said chin woman.

'Virginia! Please!'

'Yes, he's quite a good-looker,' said ear-trumpet, who seemed to have gathered the gist. 'Well-built but sensitive. Big. Sweet-looking. Just my cup of tea.' Jeremiah wasn't sure about the 'sweet-looking', but it was true, he wasn't exactly skinny. In fact, his nickname at college was 'Jellymiah', which stung a bit. But which, if publicly laughed off, stung less.

Jeremiah could feel his breath shortening and neck tightening with anxiety. 'Excuse me, aunties, and it's a pleasure to meet you and everything,' he said, starting to sidle towards the door, 'and I'm sorry not to be any help about the after-life, but—'

'But is he merely a phantasm, Mrs Champney, a chimera?'

'Try putting your hand through him, Mrs Stimples, that'll soon decide it.'

Mrs Stimples reached out with a wavy, wrinkly hand to dig Jeremiah in the abdomen. He made a dash for it.

'Woah! No thank you! Sorry, but gotta go!' He lurched towards the door that led to the stairs, knocking over the candelabra as he went. He escaped in the general kerfuffle as the women picked up the candles, trying not to get hot wax on their clothes.

'Mind you don't catch fire, Tabatha!' was the last Jeremiah heard of them, and he went quickly up the stairs towards the front hall.

Dado rails! There were dado rails all the way up the staircase. And stripy wallpaper. Stepdad Pete would be in ecstasy. The door at the top of the stairs was closed. We never close that, he thought, and then, I don't think we actually have a door there. It opened outwards into the front hall and there was an immediate change in the acoustic.

He was standing in his own front hall, but it was different. The floorboards were sanded and varnished for a start – something Pete had been meaning to do for ages – so there was a slight echo. There were some thin Turkish rugs over by the front door. A tall grandfather clock with a pendulum tocked ponderously. It was weird; this was undoubtedly his house, but all the points of reference had changed. The banisters and hand-rail were polished and fresh, and there was no carpet on the stairs, which were painted white. It was quiet, and there was a faint smell of ammonia.

At the top of the first flight of stairs stood a girl with wire-framed glasses. She was looking down at him, shocked. She was wearing an ankle-length black dress with white apron and cotton cap. Her knuckles were tight on the banister. They stared at each other for three or four seconds in silence. Then, suddenly, there were other girls with her, giggling and looking down at him too.

'Look! A man! Daisy's seen a man! Oooh!' They stayed, clustered at the top of the stairs, pointing and laughing.

'Hello,' Jeremiah managed. 'Who are you?'

The one called Daisy spoke up for them all. 'Sir? Surely, it is we who should be asking who you are, sir? And what is your business here?'

'What is he wearing?' one of the others said, which set them all off laughing again. 'He looks like a floor mop!'

'Why does he have writing on his shirt? Is he a convict on the run?'

'Ooooh!'

Jeremiah tried his most polite voice. 'I'm really sorry, but something really weird just happened. I'm not exactly sure where I am…'

'How did you get in here? You are not supposed to be here,' said Daisy.

'Yes, how did you get in?' one of the other girls said, backing Daisy up.

'I live here. This is my house. Well, it's exactly like my house but—'

He was interrupted by the loud voice of a woman calling down the stairs. 'Girls! To your rooms!' it boomed. 'What is going on?' A daunting woman in a tightly waisted skirt and blouse appeared at the top of the stairs. She stopped midflow on seeing Jeremiah. 'Young man! You must leave at once! There is nothing for you here!' Her face was dominated by a large, assertive nose, down which she glared at Jeremiah. Her voice alone would put fear into all but the largest of household pets. She came down a few steps and stood, protectively, in front of the girls. 'Girls! To your rooms!' she said again, without losing her focus on him.

'Hello, erm… madam. I'm really sorry about this, but I've just had a completely mad experience…' Jeremiah felt small.

'Go! Now! I shall call on the services of Mr Grout, if you persist.'

'I'm not persisting, honestly,' said Jeremiah, feeling the oncoming possibility of a panic attack, 'but where do I go?'

'Through that door instantly!' The woman pointed at the front door. She started to descend the stairs, meaningfully, towards him. The girls did not go to their rooms, but stayed chatting and whispering behind her. She stopped momentarily and turned back to them with a fierce look, not even needing a single word to disperse them.

They understood her message and ran up back up the stairs. No doubt the look was more frightening than the shout and meant possible punishments later. 'Yes, Miss Quentinbloom, sorry, Miss Quentinbloom, ma'am,' they mumbled as they disappeared. Then the woman turned her full attention, and her nose, towards Jeremiah and hissed, 'Be gone!' Her hostile power could be felt from all the way across the hall, and Jeremiah backed away in the wake of it towards the front door. His breath was high in his chest as he fumbled with the door catch. It was not at all like the one he was used to.

'Where's the handle?' he said, his fingers struggling with the bolt. His simmering anxiety started to boil up.

'I haven't actually been outside for five weeks…' He was gulping air now.

'Go!' the woman said quietly, proving that emanations can be more terrifying than shouts. Eventually, Jeremiah's shaking fingers found a latch which opened the door and he tumbled out onto the front steps.

FOUR

Jeremiah stood on the step gasping for air. He leaned on the metal railing.

'The only thing we have to fear is fear itself,' said Franklin D. Roosevelt at his inauguration. It's a nice phrase which might or might not be true, but can sometimes help in times of distress. What had just happened to Jeremiah was much more alarming than any of the things which he was normally afraid might happen, so much so that he stood there, confused, for a long minute, before reaching for his inhaler in his pocket. It wasn't there; he'd left it in the basement. So he focused on breathing out, as he'd been taught at the GP's: concentrate on exhaling, in long steady breaths, and try to forget about breathing in; just keep exhaling.

Then, try to think about something else other than breathing. Where's the Shard? was the first thought that came to his mind. Jeremiah liked the Shard; he remembered it going up, bit by bit, when he was a kid. It's a nice shape, like a church spire on a vast horizon. You can see it from Archway, you can see it from Richmond. It was like a homing signal to him.[2]

---

2 The only thing bad about the Shard is that it seems to have opened the door for all the other tall glass buildings with funny names. The Gherkin was first, fair enough, but since the Shard went up there seems to have been an architects'

The street was definitely Blackfriars Road, but not like it is now. There were no cars. No lorries. No buses. No tarmac surface for them all to ride on. No yellow lines, no traffic lights, no cycle lanes. No office block opposite, no concrete health centre with its windows all boarded up. What there was, was an unbelievably strong smell. It was throat-catching. Burnt rubber and horse manure. There was horse manure everywhere, in separate piles up and down the road in both directions. There weren't that many people, though. On the other side of the street a couple of boys a bit younger than Jeremiah were hanging about, staring at the house. But they disappeared down a side street when they caught sight of him.

About twenty yards away, on his side of the road, there was an old woman dragging herself down the street carrying an enormous basket on her hip. Then a horse and carriage went by towards Blackfriars Bridge. The horse's hooves and the wheels made a great racket. And in the distance another wagon with an old bloke on it shouting out something incomprehensible, which sounded like 'Yagboons!'[3]

The differences in his surroundings were obvious, but what was also remarkable were the similarities; same sky, same clouds, same temperature. There were even most of

---

feeding frenzy: the Heron, the Electric Shaver, the Pregnant Lady, the Cheese Grater, the ominously named Tower 42, and the winner of the Carbuncle Cup for the 'ugliest building', the Walkie Talkie – the one that bulges out at the top as if it had American football shoulder pads and which is said to melt the plastic fittings on cars below in the summer with its reflective glass.

3 What he was actually calling out was 'Rag and bone', which had morphed into 'Yagboons' over the decades of tramping the streets. The sound of his call had about as much connection to the original words as the street cry 'Buck Shoe' has today with the magazine *Big Issue*. Rag-and-bone men or 'bone-grubbers' were common right up until the sixties in some parts of London. They collected unwanted household stuff and sold it on to merchants. A sort of mobile recycling drop-off.

the same trees, and the same pigeons flapping about. One of them crapped on his shoulder as he was managing to control his breathing. Thanks for that. It's meant to be lucky, isn't it?

He stood there on the steps for another minute, taking it all in, controlling his breath. His hands were still shaky. He assessed the evidence in front of him, rationally and logically. There seemed to be no other conclusion possible. He had travelled in time. But not in space, obviously. He was in exactly the same place as he was before. Blackfriars Road. So, travelling in time wasn't some kind of time/space/continuum warp thing. Not like in science fiction. In science fiction there would have been a dark purple sky, and asteroids, and Zygons, Silurians or Clockwork Droids on the streets by now. No, he'd just opened a tin, seen a couple of photos and then sort of 'noticed' the past. As if it had been there all along. Well, of course it has been there all along. Stepdad Pete was right.

'Oi. You. Sling yer 'ook.' A man with a voice like gravel was suddenly in Jeremiah's personal space. He'd come up quickly and now he was at the top of the steps. His face was inches away from Jeremiah's and his breath smelt like tinned fart.

'Hello. Could you help me a minute? What date is it? Because I seem to have done something extraordinary and travelled in— Oof! What did you do that for?'

The man had punched Jeremiah in the stomach.

'You been harassing the ladies, incher?' With a voice as gravelly as this, the man could have a career in voiceovers nowadays.

'No, I'm not harassing them. Are you Mr Grout?'

'Shoo! Unless you want me to crack open your skull wiv this 'ere stick. Clear orff to where you come from.' The man was carrying a thick stick that got thicker at the hitting end. Jeremiah had not noticed that.

'I'd really like to actually,' said Jeremiah, 'but I don't know how I got here, and I don't know how to get back. Ow!'

The man punched him again and then stepped back to take a swing at him with the nasty-looking stick. Jeremiah made a run for it, leaping down the steps, falling and then picking himself up on the street. The man was after him, shouting, 'I knows you gang boys! Come back 'ere!' Jeremiah was younger and faster than Mr Grout, who huffed and puffed after him. He made a good few yards and then tried to work out where he was going. He did recognise the street layout – roughly. Pocock Street. So, there should be a dustbin alley on the right, round the back of the houses. There was. Just like nowadays. He ducked into it; it was narrow and wooden-fenced. He crouched down behind a dustbin, breathing heavily, until he heard Mr Grout go by at the top of the alley, panting and cursing. Amazing to think that the oldest trick in the book actually worked. Obviously, Mr Grout had not had the advantage of watching endless police-chase scenes on TV. The alley behind the house smelt even worse than the street, if that's possible. A dog barked from somewhere and a blackbird was singing. So much of it was familiar, but there was one big difference; there wasn't that continual, underlying judder of traffic. Basically, it was silence, with noises on top, rather than the background drone of city sounds we have now.

He waited a couple of seconds to make sure that Grout wasn't coming back this way, and carried on down the alley, counting the backs of the houses on the other side of the fence. His own back-garden gate was still there. Painted and well-maintained, not like the rotting one they had nowadays. He must remember to tell Pete – it was a sort of dark green gloss colour, with black handles and hinges. He swung the gate open; it wasn't locked. He slipped into his own backyard, closing the gate behind him, and found himself facing Daisy, the girl from the top of the stairs.

'Good day, sir,' she said, bobbing a curtsey.

'Woah! You made me jump!'

She was not so cocky now. In fact, she looked nervous.

'Are you a gentleman, sir?' she said, looking fearfully over her shoulder back at the house.

'Erm, depends what you mean,' said Jeremiah. 'Yes, I suppose, well, no, technically speaking, I'm just ordinary, but basically I'm OK...' She looked troubled. He gave up. 'Yes, I'm a gentleman,' he said; it seemed the right thing to do.

'Good. Then could you save me, sir,' she went on, quickly, 'by which I mean to imply... a rescue?' She had a gap between her two front teeth which made her lisp slightly.

He looked around. They could easily be seen from the back windows of the house, if anyone cared to look out. Daisy moved a few steps to be out of view, behind a shed, which was standing just inside the back wall. Jeremiah followed her, thinking about the shed. The shed was still there! The same shed we have! He hadn't realised that their shed was so old. There was a little space between the shed and the wall that he used to squeeze into when he was a kid. He used to hide from Ruby there. The gap at the back of the shed used to scare him sometimes when he was younger.[4]

'Perhaps you are some kind of wizard, sir?' said Daisy.

'That'd be good, but, no, I'm not some kind of wizard.'

---

4 Nobody has been able to come up with a serious answer to what it is about Sheds and Men. There is a UK Men's Sheds Association devoted entirely to the idea, and several reality TV shows have tried to make it go mainstream. But from carpentry, to making things out of matchsticks, to alcohol, to porn, no one has quite managed to put a finger on why it is that a man feels better doing it in a shed.

She seemed disappointed, but went on, 'But you did some wizardry just now, did you not? Appearing from out of nowhere. And you wear strange clothes.'

'Look, these clothes are really normal where I come from. Boring, in fact. And I'm really not anything, I just seem to have accidentally done some kind of… time-jump thing—'

Daisy cut him off. 'Sir, I only have one minute before I will be found out, so please listen.'

'OK, I'm a wizard and a gentleman and I'm listening.'

She took a big breath. 'I am in a situation that it distresses me to divulge.'

'Right. That sounds bad.'

'Please do not make me describe to you in words the wretchedness of my circumstance.' If she only had one minute, she'd already used up half of it.

'OK, I won't. So, what is it?'

She pulled aside her apron a little and arched her back, looking at him with an expression of anguish. It was fairly obvious that she was pregnant.

'Wow! Congratulations!' said Jeremiah. 'So, you've got a thing, in the… thing. Brilliant.' He was embarrassed.

'No, sir!' She tutted. 'Can you not see that I am having a baby?'

'Yuh, I knew that.'

'And when the baby is born, I should like at all costs,' she lowered her voice to a whisper, 'to keep it with me. Sir.'

'Right, OK. I don't really know how I can help with that—'

They were interrupted by the sound of a sash window being flung open and the governess woman booming down into the yard.

'Daisy? Daisy Wallace!'

Daisy called back up over her shoulder without taking her eyes from Jeremiah, 'Yes, ma'am, Miss Quentinbloom!'

'What are you doing down there? Daisy Wallace, come back in at once!'

Daisy shouted back, obediently, 'Yes, ma'am,' and then she quickly whispered to Jeremiah, 'Please, sir, tell Mrs Stokes of my condition. She will help. She is for the women.'

'Mrs Stokes?'

'The lady from the group downstairs in the basement? Tell her. She will understand.'

The Quentinbloom boom came back down to them. 'Daisy Wallace! Extra stair-scrubbing duty for you!'

'I must go, sir. Hurry. Tell Mrs Stokes. Daisy Wallace is with child.'

There was the sound of the sash window being slammed shut. Daisy hurried away, leaving Jeremiah standing behind the shed in a daze. Daisy Wallace is with child. And Jeremiah Bourne is hiding behind his own garden shed, in some alternative reality that seems incredibly similar to the real reality, but a long time ago. All he did was look at those photos. Or had he looked *through* them? And who was the scary woman in the first one? And there was that sort of fizzing air sound. How had this happened? And how could he make it unhappen? His neck was tight, and his breath was short. If only Ruby would come looking for him, saying something annoying, and Stepdad Pete would call her away and then they could all have pizza. He started to feel sorry for himself. He could feel himself swooping down, going into the shadowy part of his mind. He knew this. He'd had it before. He got it whenever he was reminded of his mum. It was loneliness, and he was used to handling it. Put it to one side, pretend it's not there and move on.

He took the only option that seemed available to him: find Mrs Stokes and tell her that Daisy Wallace is with child. He took a brave step out from behind the shed, towards the back of the house. There were three stone steps down to the back of the basement where his furniture workshop was – is – and where, in this reality, the group of old ladies had been trying to talk to the dead, wearing blue silk ponchos. The backyard was almost exactly as now, but there was a half-and-half door where nowadays there was a circular window. He must remember to tell Stepdad Pete. If he ever saw him again.

FIVE

Instinctively, Jeremiah reached into his pocket and got out his phone; take a photo for Stepdad Pete, and get some proof. There was no signal, obviously. And just the tiniest of tiny stripes in the battery icon. As he was watching it, the screen went black. So, no photos. He'd have to rely on memory, if he ever got back.

He went up to the basement window and peered in. He could see beyond the little vestibule to where the séance room was. The old ladies were standing now, their blue silk ponchos folded in a pile on the table. As she passed the window, it seemed to Jeremiah that the plainer-dressed woman – Mrs Stokes – noticed him standing there. But she did not register it to the other women, whom she was showing out of the basement door at the front. They clattered up the iron stairs to the pavement level, where, presumably, carriages awaited. He couldn't see beyond that, and now the room was empty.

'Young man, I think an explanation is in order!' The top of the half-and-half door swung open, and Mrs Stokes leaned out, surprising Jeremiah, who was still peering through the window. He jumped.

'Uh! Hello, sorry, are you Mrs Stokes?'

'And who is it that wants to know? Our mysterious incarnation? Returned for another haunting?'

'I'm not an incarnation. Honestly.'

'Come on, corker, how's it done? Mirrors? Smoke and mirrors?'

'I don't know. I just seem to have flipped backwards in time.'

'So you're a flipper. A flipper spirit.'

'No, I'm real.'

'You had better come in, then.' She opened the bottom half of the half-and-half door and stood back to let Jeremiah pass. 'And wipe your muddy shoes! You may be a magician but not a very clean one. Your shoes are covered in dirt from the yard.'

Jeremiah obeyed her and scuffed his trainers on the mat. She kept her distance and looked at his feet. 'Why are you wearing shoes that appear to be made of coloured paper?'

'These are my trainers. Quite expensive, actually. Cool.'

'So not only do they look ridiculous, but they leave your feet cool. And wet, by the look of them.'

Mrs Stokes was a good three inches shorter than Jeremiah, but she made up for it in force of character. She exuded energy like a toy car that has been fully wound back and is ready to shoot down the track. Unlike most of us nowadays, the bottom half of her was strongly connected to the top. When she walked, she walked as one piece; she didn't amble, lope or lounge. When she sat, she sat in one movement, and her back never slid down the chair. When she spoke, her voice was strong and clear and came from a well-supported diaphragm. If she was talking to you, you got her full, penetrating attention. Which she was beaming onto Jeremiah right now. He was being scrutinised.

'Sit ye down,' she said, indicating one of the chairs around the table, 'and tell me, how does a large man such as yourself suddenly materialise from thin air?'

No one had ever called Jeremiah a man, let alone a large man. They called him a lot of other things, Jellymiah for one. He was only just seventeen, so still a few months to go before losing his puppy status, if not his puppy fat. He rather liked the sound of being a large man.

'I think I've somehow travelled in time,' he started, which sounded pretentious to him as he was saying it. 'I opened a biscuit tin, looked at a couple of old photos, heard a sort of whooshing noise and that's it. I don't have a Time Machine or anything. Like Doctor Who.'

'Doctor who?'

'Like a Time Lord? OK, H. G. Wells. Do you know H. G. Wells?'

'I do, as a matter of fact. My brother Rodger has met him on several occasions.'

'Really? What's he like?'

'Well, he eats too many pancakes, ever since he was a little boy. Our mother would give the back of his hand a smack as he reached for yet another one.'

'No, I meant H. G. Wells – what's he like?'

'Oh. Well, Herbert Wells is a stickler for scientific accuracy,' she drew a chair in close to his, 'so I feel he would most certainly pooh-pooh your biscuit-tin theory.'

'Well, that's what happened. I was clearing out the cavity in this room. That cavity there!' Jeremiah got up to look at the fireplace, which was positioned in exactly the same place, of course. 'OK. Maybe the biscuit tin didn't have anything to do with it, I don't know. Perhaps I just went through some kind of multidimensional time portal?' He got down on all fours and poked his head into the fireplace. 'I wonder if I can just go through this wall, like in *Stranger Things*,' he said, bumping his head on the top of the fireplace. 'Nope.'

'Not a portal, then. Whatever are we going to do with you, Jeremiah Bourne?' said Mrs Stokes.

'How come you remembered my name?'

'It was the first thing you revealed upon your arrival among us. Mine is Mrs Phyllis Independence Almyra Stokes. My parents were free-thinkers and explorers of both the inner and outer worlds, so Rodger and I were given inspirational names.'

'Well, pleased to meet you, Phyllis…' Jeremiah bowed his head a little; it seemed appropriate, if a bit embarrassing.

'You may call me "Mrs Stokes, ma'am", until we become further acquainted, whereupon a "Phyllis" will do, if I sanction it.'

'Yes, Mrs Stokes, ma'am. You can call me Jem. Everyone does.'

Jeremiah paused for a moment, considering how to bring up Daisy Wallace, but Mrs Stokes stood up suddenly.

'Well, Jem, are you going to help me stack away these chairs or should I leave you to your ratiocinations?'

'Oh right, sorry.' The distraction of stacking the chairs made it easier to tell Mrs Stokes about Daisy Wallace and her unborn child. She listened attentively.

'The best chance of salvation for those girls is here, in this house of rehabilitation,' she said, adjusting the line of chairs so that it was exactly straight, 'where they are given a new chance in life as domestic servants.'

'Oh great,' said Jeremiah, 'so they get to be servants.'[5]

'Jem, an attitude like that is not becoming. These girls

---

5 Right up to the Second World War, nearly half of the female population of the UK were domestic servants. And most of the other half employed them. In the days before fridges, dishwashers, washing machines, vacuum cleaners and the rest, the employment of domestic servants took up a larger proportion of the economy than mining, and was even greater than the textile industry, which was huge. Virginia Woolf's famous contention that all a woman writer needs is 'a room of her own and £500 a year' presumes, of course, that the room would be cleaned, the laundry done and the meals brought to her by a domestic servant. One whose name she probably couldn't be bothered to spell correctly.

would be street orphans and fall into misery and abuse if it were not for the tireless work of their benefactor, Clementina Quentinbloom.'

'Is she the one with the really loud voice?' asked Jeremiah.

'How have you been brought up?' asked Mrs Stokes. 'By a hippopotamus? You seem not to have a good word for anything or anyone! Where do you think we women would be if at every turn we had only sour faces and negative comments?'

She took a cape off the hat-stand by the door and swirled it across her shoulders. 'Come on!' she said.

'What? Where?' he said, feeling his breath rise again.

She took a hat from the stand and placed it on her head, taking a large pin from it and securing the hat jauntily on the side of her head. It had a long, brown feather which swooped down over her left cheek.

'To my brother Rodger's house in Gordon Square; you are too interesting for him to miss!'

'What, right now? Don't you think I'm safer just staying here in the basement where it happened? What if it happens again?'

'Jeremiah Bourne, you are a puzzle and with a puzzle comes a purpose: to solve it. And purpose is something, by the look of it, that you have been lacking for some time.'

She took down a bunch of keys from a hook by the door, went over to the street door and opened it.

'Look, I haven't actually been out of the house for, like, five weeks. Apart from just now, that is...'

She looked back at him with what could have been pity, could have been mockery, he wasn't sure which.

'...because I get this thing called agoraphobia – have you heard of it?'

She nodded. 'Why, yes, I have,' she said, 'and as it happens, I know of a very effective cure.'

'Really?'

'Yes, indeed I do. Follow me, and I'll show you. Come on, chop chop!' she said, urging him towards the door.

'So, what's so special about your brother Rodger, then?'

'You are a phenomenon, Jem. And, as luck would have it, my brother Rodger and I are expert investigators of paranormal phenomena! Indeed, we are the founders of the Society for Theosophical Research and Anthro-Psychology. You've come to the right place! Or will have when we get to Rodge's.'

She held open the door and in one sweep he was outside again, in the bay of the basement, looking up at the iron staircase that led to the street. She locked the door behind them and then bustled him up the stairs ahead of her. At the top he looked around nervously for Mr Grout, but the street was mostly empty now. Attaching the bunch of keys to a large ring in her waistband, Mrs Stokes strode off ahead of him at speed. Although she was short, she could certainly move. Jeremiah had to trot to keep up.

'So, what's this cure, then?' he said, but she was already yards ahead.

SIX

By the time Artemesia Plutarch got back to her quarters – compartment, pod, flat, digs – Scoobeedoo was going crazy. He was jumping up on the sofa and bouncing off the wall. He didn't know whether he wanted to eat first or go out for a wee. He hadn't been out for over twelve hours, but he hadn't been fed for twenty-four. The correct spelling of his name was actually 'Scoubidou', after the French plastic weaving-threads toy from the seventies, not after the famous American cartoon series. Artemesia had given up trying to explain this small but important difference, when people seeing the name written down called him 'Scowbidow', which sounded like some kind of toilet brush. Not everyone shared Artemesia's obsession with games from the seventies. In fact, it'd probably be fair to say not anyone did.

Artemesia fetched down a tin of Kennomeat – another brand name from the seventies – opened it using an old-fashioned turn-key can opener, and scooped the contents into Scoobeedoo's bowl, which to her shame hadn't been cleaned for a few days. The little dog waffled it down making the sort of noise some immature people can make by squeezing their armpits for a joke. Once that was done, which was only a matter of seconds, Scoobee looked back up at Artemesia expectantly. 'OK, let's go, but I haven't got long, so it's just a short one. Only a couple of minutes. I've got to go back and be grilled again by the committee.' The

Scoob understood from the tone of Artemesia's voice that this was not going to be a big romp in the open, that his keeper was tired, knackered in fact, and also, even a bit sad. He let out a sympathetic-sounding whimper, which in dog-language actually meant: Lazy cow, there's always some excuse, isn't there, and they went out onto the landing.

Artemesia realised that she too was hungry; she couldn't remember the last time she'd eaten. Would have to pick something up on their way up to the roof. She knew that her glass-box was empty, had been for days. Nothing in there but some old fish fingers, which she dared not break the seal on, because they'd been in there for so long. Scoobee shot up the stairs immediately, so there was no point in waiting for the counterweight lift; probably broken down again anyway. Artemesia dragged her feet up step by step, hanging onto the banister; she must be more tired than she realised. Sunlight flickered intermittently across the staircases from the glass bricks in the upper wall; it wasn't too bad a day. There was an echo here in the common parts of the house and Scoobee's excited yelping as he reached the top gate could be heard three flights down. Artemesia plodded slowly behind. 'All right, Scoob, I'm coming!' she panted.

The last few minutes of the Residents' Association meeting had not gone well for Artemesia Plutarch. All this sniffing around from Super-Recall had made her uneasy; she wished they'd just move on. But the thing had now escalated into an official Super-Recall enquiry. Not good.

At the glass-box by the gate, she helped herself to a nut bar – that should keep her going. She wrote it down in the ledger, using the pencil on a string and then opened the gate. Scoobeedoo was off like a shot, into the bushes at the far wall. Artemesia sighed; it might take ages to persuade the Scoob to come back downstairs. She sat down on the green iron bench by the railings and munched her nut bar in the watery

English sunlight. From here she could see the craggy steel frames of what used to be the skyscraper blocks at Elephant and Castle, now brought to their knees and reinvented as urine collection plants for the laundry works. Cables were slung across the street from windows and redundant lamp posts, transferring electricity from generators powered by the methane gas in cow poo.[6] Buildings had vertical gardens all the way up to the roof, sprouting vegetables, edible moss and fungi. The noise of the city came up from below like low-level hiss from an old untuned radio, and was broken only by the solitary 'squeak-squeak' of the Blackfriars Road push-me-pull-you rail cart on its way south to Kennington.

A half-hearted breeze occasionally shifted the leaves of the plants and trees on the roof. They rustled and whispered pleasantly with each exhalation of the wind. A row of cabbage palms was surrounded by some tired geraniums, and jasmine engulfed one of the walls; in the centre were three maples, and over the other side, one single small birch tree, which wasn't doing too badly considering it was on a roof. No one else was up there, which was good. Artemesia sighed again; she hated breaking the rules or doing anything dangerous. Why couldn't everything be nice like it was when she was a child? Before their father got sick, and before her bloody sister started going off the rails.

---

6 One last, positive outcome from the pre-digital meltdown world was the invention of an anti-methane vaccine for cattle. A lab in New Zealand developed this in the 2020s, potentially saving some 14 per cent of human-activity-generated emissions. Meanwhile, of course, the increasingly massive data centres continued their voracious swallowing up of rare earths and cobalts, soon creating a carbon footprint far bigger than the world's cowpats. Post-meltdown, methane became popular again, as handy 'patteries' were developed to turn it into power. In a satisfying irony, banks were taken over to house cows and their excreta. Saying 'I'm a banker' to people at dinner parties carried a new and different stigma.

Her bloody elder sister. She'd always been more fiery and more trouble than Artemesia. Things came easily to Enid; the good and the bad, the boyfriends and the break-ups. Artemesia couldn't remember a time when her sister hadn't been involved in some kind of disaster. Enid was a high-risk individual. The things Artemesia had had to do to cover for her, the lies she'd had to tell their father, even early on. And when he was dying it was Artemesia who'd had to do all the final looking after, right down to cleaning him physically, and then afterwards it was Artemesia who'd done all the signing and arranging and filling-in of forms. Their younger brother, Pasteur, was doing well by then in Hyper-Organics somewhere in Norfolk and never got in touch. Artemesia was the second of the three children.

In fact, Artemesia Plutarch was one of those people who come second in everything. Never first and never last either. She'd worked hard and her results had been good, but never quite good enough. Sometimes her work could actually be better on points, she felt, but she lacked the brilliance or noticeability of, for example, a Dr Mandar Vergeelis, now head of the Morphic Resonance department at Super-Recall. Vergeelis was an ambitious woman with an upward career trajectory, a woman who could sum up a whole era in one little catchphrase which could then be used by others – others in prominent positions – and was not afraid to ask for favours in return. Even when she was young and full of optimism, Artemesia had never had Mandar Vergeelis's hunger for advancement that gets you into places. Bloody Dr Mandar bloody Vergeelis had famously got straight A-stars in all ninety subjects. Artemesia had a string of Bs. Not the pits, but not the tops.

Perhaps she lacked ambition, drive, but those who did have those qualities just seemed greedy to her. Artemesia

Plutarch – Archie – had 'promise'. She had always had 'promise' but never anything more. She was thirty-four years old now, and was still showing 'promise', when she bothered to try. But somehow, the desire to push for it, to run that last lap, had expired in her. She used to blame it on her bad luck in missing her final year in college, because of the student 'digital dependency' riots and sit-ins. She hadn't so much sat in, as sat out for the whole year. She hadn't been able to decide which side to be on, and was happier sitting on the metaphorical fence, as long as there was beer involved. The year-long turbulence had been caused by student activists who wanted to do away with what they called the 'dependency denial' of the establishment; which claimed that the meltdowns had nothing to do with human activity and were random technical malfunctions. There were nasty clashes between the Dependency Deniers and the 'Owning Our Past' contingent. In fact, some students had done quite well out of it all, making whole careers out of the protests. Conrad, the man in beige, Artemesia seemed to remember, had had some kind of student organisational role in the activism and made a lot of impassioned and angry speeches.

Scoobeedoo came dashing back to her, barking and happy. She stood up. 'OK, show me where it is,' she said and walked over to the large hydrangea where Scoobee had been playing. On the way across she chucked the nut-bar wrapper down the chute and picked up a cardboard scooper. Scoobee took her to the spot and showed her. Artemesia crouched down to dig the layer of soil underneath and chucked it all down the poo chute. People used to have plastic bags to do this, she thought; still, it's better to have an ocean and a river and put up with a bit of throat-clenching poo smell once a day. She ran her hands under the water flow and shook them as dry as she could. She could have made them a hand-drying vacuum system, she'd even suggested it once, but the Residents' Association weren't that interested in homegrown technology, or maybe they just didn't have the budget.

She liked inventing new things and fixing old ones. Like rebuilding an old VHS video machine so that she could watch TV programmes from the late seventies. She'd have loved to actually go there, but she wasn't qualified to travel, so it remained, officially at least, a dream. Any travelling she had done was well off the record and usually as a favour to do with her sister's latest misadventure. She certainly had enough info about the late twentieth century in her head, but it wasn't the sort of material that was considered worth harvesting; her speciality – entertainment factoids – was of no value in the ongoing search for historic scientific data. Her favourite module in college had been 'Pointless Toys from the 1970s', and that was still her main interest. In her compartment she had: two plastic fighting robots, a magnetic quiz robot, a KerPlunk set, two cap rockets that never worked, a SuperGraph, a Spirograph and an Aquadoodle, an empty Jubbly box, an unopened packet of Jelly Tots, a *Mutley the Dog* annual, a View-Master with no discs, an Instamatic camera and four rusty bottle openers. She also had a few cans left of Top Deck Lemonade Shandy, which she saved for special occasions, even though it tasted revolting.[7]

---

7 My editor says I'm to stop doing footnotes, especially ones that mention the fact that she exists. My editor, that is. And if I do, she threatened to cut them out anyway. So, if you do end up reading this, it may be the last one. It's been great. Thanks. Goodbye. But I did just think it would be interesting to mention the toys that Artemesia Plutarch had not managed to collect, such as Tinkertoy, early Lego – which was just random yellow, blue, white and red plastic bricks, no little people and no pre-planned design – Scalextric, Action Man and Barbie, obviously, Space Hoppers, Play-Doh. Strangely, none of these toys were connected to film franchises, as all toys are nowadays.

Right, time to face the music, or perhaps that should be: face the monotone from the man in beige, she thought. On the way back down to the compartment – to drop off the Scoob before her grilling – she stopped by the communal library shelves on the second landing. Looking around to check she was unobserved, she quickly took out from her leather satchel an ancient, creased and crumpled copy of the London A–Z, circa 2001, which was stamped with *Property of Blackfriars Road Residents' Association R and M* across its spine. She slid it onto the communal shelves next to a copy of *The Sigma Protocol* by Robert Ludlum, an equally creased and crumpled paperback from the early twenty-first century. She didn't enter the old A–Z into the ledger, as that would have led to further questions. She just had to hope that nobody had looked and found it missing while it was gone.

SEVEN

'Come along, Jem! No dallying!' Phyllis Stokes called over her shoulder, the long brown feather bobbing up and down on her cheek. 'And pull up your trousers, for goodness' sake! You seem convinced that the world should be witness to the cheeks of your behind!'

'They don't go any higher actually, it's fashion,' Jeremiah said, panting behind her.

In the distance he heard the call of the 'Yagboons!' man and his squeaky wagon. But they were leaving him and the quieter streets behind them now and heading towards town.

In this direction, the buildings soon became more closely jammed and city-like. All the houses had signs on them. Not just on the ground-floor shops, but on every floor: 'Melkin's Bookbinders and Chancery Bills' on floor one. On floor two: 'Evans Antiseptic Sundries and Fancy Goods'. Signs right up to the third and fourth floor of the buildings: 'Pearson's Pickled Tongues', and, the strangest one: 'The Lambert and Simkins Toilet Club'.

Who'd want to join that? thought Jeremiah. Men in aprons stood around outside their shopfronts. Women and children bustled between the buildings and down the side streets to the left and right. 'Seymour King's Coconut Fibre; Oilcake, Vinegar, Oakum.' 'What's oakum?' he shouted ahead to Phyllis, but she kept walking at speed. As she walked, she spoke excitedly.

'An excellent meeting was had today, Jem, because of your appearance. We in the Women's Branch of the society are making great discoveries which will soon outstrip those of the men. And about time,' she shouted. 'The Society for Theosophical Research and Anthro-Psychology, Women's Branch. STRAWB, hence the strawberry design that I have had painted on our placard. Did you see our placard?' Jeremiah hadn't. She was beginning to develop a manic tone in her voice. The long brown feather was bouncing furiously now. He started to worry. Was he in the hands of a psychopath? He was running now to keep up with her.

'Can we slow down, actually?' he said behind her. 'I'm feeling strange again. And what's this cure for agoraphobia you mentioned?'

'I'll tell you in just one minute,' she lobbed back at him.

It got busier the further north they went, past Union Street towards the bridge. Lots of people were walking in the opposite direction; mostly men, all of them wearing hats. Top hats, bowler hats and flat caps. Their boots made a tramping noise on the ground like an army of elephants.

'Who are all these people?' Jeremiah shouted above the din.

'I am afraid we must have hit the rush hour, Jem,' she said. 'It's the city workers returning home to Streatham and such.'

'What, walking the whole way?'

'Oh yes. The Underground does not serve the southern suburbs well.'[8] Phyllis happily banged her way through the

---

8 The first London Underground line was the Metropolitan from Farringdon to Paddington and it opened in 1863. It used steam trains, which must have made the air pretty unbearable down there. Electrification came in over the next thirty years or so and new lines have continued to be built right up until the present day, with the Northern Line extension to Nine Elms and Battersea Power

crowd, occasionally shouting the odd remark, such as: 'And the best of luck to you too, sir!' if anyone bumped into her.

'Are we nearly there yet?' said Jem, struggling to keep up.

'Jem! We have barely begun! I must say I am disappointed that a lad from the future should have so little fibre in him!'

'Oh look! A bus! Can't we go on that?'

It was a bus, a small one. But it was being pulled along by two horses. There were about five people inside it, and a winding stair at the back led to an open-top roof on which two or three men were sitting precariously, hanging onto a rail.

'No, Jem, we cannot,' said Phyllis. 'All the places are taken, even those on the roof.'

'But I'm really suffering here,' said Jeremiah. 'What if I have a panic attack?'

Then a claxon hooter sounded behind them, making him jump. The people on the pavement moved back. A rickety little car came chugging up behind them. It had a thin canvas roof and big, pop-up headlights, like searchlights, on the front. Inside was a man wrapped in scarves.

'Look at that, Jem! A motorised vehicle. No horses!' said Phyllis, who had stopped to let it pass. 'So clean! So much better for the air! That's the future, Jem, you mark my words. On second thoughts, *is it* the future? You would know.'

Station, opened in 2021, and the Elizabeth Line in 2022, although that is not officially an Underground line. I find it peculiar to imagine Queen Victoria on the Tube, something she never actually did, although she could have. Though she would have had trouble managing the fifteen-minute walk changing from the Hammersmith and City to the Bakerloo Line at Paddington. She lived for forty years after that first line opened.

'Yeah, it's the future all right. But it's going to make the air really toxic and polluted.' The crowd gave a small cheer as the car moved through them and turned a corner up ahead, tooting its horn all the way.

'More so than this?' said Phyllis, looking upwards. The air was foul and sticky with dark grime. Chimneys on the skyline behind them to the right belched dark clouds into a deep indigo horizon. 'And is the south side of the river still a place of skulduggery and throat-cutting?' she said, moving off at speed again.

'And bankers. Luxury flats for bankers,' he said, setting off in pursuit of her. 'Coh! What's that smell? That's disgusting.'

A wave of seriously fetid air from downriver hit them in the face as they fought their way towards Blackfriars Bridge.[9]

'The tanneries at Bermondsey. Turning cowhides into leather. One grows accustomed,' said Phyllis, barging a path for them both.

To his left, he recognised the Rose and Crown pub, which is currently a lonely slice of nineteenth-century brickwork lost among the twenty-first-century glass and concrete. There it was, the old Rose 'n Crown, exactly the same building, but part of the original terrace of small houses. Two old blokes in hats sat outside on the bench, drinking from tall pint glasses. He remembered getting caught in that beer garden with his mates, when they should have been in a revision period for GCSEs. He wished he'd done more revision now, so he wouldn't be having to do Year

---

9 Most of south London smells nearly as bad nowadays as it did 150 years ago due to the common use of skunk, a genetically modified form of marijuana. The clue is in the name. It can commonly be smelt – tasted almost – throughout London, not only in the city parks where it is rife, but emanating from the housing terraces and estates of the rich and poor alike.

Eleven again. All of the others had passed, so he'd also lost his friends as they moved on to sixth form, or worked for their ACE certs. Now his only friend seemed to be Nandy Banerjee, who came over to Blackfriars Road once a week to do extra maths home-study with him. The fact that she was in the year below him was a bit humiliating at first, but not as humiliating as the abject failure of his grade. Perhaps he'd just assumed that with his memory, he'd be able to trigger off all the answers on the day.[10]

Phyllis fought her way onto the bridge and they arrived at one of the stone alcoves above the main struts, where, finally, she allowed Jeremiah to stop for a rest.

'There! Look at that!' she said, gazing in the direction of the Houses of Parliament. 'What do you think of our river, Jem?'

Jeremiah sat on the cold stone seat and looked out over the familiar stretch of water, sludgy brown and churning as it flowed. Underneath them, an enormous barge was emerging and gliding upriver like a giant dead beetle. Its masts – set at an angle to get under the bridge – looked like the beetle's legs sticking up. There were boats all along the shore, a great, spidery tangle of ropes and masts bobbing at different angles, or just tilted in the mud. And the smell here was of fish, old rope and the yeasty whiff of beer being brewed.

In the other direction, towards St Paul's, Jeremiah recognised the huge, brightly painted insignia saying

---

10 There are all sorts of tricks you can use to aid memory, triggers that you can pull. There was an urban myth a few years ago that children were no longer being allowed to take Starbursts into exams. Not because of the sugar content, but because of the different coloured wrappers. If every time you revise your verb conjugations, you take out an orange Starburst, say, then in the exam, you take out an orange Starburst, it will trigger the memory of all the tenses you learned. There, I'm allowed to do a footnote if it's 'sensible and interesting'. That's what I was told. Didn't say it actually had to be true.

'London Chatham and Dover Railway 1864', which still stands there today on the old abutment, alone, magnificently, but pointlessly, as it no longer supports the original railway bridge fifty yards east of Blackfriars Bridge.[11] The railway bridge that Jeremiah saw was a superb piece of engineering, spanning the river, where nowadays stand its eight red supporting pillars, sticking up out of the river, attached to nothing.

'How is your condition?' asked Phyllis. 'You have made it in one piece thus far, so I see no reason for you not to continue.'

'Yeah, I know, but you said there was some kind of cure?'

'There is indeed, and this is it!' Phyllis started off again.

'Ah, that's such a dodge,' said Jeremiah, forced to get up or lose her. 'You were just tricking to get me out of the house...'

As soon as they arrived on the north side of the bridge, the noise and chaos seemed to clear. The roads were wider, and the main sounds were the clop of horses' hooves and the grind of the steel-rimmed wheels of the carriages they were pulling. Phyllis slowed her pace and they walked side by side up the hill, turning left into Bride Lane, past the wedding cake of a church spire, crossing Fleet Street and into Poppin's Court (yes, Poppin's Court, still there now). The busyness of the day fell away with each corner they

---

11 Work started on Blackfriars Bridge in about 1760 and it was opened in 1769. How they managed to drive piles into the bed of the river without heavy pile-drivers, fork-lift trucks or electric diggers is confounding. But perhaps the river didn't flow quite so furiously there before the embankments were built up in the 1860s by Joseph Bazalgette. The embankments were built to house London's first proper sewage system and Bazalgette became known as 'The Sewer King'. His great-great-grandson, Peter Bazalgette, carrying on the family tradition for innovation, brought the reality show *Big Brother* to British television.

took, until they were passing among the grander terraces of Holborn and the gardens at Coram's Fields.

A raggedy girl with a tray of flowers slung around her neck came by, shouting her wares. 'Roses is red, violets is blue, one fer a penny, 'n tuppence fer two…' she cried, 'Give us a shillin', give us a parnd, or 'arl put the 'ole lot of 'em back in the grarnd…' She didn't look healthy and sweet like the flower sellers in the film of *Oliver!*; she looked rancid and weather-beaten, more like one of the rough sleepers you might see in any part of London today. 'Oi, Abercrombie!' she shouted at Jeremiah. 'Wanna buy a lovely flower?'

They turned into Gordon Square. On all four sides of the grassy square, four- and five-storey houses were laid out in terraces. The central square had trees and bushes in it and black-painted railings all the way round, just as nowadays.

'You must explain to me, Jeremiah, why you are wearing a jersey that has the name Abercrombie written on it, when, as you say, your name is Bourne.' Jeremiah tried to explain the concept of designer labels to her.

'So, you pay extra, well over the odds apparently, for an item of ordinary clothing, and then you walk around with the name of the person who hoodwinked you emblazoned on your chest, as if to announce, "I am proud to have been robbed by Mr Abercrombie"?'

'Basically, yes,' said Jeremiah.

'I'm sure my brother Rodger will lend you a proper suit and tie with a stiff collar, for which he has no use any more.' She stopped at number 49 and walked up the stairs to the front door. 'And here we are!' She pulled on a metal handle hanging down to the right of the door like an antique toilet flush. There was a distant muffled clanging and the sound of steps in the hall. 'In fact, as you will find out shortly, my dear brother Rodger no longer has any use for clothes at all! A word of warning: don't stare.'

EIGHT

The large front door swung open slowly to reveal what looked like a ghost, peeking out timidly from behind it. An extremely thin woman in a traditional maid's uniform – white apron and long dark dress – stood motionless and expressionless in the half-light beyond the open front door.

'Ah, Janet dear! Is he in?' Phyllis shouted at her across the threshold. Without uttering a sound, the maid nodded and stood back to let them into the hall, closing the door behind them. From somewhere inside the house came the largest voice Jeremiah had ever heard.

'Halloo Hallay! Do not delay! Janet? Show them into the withdrawing room and do try to smile if we have guests!' The voice was like a trombone at full blast; it had rich, actorly tones to it. It was a voice that could have encouraged nations in the low period after the Second World War. A voice which, if it was your own, would be impossible not to like the sound of.

'Do come this way, Mrs Stokes. Sir Rodger will receive you now,' said Janet in a mousy whisper. As they walked past her, Janet stood up straight and tried to crease her face into the memory of a smile.

Suddenly, Sir Rodger himself was in the hallway with them. The person was as large as the voice. A huge, whiskered man with a beaming smile on his face. He was wearing a small red velvet cap, socks and a pair of crested leather slippers. And that was all. 'There, that didn't hurt, did it? Well done for trying, Janet!' he boomed. 'Ah! Phyllis, my conscience! My jewel! Come!' And he beckoned them into a room at the front of the house. They followed, Jeremiah looking around, anywhere but at Sir Rodger's receding buttocks.

Jeremiah checked his breathing. Perhaps Phyllis was right: he had got this far and technically speaking he was indoors again, not outside. Involuntarily he checked his pocket for his inhaler. He knew it wasn't there. He'd have to do without it.

Sir Rodger's withdrawing room was like an abandoned junk shop; three-legged tables with red tablecloths supported lamps with big embroidered lampshades. There were upholstered chairs with throws over them, a doll's house balanced on a child's chair, a chaise longue that had one leg propped up on books, and every surface cluttered with boxes and books and piles of papers bound in string. There was one big shaft of light coming in from the tall windows, leaving half the room in shadow, the other half dazzlingly bright with dust particles floating through it. In the shadowy half, Jeremiah could just make out an ornate birdcage on a stand, with what appeared to be a parrot perched in it. Although whether alive or stuffed, Jeremiah could not be sure; if alive, the thing was keeping preternaturally still.

'Come in and rest thy pins!' Sir Rodger waved expansively around the room, indicating several possible seats at once. 'And whom do we have here?' he said, peering down at Jeremiah from eyes set deeply under a pair of eyebrows that reminded him of a squirrel's tail.

'Dear Rodge,' said Phyllis, making the introductions, 'this is one Jeremiah Bourne, who has certain supernatural qualities which I suspect will interest.'

'Does he, by gosh? How do you do, Bourne? Rodger Allcott Standish. Magistrate.' Sir Rodger reached out with an enormous hand and shook Jeremiah's in a vigorous and enveloping grip.

'Hi,' said Jeremiah, as casually as he could. 'Are you a nudist or something?'

Phyllis came to his rescue. 'My brother Rodger decided recently to dispense with all clothes so that he could—'

Sir Rodger interrupted her. '—feel the skin touched by the air, soul free of the restrictions of trousers and buttons! I feel I have spent half my life in the doing and undoing of buttons! If I counted up all the time I have spent fiddling with the damn things…'

Janet, the whispering maid, spoke up. There was a hint of disapproval in her voice. 'Would you like tea here in the withdrawing room, Sir Rodger?'

'Aye, say I!' he said, throwing himself into one of the upholstered armchairs, which was a relief to Jeremiah. Janet made a cursory nod and slid out of the room. 'Might get a bit chilly come November, but hey ho, nature's the thing! *Naturalis ante lapsum,* eh? Before the Fall. Eh, Bourne? Sit! Sit!'

Jeremiah didn't know which seat to sit in, so he sat on the nearest piece of furniture he could find – the chaise longue, which swallowed him up like a sea monster; its cushion pad felt like a sponge wafting on the ocean floor. This could do with some work, he thought, and couldn't help himself from making a quick calculation of how many hours such a restoration would take him. Phyllis sat upright on an austere oak chair.

'So do crack on and tell us, while we wait for tea. What "supernatural qualities" do you possess?'

'Sounds impossible, but I've travelled in time, and your sister thinks you might know how I did it…'

'I see, I see,' said Sir Rodger, nodding intensely.

'He appeared out of thin air while our society was holding a séance,' said Phyllis. 'Claims he has arrived from the future, and I am inclined to believe him.'

The quiet of the room was suddenly pierced by a screech. 'Oooo, aaargh! Thinn air, thinn air! Ooo, I belieeve 'im, I belieeve 'im!' The parrot had woken up.

'Be quiet, Dryden, or I shall put your hood over your stand,' snapped Sir Rodger.

The parrot gave a smaller squawk, a half-hearted, resentful apology, and Jeremiah could just make it out, hopping from leg to leg on its perch in the gloom.

'Has your special society thing ever come across anything like this before? And like, how do I get back?'

Sir Rodger coughed and then swallowed, momentarily lost for words. If it hadn't been for his air of confidence, Jeremiah would have said he was out of his depth. Then he turned to his sister. 'So tell me, why would the boy go to all the trouble of transtemporisation, only to appear in the *Women's* Branch of the society? It doesn't make sense.'

'So far, no scientific explanation,' said Phyllis, bristling at the put-down.

All his adult life, Sir Rodger Allcott Standish had been aware of the burden of responsibility on his shoulders. He was an eldest son. He was a Sir. He was a magistrate. People looked to him for a decision. He was supposed to know the answers. He could always come up with a decision, any decision, and push his eyebrows up and down with authority; he didn't have a problem with that. It was understanding what they were talking about that floored him. Since he was a boy, his mind would just go blank if asked a direct question. Still, he was large and had a large voice, and so far, he felt, he'd got away with it. No one had perceived the internal panic.

'It so happens we have an eminent scientist in our midst today: Dr Henry Davenant Hythe,' said Sir Rodger. 'He's in the library, preparing a lecture for the Royal Society. Perhaps he can throw some light.' He strode between some double doors to the back half of the house. Jeremiah pulled himself out of his clam of a chaise longue and followed, as did Phyllis.

They were now in a room with a much higher ceiling than the withdrawing room. It was octagonal and all the walls were covered in books, some neatly behind glass casing, others just rammed any old how onto the shelves. There was a round ceiling window, from which came light dappled by the leaves of what must have been a very sizeable tree outside. Against one wall was a ladder, and at the top of the ladder was a man, leaning into the bookshelf. Sir Rodger stood at the bottom of the ladder and gave it a little shake. The man at the top of the ladder had to grab at the bookcase to steady himself.

'Henry? Come down here, someone I want you to meet,' Sir Rodger called up to him.

From above them came a scratchy, thin voice, with a slightly less posh accent than those of Phyllis and Rodger. 'You have nothing under "Blastocyst" in your library, Rodger.[12] An egregious oversight. And precious little on "Splitting of embryos".'

'Sorry, old boy,' said Sir Rodger, giving the ladder another jerk, 'come down! Chap here says he's from the jolly old future. Says he's from...' He turned to Jeremiah. 'Sorry, when are you from?'

---

12 A blastocyst is the little sac which forms around a fertilised egg for about six days, before attaching to the uterus and going on to become the sac for the embryo. It's handy to know about it in IVF treatment, as it can be freeze-dried for later use. Of course, it's not, strictly speaking, essential to know this; in fact, my editor said, 'People won't want to know all that,' but I thought I'd put it in, in case Ed. is wrong. Which wouldn't be the first time.

'The twenty-first century.'

'Says he's from the twenty-first century. Do come down here and join us, need your expert opinion. Where does science stand on temporal shilly-shallying?'

The man came a few steps down the ladder and scrutinised Jeremiah. 'Time traveller, eh? What are you staring at, boy?'

'Nothing,' said Jeremiah. 'Just kind of relieved you're not all nudists.'

'Ha!' The man cracked a humourless laugh. He was wearing a three-piece suit in a tweedy brown, with a stiff, detachable collar and tie, and had heavy leather toe-capped shoes which looked as if they had served several generations of his forefathers. He was a smaller, thinner man than Sir Rodger, with a moustache that seemed to grow horizontally out from his face. 'No. No naturist, I. Neither am I a vegetarian, nor a Theosophist.'[13] He gave an admonishing look at Sir Rodger, came down to the bottom

---

13 OK, Theosophy. Ed. reckons I don't need to do this one either, but Ed. has been going a bit flaky recently, so just in case, here's a quick résumé. Theosophy was started in 1875 by a Russian émigré, Madame Blavatsky. Theosophists believed there are 'masters' who live in Tibet who have superpowers and want to revive the ancient wisdoms of the East. So what these 'masters' did is set up a society and have a lot of meetings and produce pamphlets. No explanation for why they used meetings and pamphlets as their method of spreading the word. If they had superpowers, they could have used telekinesis, for instance, but there we are. They did stimulate general interest in concepts like reincarnation and karma, and might be responsible for subsequent misunderstanding by the West of all things Hindu or Buddhist.

Telekinesis – now this one, surely everyone does know? But no, evidently not. Perversely, Ed. thinks this is the one that needs explaining. 'Telekinesis is the supposed ability to move objects at a distance by mental power.' There. Perhaps I should have asked for an editor for my editor. I wonder if editors are on zero hours or are salaried employees. Perhaps my normal editor is on 'Annual Leave' and had a sub take over today. Perhaps some old retired person who needs the two days' work a week just to feel vital and alive again. I feel bad now.

of the ladder and continued. 'And nor am I a believer in what is laughingly called the "alternative realm of illusion", like the Allcott Standish siblings here.'

'Unfair, old boy. Low blow,' said Sir Rodger. 'I contend that this young shaver may not conform to your narrow way of thinking.'

'Is it scientifically possible to travel backwards in time?' asked Jeremiah, but the two men carried on as if neither he nor Phyllis were there.

'Since it was in the middle of a séance that the chap appeared,' said Sir Rodger, 'we must admit that he may have been summoned there by forces beyond our knowledge.'

Henry Davenant Hythe let out a derisive snort. 'Not very empirical, Rodger. What's more, I fail to see what good your supposed supernatural phenomena will do in the real world, nor how they will alleviate the suffering of the masses.'

'Hello?' said Jeremiah. 'I thought we were going to try and work out how I got here, not have some philosophical discussion?'

They all stopped to look at him. Phyllis leaned across to Jeremiah and said, quietly, 'Dr Davenant Hythe does a lot of work in the field of eugenics, you know. To help those who are born with less.'

Jeremiah looked at Henry. 'Eugenics? Isn't that the Nazi one?' he said.

Davenant Hythe tutted. 'If we can discover the genetic causes of disease, disability and birth defects, we can create superior, stronger people and a more stable society – free from the unfair inheritance of inferiority.'

'Are you sure? Because I did the Holocaust at GCSE – in fact history was the only good grade I got – and eugenics ended up with six million people being gassed to death.'

'Oh dear,' said Phyllis, 'I'd better write to George Bernard Shaw and warn him. He is a keen eugenicist.'[14]

'GBS wouldn't buy any of these supernatural phenomena, and neither do I,' scoffed Davenant Hythe.

'Yes, Phyllis dear, shall we leave dear GBS out of the equation, just for now?' said Sir Rodger, turning back to Davenant Hythe. 'What about when a thing-me-jig just can't be explained by your scientific rigmaroles?'

Their debate was interrupted by Janet. 'It is three o'clock, Sir Rodger. Tea is served in the withdrawing room. As requested.' She stood in the doorway for a moment, and then disappeared silently into the shadows.

'Thank you, Janet, thank you. Come along, chums, tea!' Sir Rodger strode after Janet. 'Janet? Will you join us for tea?'

The others came through into the shadowy front room, where Janet had cleared a space on a low table and placed a tray with matching cups, saucers, teapot, milk jug and sugar bowl with silver tongs. The whole kit. She was standing in the doorway, looking horrified at Rodger's suggestion that she join them.

'Oh no, sir! I will not! Please don't ever ask such a thing again!' She left, sharply closing the door behind her.

---

14 The socialist writer George Bernard Shaw was indeed an advocate of eugenics and was also a vegetarian and sometime naturist. But actually, it's unlikely that he would have changed his opinion if Phyllis had warned him of the Holocaust. He was quite open about the benefits of exterminating those he called 'Not Fit to Live', by which he meant those unable or unwilling to make a contribution to the 'Socialist State'. 'If people are not fit to live, kill them in a decent way,' he was to write in 1934, and '...to kill them is quite reasonable and very necessary'. In an article published in the *Daily Express* in 1910, where we are now with Henry and Rodger and Phyllis, Shaw wrote, 'A part of Eugenic politics would finally land us in an extensive use of the lethal chamber.' An ominous turn of phrase – and a process which he also described as 'weeding the garden'. And he didn't change his mind decades later, when in 1934 he wrote in *The Listener*, 'I appeal to the chemists to discover a humane gas that will kill instantly.'

NINE

'Did you see that?' said Sir Rodger, sitting back down in his large chair and reaching across to arrange the tea things. 'A few short years ago, a servant would never have spoken out for themselves like that. The human character is changing, Jeremiah, and I for one am all for it! Bravo, Janet! How many sugars?' He managed to be both generous and condescending at the same time.

Jeremiah grew impatient as they went through the process of pouring tea and making sure each had a cup. 'Milk in first?' and 'How many sugars?' said Phyllis, who had taken control of the tray. Jeremiah's foot was beginning to twitch and his knee was tapping up and down involuntarily. 'Jem!' Phyllis scolded, looking down at his leg, which was banging the small side table. He stopped it and took his delicate china cup from her.

The tea was a little thicker than tea is nowadays, but Phyllis had put in a large quantity of raw sugar, so perhaps it was that. Finally, Jeremiah was able to gain their attention enough to go through what had happened to him, step by step. The biscuit tin, the pictures – one of which had seemed to be of Phyllis's séance and the other, unsettling one, of the tall woman with long hair – the whooshing noise. Henry interrupted him when he got to the bit where he had tried to take a picture of it on his phone.

'Just one minute. You attempted to take a photograph using a "phone"? A photograph, on a telephone?' said Henry.

'We haven't had a telephone installed here,' said Sir Rodger, pouring his tea into the saucer to cool it, and then slurping it up. 'I don't think it's a fad that is going to catch on.'

'Yeah, look,' said Jeremiah, taking out his phone, 'it's, like, a phone, but it's got all these other things on it. You know, like music, messages, apps...'

They stopped sipping their tea and were transfixed by the phone, making 'ooh' and 'aah' noises as if they were on a TV cooking show. 'Well, I'll be...' said Sir Rodger.

'Jeremiah! You never showed me this!' said Phyllis, almost indignantly. 'This may be the answer. A black glass!'

'Well, it's black at the moment because it's run out of battery,' said Jeremiah, 'needs a recharge, but normally you can see loads of stuff on it.'

'So you are a Necromancer!' said Sir Rodger. 'This explains a lot.'

Phyllis went on, 'Black glass has been used for centuries, Jeremiah, to see into the past, to talk to the dead.' She and Rodger were excited.

'Yeah, but my phone had nothing to do with that,' said Jeremiah.

'The first black glass we know of was that of Pliny the Elder, Jeremiah,' said Sir Rodger, sitting forward eagerly on his seat. 'You've heard of Pompeii? When the volcano engulfed the city of Pompeii, it covered Pliny the Elder in ash and finished him off, but not before he'd amassed an enormous collection of artefacts from the ancient world, and left them to his nephew, Pliny the Younger. Among his collection was his famous black glass which had reputedly come from ancient Egypt—'

'Yeah, look, thanks for the tea and everything, but—' said Jeremiah, standing up. They ignored him again.

'Have you quite finished with your fanciful hogwash?' said Henry Davenant Hythe. 'Necromancy, séances, ancient wisdom, black glass? Forgive me, Phyllis, all hokum!' He put his teacup and saucer back on the tray. 'Here, boy, give it to me.' He reached out his hand, expecting the phone to be given up instantly. He may have had a slightly less privileged upbringing than the other two, but he was just as arrogant. Jeremiah handed over the phone. Henry held it up and gazed into the screen for quite a few seconds. Then turned back to them without handing the phone back.

'There! I have looked into it, I have gazed into and beyond its mysterious black surface, and no… nothing,' he declared. 'I have not seen my dead grandfather. Neither have I seen William the Conqueror. And nor, most importantly, are any of the hundreds of poor orphans out there one single jot better off. We should be using our scientific abilities to try to improve the lot of the human race, not peering through a looking glass for spiritual gratification.'

But Phyllis was not giving up on the spiritual gratification. She mentioned the famous black glass that had belonged to Dr John Dee, Queen Elizabeth I's chief scientist. 'Scientist? Huh!' spat out Davenant Hythe. 'Alchemist and charlatan more like.'

'Dr John Dee's black glass is on display in the British Museum, Jem; you should go, when you find the time, to have a look at it,' said Phyllis, reverently.

'Look, do you people actually know anything about how I got here?' Jeremiah shouted. 'It wasn't my phone that did it, OK? It just ran out of battery!' There was a small pause while they all stared at him, hurt. He sat back down.

The brief silence was broken by Sir Rodger. 'Why not give it a try, Jeremiah? The black glass "phone"? Eh? Right now. Right here. Look into it deeply and see what happens. Dare you?' For a moment Jeremiah felt he might be in some sort of trap, like in a psychological horror movie. Sir Rodger and the others had gone creepily quiet. Did his phone actually have hidden powers? Was Sir Rodger about to sprout tentacles and transform into a vengeful demon? Henry Davenant Hythe pushed the phone towards Jeremiah in a mocking gesture.

Jeremiah took the phone off him, not actually looking into it. He felt stupid getting spooked by them. 'Like I said, it's more likely to have been the biscuit tin.'

Henry gave a childish laugh. 'I'm sure Rodger can provide us with a biscuit tin, eh, Rodger? Can you oblige?'

'It wasn't just any old biscuit tin, it was a really old one, with those photos in it—'

'And plenty of old photographs here too, eh, Rodge?' sneered Henry again. 'If you like, I can take your "phone", hold onto it myself for a while and conduct some proper scientific experiments on it, to test its so-called psychic power.' He put his hand out again for the phone, trying to look as if he was casually doing Jeremiah a favour, but Jem could sense more desire in him than he was showing. He noticed a slight twitch in Davenant Hythe's right eye.

'No, thanks. I'm good, thanks,' he said, putting the phone back in his pocket. Davenant Hythe withdrew his hand.

After a pause, Sir Rodger spoke up. 'Well, I'm so glad we've thrown some light on the subject – or should I say, some dark on the subject! Black glass? No?' He laughed hugely at his own non-joke, and then slid back into contemplative silence.

Suddenly there was a noise from the front hall: shouting and slamming of doors.

TEN

They could hear Janet's squeaky voice being raised to the level of a fighting street cat, while whoever she was with had more of a low dog-like bark.

'Mrs Jarvis! Please stay!' they could hear Janet plead. 'Don't leave me to manage 'im all by misself!'

The lower voice came back at her, 'I'm done and there's an end to it! I'll go and live with my sister Mavis in Mortlake!' Another door slammed.

Sir Rodger looked embarrassed. There was a timid knock on the door. Janet pushed it open a fraction and spoke from the crack. 'Please, Sir Rodger, sir, Cook is leaving, sir. She said she will not stay in your employ a moment longer unless she may wear a proper cook's uniform and she said she don't like working for a nudie. She packed her case 'n all.'

Sir Rodger sighed a big sigh. 'Oh dear, not again.' He stood up out of his chair, to his full height. 'I am not so good with the emotions of the staff. Well, with emotions per se, really. Would you excuse me a minute?' And he left the room. Janet crept quietly into the room and began to collect the tea things.

'Janet, you may leave them,' said Henry Davenant Hythe, irritated by her presence. But she carried on clearing them away. From outside in the hall Sir Rodger's voice could be heard, pleading with Mrs Jarvis, the cook.

'Cook! Jarvis! Please stay! I cannot manage without you and think of poor Janet all by herself! You may wear whatever uniform you choose!'

'With a starchy apron?'

'With a very starchy apron.'

'All right, but I shall need a proper list of duties and no more… Bohemianisms.'

'Thank you, thank you, thank you, Cook. You shall have whatever you ask. You are a darling.' Sir Rodger came a little way back into the room, his normally red face now a deep hue of purple. 'For the sake of peace in this house, it seems I must retire to the dressing room momentarily to put on some clothes.' And he disappeared again.

There was an uneasy silence which Jeremiah broke. 'And what about that girl I met, Daisy Wallace?' he said to Phyllis. 'She was really distressed. She thought you would do something to help her, but you don't seem that interested.'

Janet dropped a cup, breaking its handle. 'Sorry, sir. Sorry, ma'am,' she said, bending to the floor to pick up the pieces. It seemed to Jeremiah that Janet was going as slowly as possible, so that she could listen in to their talk.

'Daisy? One of the fallen girls?' asked Davenant Hythe. 'I'm afraid women like that, from the lower orders, so often need saving from themselves. Wouldn't you say, Phyllis?' His belief in his own benevolence was unshakeable.

Janet finished putting the crockery on the tray. She headed towards the door with the tray but stopped there and turned back. 'Beggin' pardon, sir, ma'am, but if 'n when they're given a chance, like, women like that can make a decent go of it, I says.' She quickly left, closing the door behind her.

Henry Davenant Hythe burst into laughter. 'Goodness, quite the little Socialist!' he said, winking at Jeremiah. 'What do think of that?' and then to Phyllis: 'Are all the girls from the Quentinbloom establishment as feisty as that?'

Phyllis's back straightened. 'Well, I happen to agree with her,' she said, stiffly.

The door was flung open, and Sir Rodger took a bold step in. He was wearing a rustic costume, with a floppy shirt that had peasant embroidery on it. There were tassels on his trousers and bells on his wrists and ankles. He looked rather like an over-decorated Christmas tree with washing hanging off it.

'I'm afraid I have grown somewhat larger in the short time since I last wore trousers, so this is all I could find to fit. I got it from a Peruvian llama herder while travelling in the Chincha Huaca,' he said. Then, holding out a jacket and trousers and waving them at Jeremiah so that his bells jangled, he continued, 'Now, Jeremiah, would you be interested in inheriting this old tweed suit of mine? From my student days, when I was, ahem, svelte. As you can see, even taken out fully, it would not go around my middle.'

'Er, that's very kind of you, thanks,' said Jeremiah, taking the suit off him, 'but what I really want is to get back to Blackfriars Road, now?'

'So soon?' said Phyllis.

'Look, when it happened, I was in a different time, yes, but in the same place exactly – your meeting room, my basement workshop, right? So, whatever it is didn't move me in space, just time. So, I think I should go back there. Thanks for all your help, and really interesting hearing all the different theories and everything, but—'

Sir Rodger picked up on this. 'So what you're saying is that, were you to succeed in returning to your own time, you should be very careful *where* you make the attempt from,' he said.

'Exactly,' said Phyllis, 'he's right. He might suddenly find himself in the future, for example, standing in the path of an oncoming train.'

'Bunkum!' said Henry.

'Yes, indeed,' said Sir Rodger, 'or buried alive in a block of reinforced concrete.'

'Thanks, guys,' said Jeremiah, 'so now I can go from having a fear of panic attacks, to having actual, real panic. Nice one.' He stood up and started gasping for breath again. 'I need to go home to Blackfriars, now? I mean, like, right now? Thanks for the tea.' He moved towards the door.

'How will you know the way?' asked Phyllis.

'It's OK, I remembered it. I got this really good memory for directions from my mum.'

'No, no, not at this time of the evening! You cannot possibly walk out alone, particularly south of the river! We can order up a carriage whenever you like, I insist,' Sir Rodger said.

'What, like a sort of Uber? Great. How long do you think it'll be?'

'They're very good these days,' said Phyllis, 'he should be here within an hour or two.'

ELEVEN

'Look, I only bumped into Enid on the landing once or twice,' said Dickensian, the oldest member of the Blackfriars Road Residents' Association sub-committee. His round glasses glinted in the flickers of sunlight playing through the plane trees outside. 'I can't remember every little thing she said at every single encounter.'

'Well, try harder!' said Conrad. He was getting frustrated with them all. He adjusted the cuffs on his pale beige shirt.

Dickensian looked across to Toto Chairman for support, but she said nothing. This was now Conrad's gig; her authority here had been 'relaxed down'. Toto Chairman sat back, relieved to have nothing to do with any of it. She shrugged at Dickensian and carried on sucking her mint.

'Enid did a very good job on vitrification ingress on my floor a few years back, if that's any help?' said another committee member, the large-boned woman with very short hair called Ordnari Cervantes, whose earrings clinked noisily on her shoulders. Despite claims from the manufacturers, the vitrification process did not always prove 100 per cent impermeable. Often it absorbed moisture – especially if not maintained properly. A frequent problem here in Blackfriars Road.

'Oh yes, I think I remember that,' said another member, Half-Dante Kwei, a small, balding man, 'but she was unco-operative when it came to the steam doors.' He had tried so many times to get the steam doors fixed, he had forgotten what was wrong with them in the first place.

'The glazier came over in two hours flat!' said Ordnari Cervantes. There was a general murmur of approval. 'Two hours! That's good!'

'Can you recall the glazier's number?' said Dickensian, in his high-pitched drone. 'Two hours is excellent. I always have to wait for days. Toto Chairman? Can we circulate the glazier's number to the whole group afterwards?'

'No! We can't! Can we stick to the point, please!' interjected Conrad. This was nothing like the revolution he'd dreamed of when he was a student. He'd imagined that having a little bit of authority would be sexy and radical, not petty and exhausting. 'Exactly how many years back were these encounters on the landing?' They all fell silent again. Despite having passed their memory exams, some of them with honours, they sat there like dogs who have been taken on a major walk and now just want to chill.

The thing that annoyed Toto Chairman about the Super-Recall investigation was that she'd had to give up her chair. Now she had to sit on an old school bench at the back, while Conrad lounged in her 'Armchair de Régence' at the head of the room. She'd resented that chair for seventeen years; it was her prerogative to resent it if she chose, and she missed both the chair and the resenting of it. And her knees had flared up again. It didn't look as if this intervention from Super-Recall was going to go away any time soon.

Artemesia Plutarch came in quietly and slipped onto the bench at the back, next to Toto Chairman, hoping not to be noticed.

'Ah, there you are,' said Conrad, looking at his wristwatch, 'late again. Do you have a problem you want to share with us?'

'No. Just the dog, you know. Sorry,' mumbled Artemesia.

'Your dog is a problem you'd like to share?'

'Well, no, obviously,' Artemesia gave a half-laugh, 'unless anyone likes picking up poo in cardboard scoopers.'

'Is there a problem with our cardboard scoopers?' asked Conrad. He was not a man who got a joke easily, in fact he might be described as joke-lexic.

'Can I just mention the new sound-proofing in the lobby?' said Half-Dante Kwei. 'Does anyone else find it still too echoey?' There was a murmur of agreements and disagreements.

'No. You cannot,' said Conrad, trying to keep hold of his agenda. Toto Chairman snorted a laugh. 'Yes? Toto Chairman? Do you have anything to say about the sound-proofing in the lobby? Or may we carry on with matters under review?'

Toto Chairman shrugged as if to say, 'You're in charge, mate, you do what you want.' What she actually said was: 'Apols, Conrad-ji. Mucho apols. Carry on.'

Conrad gave a disapproving sigh and looked around the room at all the bored faces. It had been so much more fun in the year of the student sit-ins, when he could make a rousing, angry speech about the iniquities of digital dependency denial that no one would dare disagree with, and then not have to actually fix anything.

He went on, 'So. Can we all now put our minds to item two? It appears that there's a boy.'

Artemesia winced. She'd hoped it wouldn't come to this. She looked at the floor.

'It seems he has acquired some kind of Recall – illegally – and he's running wild.'

'A boy? What kind of a boy?' said Ordnari Cervantes.

'A local boy, obviously, so it concerns us all.' Conrad looked hard at each of them individually for signs of discomfort, such as looking at the floor.

'And when is he meant to be from?' There were mutterings of incomprehension.

'We're not sure. He keeps jumping about. We don't know when he's from. And it's possible that neither does he.'

'How do we know he actually exists?' asked Dickensian, always ready for a conspiracy theory. 'Do we know who it was that saw him? Did they actually *see* him?'

'It's reliable,' said Conrad, 'there's been reported sightings in the early twenty-first, and early twentieth.'

There were some impressed mumbles from the meeting.

'Now, Super-Recall are keen to get hold of anything we have on him. Sightings, anomalies...'

'Has he been trained?' asked Faraday Tang, an elegant woman with large teeth. She was the quietest member of the sub-committee. She unfolded the woollen collar up around her neck. It was getting colder. The leaves on the plane trees above their heads would soon be drying up and browning.

'Don't see how he could be travelling without being trained,' said Beatlejohn Basho. He was the youngest member of the sub-committee and was put out. The thought of someone younger than him jumping about in time, with no qualifications, made him cross.

'Did this boy put in the sound-proofing in the lobby? I don't understand,' said Half-Dante Kwei, who was often a sentence or two behind.

'Artemesia Plutarch?' said Conrad. The floor had not conceded to Artemesia's desire to be swallowed up by it. 'Do you have any light to throw on this?' Eyes turned to Artemesia. She would have to say something.

'Well...' She paused, grabbing at anything she could think of. 'He's... he's just young, you know... so...' She hoped this would suffice.

'So, you know him?' Conrad lasered her.

'No, no,' Artemesia added quickly, 'it's just, you said he was a boy, so, I assumed...'

'So, is anyone covering this?' said Toto Chairman, partly to take pressure off Artemesia; she'd always had a soft spot for her. It was the first contribution she'd made to the meeting and the members were so used to her voice being the decisive authority in the room that they were silenced and looked expectantly to Conrad for an answer.

'Yes. Of course,' said Conrad, after a pause. 'The report has come from one of our world-beating retrievers, who is on the case right now. Someone with experience in both of those eras and an unbeaten record. Perhaps you've heard of her? Dr Mandar Vergeelis.'

Who else? thought Artemesia. Mandar Vergeelis, smarty-knickers. Winner of three Disruptor of the Year Awards in a row.

'I still don't see what this boy has to do with the echo in the lobby. I think it may be caused by the steam doors,' opined Half-Dante Kwei. 'Wasn't that what we were all supposed to be here to discuss?' He was shouted down by all in a general melee and the meeting of the Blackfriars Road Residents' Association sub-committee for Recall and Maintenance lumbered forward to its inevitable tea break.

'Hello, who is that?' A voice on the end of the phone was met with silence. 'How did you get this number?' More silence. 'Is that you? Pete?'

'No, it's me, your loving sister, you pillock.' Artemesia's voice was muffled, as if she were cupping the handset.

'Archie? Is that really you, my love?'

'Who else is it going to be? So look, I've come all this way back to warn you...'

'What are you doing on Pete's phone? Are you with Pete?'

'No, 'course not. I've just come back so I can use his mobile phone. He doesn't know. You haven't exactly made getting in touch easy, you know. Where are you?'

'Where are *you*?'

'In the bloody basement in 2019, that's where I am and I've only got two minutes. So listen—'

'Have you seen Jem? What's he up to these days? Is he OK?'

'What, like you care all of a sudden?'

'How could you say that! I'm only doing what's best for him—'

'Look, I'm in deep doggie-doo as it is, so listen—'

'I do care about him, you know.'

'Yeah, sure you do, whatever. Listen, they're onto you again. They know roughly when you are now. And they know about Jem.'

'What? How?'

'I don't know. But they've put Mandy the Virgin on it now, so watch out. She's good. And Jem's been stumbling around doing a bit of the old Time Warp Shuffle himself, so—'

'What? How's that possible?'

'Don't ask me, he's *your* beloved offspring. You know any early Nineteen Hundreds?'

'No.'

'Nor me. But that's where he is. You're gonna have to do some revision.'

'How in God's name did he get there?'

'Gotta go, Een. Look after yourself.'

'Hang on—'

'No, really can't stay. Be seein' yer.'

Artemesia tossed Stepdad Pete's mobile onto the half-upholstered armchair and, with a quick fizzing sound and a rush of air, remembered herself back to where Scoobeedoo was waiting for her: tied up to the railings outside, in the basement bay of the house. She undid his lead and they nipped up the outside stairs to the front door. 'Sorry, Scoob. I'll make it up to you tomorrow with a proper walk in Little Dorrit Park.' She pushed against the malfunctioning steam door with her shoulder – it worked if you knew exactly where to shove – and they sauntered into the lobby as if they'd just been out for an evening stroll. There were a couple of lads hanging out by the row of drinks dispensers in the front hall, but Artemesia and Scoobeedoo walked past them unnoticed and up the glass stairs to home.

TWELVE

So, there's nothing very intrepid about time travelling, thought Jeremiah, as he looked out of the window of the very bumpy carriage into an almost black London night. Phyllis had nodded off on the seat next to him. They were squeaking and heaving their way back south of the river and, beyond the window as they crossed Blackfriars Bridge, the water glistened like an oil slick. They passed the 'London Chatham and Dover Railway 1864' insignia, whose colours had homogenised into a dull browny-purple in the darkness. Time travel is not even travelling as such, he thought, because you don't go anywhere. You stay exactly where you are – but backwards. He wondered, if he ever did get back to 2019, whether it would be like those kids' books and comics, where you can go away for years, but no time has passed when you get back. Was he going to grow old here, and then somehow one day suddenly find himself back in Stepdad Pete's workshop, wire-woolling that same chair, with Ruby messing with his mobile? It didn't feel like that; it felt as if, minute by minute, second by second, time was just passing normally, irrevocably.

When they arrived back at Blackfriars Road, Phyllis woke up with a jolt and within a second was fired up, fully charged, issuing orders and making demands. 'I will leave a note for Clementina and Mr Grout, explaining your presence. We have a guest!' Telling the coach man to wait for her, she unlocked the basement. It was freezing in there. She knelt down and filled the cast-iron stove with wood from the pile, lighting it with a long match from a box on the side.[15]

Jeremiah was glad to be back, although it was not exactly welcoming. Phyllis had offered to stay with him, but he'd turned her down. Now that he saw the dark cavernous space with all its stacked chairs, he half wished he'd accepted, but he was too proud to change his mind and ask. Phyllis showed him how to work the oil light. It cast a yellow canopy of dingy light, leaving the outer edges of the room fuzzy and mysterious.

They'd asked Janet to prepare a wrapped cloth of biscuits for him, which he was grateful for. Phyllis found some bedding in a cabinet drawer and helped him make up a bed on one of the old benches. He wondered to himself if the bench was still around today, somewhere. Probably been repainted a hundred times and sitting in some hipster café in Shoreditch.

'Now, you are quite comfortable? And you are no longer nervous?' Phyllis said from the door. 'You will be able to get a good night's sleep here.'

It was true, his anxiety level was strangely low and he could feel an envelope of sleep closing on him.

---

15 It doesn't take a huge amount of imagination to get a feel of what breathing would have been like in London when domestic wood stoves were the norm. The smell sticks to your clothes and skin for days, like a zombie, or what I imagine a zombie would smell like. In fact it's been discovered recently that, even in the twenty-first century, when users of wood-burning stoves have dwindled to just a few odiferous style victims, domestic wood burners are causing more 'small particle' pollution than car traffic. Only the trendiest 8 per cent of the population use them any more, and, despite their claims that wood burners will enhance your mindfulness, decrease your carbon footprint and impress your dinner guests, it seems domestic wood stoves are responsible for 38 per cent of the low micron, small particles in the air – the stuff that gets in our lungs and blood.

'I put a few drops of laudanum[16] in your tea earlier, which should smooth the path to the nether world,' she said, gathering up her things and pinning her hat with its feather back on.

'You mean you drugged me?'

'Oh yes. I sometimes slip a few knockout drops into Rodger's brandy when he is becoming overexcited and noisy. Always works wonders.'

As she was leaving, she said, 'If you do succeed in getting home, remember to come back to us here, and bring some proof, so that we can convince Henry.' Then she was gone, and he was alone with his thoughts.

The biscuits didn't last long after she'd gone and he sat there in the half-light, trying to keep his eyelids from dropping shut. Around him were the ghostly shapes of antique chairs, the table, an antique desk and, barely visible in the corner, the candelabra. So this is what it feels like to be an antique, he thought, waiting around for someone to sit on you, freezing cold and it smells like my primary school.

The official definition of an antique is 'something desirable because of its age'. And that has to be 'at least one hundred years old'. There are loads of reproductions and fakes around, of course, and category errors: things

---

16 Laudanum is basically opium. It was freely available in chemists without prescription until well into the twentieth century and very widely used, including dosing children and animals with it. Farmers would go into the apothecary for 'a h'a'porth of stuff' and then go back to their fields, out of their heads, and fall asleep on their hoes. It was sold in a solution with alcohol, so there is a small question mark over the florid withdrawal symptoms described by Thomas De Quincey in his *Confessions of an English Opium-Eater.* Was he, in fact, unknowingly describing alcohol withdrawal hallucinations? Likewise Samuel Taylor Coleridge and his poem *Kubla Khan,* which is assumed to be about a laudanum addict's visionary dream, but which might have had more to do with the booze he was getting through – a few bottles of claret a night, it is thought.

that have been cobbled together out of other old bits of furniture – like the carved legs of one piece stuck on a completely different piece. I wonder if that's what I am? he thought, as he curled up under the blankets and an opiate sleep crept all over him. Like I'm one of those cobbled-together bits of furniture; the legs from one time and place and the brain from another. Maybe there are bits of me that are a hundred years old. I'm a category error.

He was with his mum, they were coming away from karate club, she was picking him up in her taxi as she always did. The taxi was parked a few yards away and they were walking towards it along the street, hand in hand. But as they got to the car door, suddenly a cold fear tightened his mum's grip and she walked straight past the vehicle, pulling him with her, as if her taxi had nothing to do with her. Then she let his hand drop from hers and told him to walk home on his own, as if he also had nothing to do with her. When he asked what was happening, she told him not to look behind. But of course, he did. There was a woman following them; it was the woman with long hair from the photo in the biscuit tin. Then Mum nipped across the road at a trot and disappeared, weaving her way into the crowd. The woman with the long hair followed her; her long hair was an auburn red. He felt the immediate jolt of an existential fear; nine years old and suddenly alone on a crowded London street, frightened and angry that his mum had let him down. What about Mum's taxi? Our taxi? He left it there and tried to run, but the air was like glue and the ground seemed to recede under his feet.

He woke suddenly as if from the bottom of a deep well. A noise had startled him in his sleep. The oil lamp was still giving off a dull yellow glow.

There was the noise again. A clanking of keys in the outside basement door, a chinkling of chains and a sliding of bolts. Jeremiah was immediately awake. It was still night, so he didn't think it could be Phyllis already.

'Hello? Who's there?' he called in a shaky voice.

The door swung open and in two strides Mr Grout was in the room and had grabbed Jeremiah by the neck. 'Gertcha! Gertcha, yer little runt! Not lettin' yez off so lightly this time!' He hauled Jeremiah up to a sitting position. Jeremiah could only splutter and grunt. 'You're comin' with me, laddio, 'n I want to know all about it!'

'I've got a letter from Mrs Stokesss…?' Jeremiah managed to squeak through his clenched jaw.

'Trousers,' growled Mr Grout, nose to nose.

'Trousers?'

'Put 'em on!' Mr Grout had grabbed the tweed trousers that came from Sir Rodger and thrust them in Jeremiah's face. 'And sharp about it!' He threw Jeremiah down and stood over him with the trousers. Jeremiah figured it was best to put the trousers on; he'd been sleeping in his pants. He slid the trousers up past his knees as quickly as he could. The material was unbelievably scratchy; he'd never felt anything like it.

'There's a letter to you from Mrs Stokes—' he tried again, but Mr Grout gave him a cuff across the top of the head which set him off balance with the trousers still not done up. He hopped away and sat on the bench to finish.

'Will you stop hitting me!' he said, as assertively as he could.

'Ar'll stop whacking yez on yer bonce, matey, when you tell me the names of all yer confederates and scoundrels in yer gang. 'N we can round up the lot of yer.'

'I'm not who you think I am, you know, Mr Grout,' said Jeremiah, having trouble with the buttons on the flies of the trousers, which were stiff. Mr Grout whacked him on the head again, which made the job more difficult.

'Oh really. And who d'yer think I think yez are, then? Johnny Gerrin? Kid McKoy?'

'Who? Look, I've no idea who they are,' said Jeremiah, then, 'There. I put the trousers on. Now, over there, somewhere, is a letter from Mrs—' Mr Grout smacked him again.

'Right! You're comin' wiv me, matey boy!' said Grout, grabbing hold of him.

Jeremiah pulled back long enough to snatch the contents of his jeans pockets and shove them into the long tweed pockets, which seemed to go all the way down to his knees.

Holding Jeremiah's shoulder, Mr Grout made him put on his shoes and then, with a fierce pincer grip on the elbow, propelled him towards the door. 'How d'yer get in 'ere anyhows, yer layabout?' he said, as he reached for the door with his other hand and swung it open.

'I told you. Mrs Stokes said I could stay. Ow!' Another whack.

Somehow Mr Grout managed to drag him out into the under-stairs area, lock the door behind them and bundle him up the steps onto the pavement without letting go his grip of Jeremiah's elbow.

'Yez one o' them Elephant Boys, incher? From round the back of the Elephant and Castle. Or one o' the Forty Thieves, one or th'other!'

'I don't even know who they are, I've never heard of them, and can you stop spitting in my face?!' said Jeremiah.

Mr Grout stopped on the pavement and pointed to the railings along the front of the house. 'See this? This chink 'ere in the railings? That's pistol shot, that is! Pistol shot. Poor Miss Quentinbloom nearly got caught in the crossfire last month. Well, let me tell yer this, smiler. We're not 'avin' it no more. Understan'? You gang boys 'n girls, fightin' it out on our street.'

There were a couple of gashes in the railings, it was true. Jeremiah made a mental note to check if they were still there nowadays, painted over, if he ever got back. Mr Grout dragged him along towards the house next door. Where, waiting by the steps to the basement of the next-door house, was a squat, round woman in a long and frayed skirt.

'Yer got 'im, Mr Grout! Yer got 'im!' Her voice sounded as if it was being pulled through a tin can full of gravel.

'I got 'im, Mrs Grout.'

'Ar'll 'old the door for yez,' she growled. If anything, her voice was even deeper and rustier than Mr Grout's. 'Bring 'im darn 'ere 'n we can shove 'im in the coal 'ouse.'

'Yeah, we can shove 'im in the coal 'ouse, like I said,' said Mr Grout, struggling to shunt Jeremiah down the steps. Mrs Grout bobbed down the stairs in front of them, unlocked a door in the basement area and held it open. There was a lamp over the door into the basement and Jeremiah caught sight of Mrs Grout's face as she swung open the coal-cupboard door. It was a big, round, crumpled face with the most turned-down frown he'd ever seen. Her skin was creased like the top of a crusted loaf. You could hardly see her eyes.

'It's not me!' he shouted, in a last vain attempt not to be locked in the coal cupboard. 'You've got the wrong guy. Help!'

'Give 'im a while to consider 'is wrongs,' said Mrs Grout, 'and come up wiv some names.'

'Right. Goin' ta give yer a while to consider yer wrongs, and come up wiv some names,' said Mr Grout, throwing Jeremiah down on the floor inside the cupboard. Mr and Mrs Grout stood in the doorway above him blocking the entrance.

'Yeah. Yer can stew 'ere 'n contemplate yer fate till then,' said Mrs Grout.

'Until then, yer can stew, like I said,' said Mr Grout.

'Hard labour. Four years, thass what you'se lookin' at,' said Mrs Grout.

'All right, Mrs G. I'll take care o' this,' said Mr Grout, and then, 'Hard labour. Four years, that's what you'se lookin' at.'

'I hope yer find the accommodations suitably uncomfortable,' said Mrs Grout and gave a short exhalation that may have been a laugh. 'Right yez are, Mr G. Come along!' And the Grouts left, slamming the coal cupboard door behind them and locking it noisily.

Jeremiah shouted after them, 'You got the wrong guy, please!' But it was no use. He slumped down on the floor; it was cold and damp and covered in sand. Not coal, at least that was something. He was in a basement box room, under the pavement, with one tiny window with bars on it in the corner of the ceiling. And he was wearing a pair of trousers that felt like sandpaper. Great. Fantastic. He was just thinking – What happens when I need a wee... when there was another jangling of padlocks and the door was opened a fraction. Mrs Grout's voice came through the crack. 'And 'ere's a chamber pottie if you needs to go. No doingses, mind. Let me know when yerv bin.' She shoved an old china chamberpot with a broken handle through the door at floor level, and then shut the door with more chain and padlock jangling. The pot was cracked and yellow around the edges and smelt of something more like a dead animal than urine.

'Thank you, I suppose,' Jeremiah called after her.

THIRTEEN

If sitting on the floor of a cold, damp cell for hours with a wet bum is a form of Zen meditation, Jeremiah felt, he should be a Master. But this didn't feel like nirvana. His thoughts were running wildly. How had this happened? What was the date? Not 21 October; that's the date Marty McFly travels in time in *Back to the Future.* There had been no Tardis to take him into another dimension, no Platform 9 ¾. Just ordinary life, going on as before, except, a very long time before. Then he thought – If I do get back to 2019, and then come back in time again to here, would there be another Jeremiah in this little cupboard prison? What if they both came back to nowadays? What if there was a Jeremiah living my life nowadays – like I've split in two and nobody will even know that I've gone?

The laudanum must have worn off, because, unable to sleep, unable to think clearly, his ranging thoughts kept him semi-conscious for hours. Until there were noises from the other side of the door. The scraping of furniture on a stone floor, the chatter of children and a few muffled shouts: 'Oi! Jolly! Samuel! 'Op it! And James, finish yer porridge!' Mrs Grout's voice. It must be morning; he must, somehow, have slept. There was a jangling of chains and the door creaked open about six inches and Mrs Grout's face filled the gap.

'Some porridge left over. Yer swear on the Bible to behave, yer can 'ave it.' A few other faces crowded in behind her, children of all ages, some by her knees, some leaning above her. 'Ain' 'e got funny 'air,' said one. 'Looks like a puppy dog,' said another. Mrs Grout shushed them with a grunt and a severe look back over her shoulder.

'Yeah. All right. Thanks. I swear. To behave, I mean,' said Jeremiah, suddenly realising how hungry he was. A bowl with a wooden spoon in it was pushed across the floor to him, all eyes staying on him as he bent to pick it up and take a mouthful. The grey gunk in the bowl was thick and lumpy. The taste of it never got to the back of his mouth; its mere smell, as he brought the spoon to his lips, was enough to make him retch. It was foul. Not Tesco's Finest muesli mix by a long way. More like some kind of stew made from chopped-up trainer insoles.

'Urrghlch!' he said, unable to do this politely. 'You wouldn't have any toast, would you?'

The children around Mrs Grout giggled and chattered: 'Oooh, toast!' 'What's toast?' and 'Can *we* have toast?' Mrs Grout gave another blunt noise to shut them up.

Jeremiah tried again. 'I mean, thanks very much and everything. Mrs Grout, ma'am. Madam...' He ran out of things to say. The children exploded into laughter at 'madam' and were swiped at by Mrs Grout.

'Shut it, you lot, 'n back to work. Dolly, Tess, stop starin'. 'S only a man!' As she reached for the chain to lock him back in, other voices were heard.

'He's in 'ere, Miss Quentinbloom, ma'am.' It was Mr Grout, and behind him, Clementina from next door. Mrs Grout opened the door wide enough to let them both look down on Jeremiah. Instinctively, he stood up.

'Oi, you! Get up!' said Mr Grout, too late to assert his authority. 'Yer got a visitor!'

'Yes, thank you, Mr Grout. And good morning, Mrs Grout.'

'Morning, ma'am.' Mrs Grout gave an ungainly curtsey.

Clementina Quentinbloom had adopted a severe, school-marm manner early on in life, as a way of coping with expectations and assumptions that were made of her as a woman. She'd decided as a teenager that – rather than seek out a suitable husband as her peer group had, and lead the normal life acceptable to society: wife, mother, caterer, with a nice sideline in embroidering cushion covers – she would go out in the world and do good. She'd nursed her mother before she died, so she'd missed the best marriageable years anyway. Not that she was what we would call, by modern standards, old. But being a single woman in her mid-thirties meant that she was now considered past it, and would have to be a governess or teacher. Or go to India to try to find some poor, sex-starved civil servant and run his estate while he drank himself to oblivion in the heat. No, here in the poorer areas of London was the place where a woman could have the most impact and feel that she was saving souls. And there were enough around here who needed saving, particularly the girls, who were like lost, sodden fledglings before Clementina took them in, fed them, gave them discipline and duties and a start in life. Just as there would forever be a plentiful supply of the unwanted and unwashed, she thought, so would the demand for domestic servants to the middle classes never dry up. But to maintain her position she had to appear strict.

She looked Jeremiah up and down without saying a word and without allowing her face to give away any sign of thought or feeling. The power of silence to unnerve an opponent was a useful tool she had practised on the girls for years. 'Yes, Mr Grout. This is the man who intruded on our sanctuary,' she finally said, after a long, penetrating pause. 'Better dressed than yesterday, but without doubt this is he.'

Jeremiah was indeed thoroughly unnerved. It worked. 'OK, look, I know it must seem suspicious to you, but I'm not part of a gang or anything,' he stammered. 'My name's Jeremiah Bourne, and, and…' he searched for something he could say to win her over, '…the only person I know round here is Phyllis Stokes, and she wrote me a letter, which you'll find in her basement, saying it was OK for me to stay there.'

'Really,' said Clementina. It was not a question.

'Yes, really. And she's got a brother, Rodger. He's a magistrate, Rodger All-something Something? And they've got a friend, Dr Henry…' He was so rattled that his normal powers of recall had abandoned him. He petered out into lame muttering under her gaze.

'Those are the names on the Theosophical Society noticeboard outside this house. Well done, my lad. So at least you can read.'

Mr Grout took out a piece of paper from his pocket – presumably Phyllis's letter – and tore it into four pieces, then scrumpled the pieces and put them back in his pocket. He then laughed as if Clementina had cracked a great joke. She looked swiftly across to him and he stopped instantly.

Jeremiah searched desperately for something to alleviate the situation. 'Daisy!' he said. 'Daisy Wallace! That's another name for you!' Clementina instantly froze on him.

'Which one's Daisy Wallace?' Mr Grout looked at Clementina.

'She's the black girl with the glasses,' said Jeremiah.

'She is the dark-skinned girl, the one who lost the spectacles we gave her, Mr Grout,' said Clementina, 'so we had to get her a second pair. And what is your business with Daisy Wallace?' she shot at Jeremiah, keeping very still.

Jeremiah blurted out the only thing he could thing of. 'Nothing really. Just… she's pregnant and she wants to keep the child…' The moment he said it, he knew it was a mistake. Idiot. He was just trying to get himself out of trouble, like a coward. He wished he could go back in time, if only a couple of minutes, to the moment just before he'd said it. But it was out there now.

There was a long smooth intake of breath from Clementina and then, surprisingly, she lost her poise. 'How dare she? Go behind my back! Little Daisy! After all the efforts I have made on her behalf!' Her face flushed red and furious. 'Mr Grout, I suggest you lock up this no-good fellow until further notice. And I shall go immediately and have words with the young lady in question!' She turned and left, more hurt than offended.

The Grouts moved in on Jeremiah. 'You're a very unlucky man. A very unlucky man indeed,' said Mrs Grout. Mr Grout was breathing in Jeremiah's face again. Jeremiah winced.

'You're doing that breathing in my face thing again,' he said.

Mrs Grout moved in from behind and stuck her face in between them. ''E can breve as 'n where 'e wants.'

'Exactly. I can breve as 'n where I wants.'

''E could crack yer 'ead open like an egg for 'is breakfast if 'e wanted. Wiv this bit o' wood 'ere.' She passed Mr Grout his knobbled stick, which had been standing in the doorway.

'Thank you, Mrs Grout. I'll take care o' this one,' he said, glaring aggressively in Jeremiah's face all the while. 'See, I could crack yer 'ead open like an egg for my breakfast, but I choose not to. I choose…' he grabbed Jeremiah's neck and pushed him back into the coal cupboard, 'to eat my breakfast all calm and peaceful like, with bread 'n drippin' soldiers for dippy dip. D'you 'ear me?'

'Yes, of course,' said Jeremiah, 'hard not to, when you stand so close.' The constant bullying and pushing had wound him up into a state of not caring any more.

'Those are my girls to protect, d'you understand?' Mr Grout snarled at Jeremiah.

'Yes, yes, whatever you say,' said Jeremiah through his tightened throat.

'Mrs Grout? Lock 'im up!' said Mr Grout dramatically, dropping Jeremiah back onto the floor and striding towards the door.

'Right y'are, Mr Grout,' she said, reaching for the chains and keys hanging from her belt, 'but we ain' got no drippin'.' And then, when the door was closed on him, Jeremiah heard her say, ''Ain' got no bread neither.'

FOURTEEN

If you've lost everything – your family photos, your passwords and accounts, your ID documents, your music playlists – then the fact that so has everyone else might bring about a new sense of community in you. Either that, or a new licence for your inner criminal.

When information is digitised and becomes a stream of data, its value – not its financial value, but its usefulness, its emotional significance – can become equalised. Like an orchestra recorded with audio-compression software, each instrument has the same rating. When everything is reduced to a series of binary indices, who is to tell the difference in intensity between the speeches of Barack Obama and the specifications of the nine different kinds of non-stick oven trays available?

When presented with the raw digitised data, how would you tell the difference in emotion between, say, *Love Island* and the love letters of Hitler and Eva Braun? Between the score of Handel's *Messiah* and the football league scores for 1962?

OK, I'm overdoing the point here, but it's important to see that although information is power, too much information is a headache. So what we do is tend to rely on opinion. The opinions of other people who will undoubtedly have an agenda. People do.

If your job was in Super-Recall and Retrieve – like a content monitor in one of the big tech giants nowadays –

you would get to make value judgements. Which piece of history, of science, of human knowledge would be worth going back there to get, now that all of it had been wiped? What to recall, what to retrieve? What could you get away with and, most importantly, what's going to get you promoted, while your colleagues and competitors dwindle?

Dr Mandar Vergeelis, soon to be Professor Dr Mandar Vergeelis, had chosen twentieth-century innovations as her specialist subject and had written her A-starred thesis on 'Things that went wrong in twentieth-century thinking'. She had a lot of material. She covered the period from about 1880 to 2020, what's called the 'long twentieth century'. This had qualified her initially for a position in the Breach department at Super-Recall and Retrieve, from where she'd graduated to Data Harvesting, both basically office jobs in the old County Hall building, beside the Thames at the south side of Westminster Bridge, near the rice paddies at Vauxhall. Occasionally the monotony of the days was brightened by breach hearings, which took place in the circular debating chamber on the ground floor, in which those who had breached were sent back into Refreeze, which might mean a year or two's Tralezepam, or 'Trallypaz', sentence. However brilliant your recall, it could always be blunted by enforced, regular doses of benzodiazepines, which obliterate memory. Like a sort of Rohypnol house arrest.

Laboratory chemistry was one thing that had not vanished in the data loss. Chemistry like it used to be, bubbling test tubes and round-bottomed beakers, had thrived since the DigiMelts. Remembering the Periodic Table was the first qualification for entering primary school at age five and separated the likely 'Recallers' from the 'Can't be arseds' into streams that would brand them for the rest of their lives.

If they pushed the right buttons and knew the right people, particularly high achievers from Data Harvesting were sometimes sent on Research and Retrieve missions. Basically, field work where you could act on your own initiative and form your own opinions as to what, in the past, had value. And this is where Dr Vergeelis saw opportunity.

Since the abolishing of the Greater London Council in 1986, the sprawl of buildings at County Hall have gone through a humiliating turn-around of new usages, all taking place in one or other vast-ceilinged room at the end of winding corridors: an aquarium, two Japanese restaurants, flats, a patisserie, a gym, a swimming pool, a luxury hotel, a not-so-luxury hotel, a cinema museum, film-production offices and, in the former debating chamber, a theatre. An ideal space for courtroom dramas, the massive debating chamber is circular and has a tall wooden throne at one side. The bench seats are like parliamentary pews; the acoustic is terrible.

Mandar Vergeelis's fascination with breach hearings began when she was a student. She liked to go in there on her breaks to hear the new cases, perhaps on the off-chance of something coming up that might be useful to her later on, or perhaps because she just liked seeing people being punished. She found it soothing to see the dignity, or lack of it, with which they received their sentences. She took her sandwiches in with her – you were allowed to – and helped herself to a cup of tea from the urn. Her favourite judge was O'Devius Grimkandy, a hard bastard whose specialist subject as a Recall student had been 'Hanging Judge Jeffreys', the English Civil War judge responsible for sending over 250 people to the gallows.

She sat in the upper back row and focused on the ongoing case of a woman who had done a runner rather than finish a Trallypaz sentence. Although this woman was a super-memoriser, she hadn't even bothered to qualify; she was a drop-out. Applying for Super-Recall and Retrieve was a privilege that had to be earned and was not to be abused, but this renegade had squandered her talent, ignored her responsibilities and done, basically, whatever she felt like. She'd disappeared a few years ago, and Mandar Vergeelis, listening carefully to each detail and filing it away in a locked cabinet in her mind, never sharing information, never chatting idly, now had a pretty good idea of when to find her.

Mandar knew she would need something big if she was to get to the top, not just of Data Harvesting but of Super-Recall itself; that's where the real decisions were made. The runaway woman wasn't big, but she might lead to something big.

If Mandar could bring back that something – something from her prize-winning thesis on what went wrong in the twentieth century, perhaps – then she would never have to bother with breach hearings, or departments, or feedback reports ever again. She could be her own department; she could change the course of history.

FIFTEEN

There's a long and honourable history of really bad ideas that caught on, and a lesser list of good ones that didn't. In the bad-ideas-that-inexplicably-got-taken-up corner sit things such as: cutting down all the trees on Easter Island to make the big statue heads, so the entire population had to vacate the island for want of an ecosystem. Right up next to that sits the Xhosa prophet who had the brilliant idea that the Xhosa should kill all of their cattle to bring about a resurrection of her people – the cattle were duly slaughtered, and by 1857 upwards of 50,000 Xhosa died of starvation. Of course, there are plenty of bad ideas that do almost catch on, but are thankfully prevented from coming to fruition due to complete incompetence in their execution; the CIA score particularly highly in this category. Not to be confused with the recent 'Birds Aren't Real' prank: the CIA's 1956 attempt to kill all the birds in America and replace them with flying robot spy-cameras happily never got off the ground. And nor did their attempt to assassinate Fidel Castro by poisoning his socks.

In fact, it's amazing that any kind of scientific progress is ever made. When you consider that in around 60 BCE, Lucretius wrote, in his poem *On the Nature of Things*, a complete and accurate description of the atom, its nucleus with electrons revolving around it, as well as explaining how the planets revolve around the sun. But would they listen?

Of course not. People seem to have a homing instinct for bad ideas and just get bored with the really good ones.

But leaps and bounds forward in knowledge and its application do happen, sometimes in very quick succession, or even at the same time. You can wait around for centuries for an innovation and then, like the proverbial number 9 bus, or sugar-free drinks, two or three come along at once, all in the same year. Almost as if the new idea is sitting there in the ether, waiting for human beings to recognise it. Perhaps it's morphic resonance again.

The years after Jeremiah's mum disappeared were particularly good years, for example. Or to be more accurate, the time between 2014 and 2016. There were advances in Higgs boson particle physics, retroviral drugs for HIV and Ebola, and DNA discoveries which showed what colour dinosaurs were. But the ideas which perhaps people didn't realise at the time would catch on quite as much as they were to later, were in the field of cryogenics. Freezing things. The UK was particularly strong here. Scientists in Oxfordshire working with liquid xenon managed to cool wind turbines, make advances in MRI scanning and wipe out most of the nasty campylobacter gut infections with something called 'rapid surface chilling', which sounds rather nice, actually. But not all freezing requires cold temperatures. Vitrification, as mentioned before, is where liquids and gases are solidified and preserved without using ice. And it may seem as if I'm wandering off the point here – having left Jeremiah sitting miserably in his coal cupboard in 1910 – to hold forth on ultra-fast cooling rates and cryo-preservation, but the reason for this side-track is that there are certain years which might be of more interest than others to people who want to gain, or gather, knowledge. Particularly knowledge that may have subsequently been lost in some massive data-drain-type disaster, or meltdown, for example. And those people might go a long way to get that knowledge, to harvest it, if you like. Like police on the trail of a cold case. And so, if for whatever personal reasons of your own – such as having a child illegally with someone from another century, for instance – you didn't want to be found by those 'harvesting police', you might want to make yourself scarce at such times.

If Jeremiah's mother had taught him how to remember the code for making genome edits (via CRISPR-Cas9,[17] another 2015 triumph from Oxford) instead of how to get from Campden Hill Square to Highgate via Baker Street, he might have been more useful to anyone from the future who might be prying into her situation. But science wasn't her best subject, and anyway, she didn't want anyone to even know Jeremiah existed. She wanted as quiet and normal a childhood for him as possible. Obviously that plan was unravelling quite fast now, what with him stumbling through time like a bull on acid.

She did leave him a note on a card. Not exactly sufficient, but it was the best she could do under the circumstances. Thinking of the right thing to put on it was hard. And she regretted forever afterwards that she'd tried to keep it light. 'Like the Terminator, I'll be back' now seemed such a dumb thing to end with. Still, she had managed to get in that she loved him – she didn't regret writing that three times. 'Luvya, luvya, luvya.' She had forgotten the exact phrasing of the feeble excuses she'd written before that, the attempts at being sensible; the 'it's for the best if you knew the alternatives', and 'in the long run', and 'better for you in the future'. She had drawn the line at claiming she was only doing it for him, even though that was the

17 Probably best to google that one.

truth. She'd felt that would be too much weight to load onto a nine-year-old boy. But she knew what she was doing, and there really weren't other alternatives open to her. And Stepdad Pete was a good guy, she kept telling herself, he'd see Jem all right. Which he did.

You know how when you're watching a really good film, a few hours can go by without you even thinking about the time? Well, Jeremiah had the complete opposite of that feeling, sitting in that coal cupboard under the Grouts' stairs. It was as if he was sitting in an exam, but the clock just didn't move forward and he just kept staring at the same blank piece of wall. Every now and then there would be the sound of leather shoe soles on the pavement above and then it would go silent again. He thought about Daisy Wallace. He'd really dropped her in it, he knew. He wondered what kind of ear-bashing she was getting right now, and it was his fault.

There was a scraping noise from above, which he noticed only when it stopped suddenly. It had been going on for a while; he couldn't remember it starting. It was now replaced by a clanking. Someone was heaving at the bars of the skylight window above his head. After a few small bangs, there was one big clonk and the bars came free, the window swung open and a face appeared in the gap.

''Ello, me old cock!' a voice came down to him. 'Are you in va league?' It was a young man's voice, with a husky, twin sound like a split reed on a saxophone.

'What? Who are you?' Jeremiah shouted back up at the face. 'And what did you just say? Would you mind repeating it?'

'You got an 'and in va glove, 'ave yer? Eh?'

'A hand in the glove? Is that what you said?'

'Less put it lark viss. Where yer from? Rarnd 'ere?' The

head leaned in further to reveal the torso of a bloke about Jeremiah's age, or perhaps younger, wearing a collar, tie and jacket.

'Oh I see,' said Jeremiah, who was finding it almost impossible to understand his congested London accent. 'Well actually, yes, I am from round here. Next door, as it happens.'

'Is vat so? Ven we may confederate. Annuver Eliphant Boy! Please to meet 'n all vat. Ed Viney's ve name,' and he shoved an arm down towards Jeremiah. 'Come on ven, look sharp!'

There was a pause while Jeremiah stood and looked up at him blankly.

'Carm orn, matey! You bin sprung! By yours truly, Mr Ed Viney.' He slid most of his body down towards Jeremiah and was almost in touching distance now. 'You doan wanna stay 'ere cooped up inner clinker, duz yer? Less be away wiv yer!'

'I'm sorry,' said Jeremiah, 'I can hardly understand a word you're saying. I never thought people actually talked like that, except in old movies. You're talking in, like, real clichéd cockney.'

'Vass good. Vass very good va' iz,' said Ed Viney. 'Ed Cleeshay arl call misself from nar on. Sarnds Frenchy. Parlez-vous Ed Cleeshay? Formidiabolo!' He grabbed Jeremiah's wrist and gave him a big tug upwards. Jeremiah pulled back from him. 'Carm on! Carm on! Grab 'old o' me wrist!'

Ed Viney took hold of both of Jeremiah's arms and pulled him upwards towards the skylight window. He had an iron-like grip and was very strong. Jeremiah was escaping from jail whether he liked it or not. With a lot of grunting and flailing, and a scrape on his ribs as he pulled himself through the narrow window, Jeremiah was out on the pavement on his hands and knees, panting. Ed Viney was already up and dusting himself down. He had on what must once have been a reasonably sharp suit but was now grimy and shredded at the cuffs. He held Jeremiah by the elbow and pulled him off towards the other side of the road.

He was a lot shorter than Jeremiah, but his grip was tight and his arm was steely. He appeared to be made of heavy-duty wire. He had a strange lollop to his step, which made him seem like a wounded animal. He pulled Jeremiah swiftly over the road and down a side street, trotting along faster than a walk, but not quite an actual run. 'Carm orn, matey, less 'opp it, sharpish!'

'I don't feel good being outside,' said Jeremiah, 'in the street, I mean. I'm not comfortable going out.' He wished he had his inhaler.

Ed Viney croaked with laughter and pulled Jeremiah's hair in what was meant to be a playful way, but hurt a lot. 'And I'm not 'appy vat ve King gorn 'n died, niver,' he shouted back, ''e was a Eddie, jess lark me. Come orn!'

SIXTEEN

The positions of the alleys around the back of Union Street were familiar to Jeremiah, but it was strange to recognise where you were while the details were so different. There were a couple of men rolling barrels out of a warehouse where the fitness centre is now, but apart from that nobody would have seen the two of them hurrying eastwards through the streets. The only other witnesses would have been the rats. The rats seemed to be running around quite confidently, in and out of doorways, sniffing out a few crumbs or any rotting vegetables, stopping for a little chat with other rats, perhaps. 'Hello, spread any good diseases lately?' There are still rats there nowadays of course, but they tend to behave a little more discreetly in case the pest-control people get wind of them. Unlike the foxes. Nowadays the urban foxes wander around these streets as if they own them – they don't bother to stay out of the way of humans, they just pad around minding their own business, which consists of tearing apart any rubbish bags that have been left outside, pulling left-over takeaway food cartons all the way across the pavement, and occasionally having incredibly noisy parties where they scream abuse at each other.

'So, whass yer nime, matey?' shouted Ed Viney as he yanked Jeremiah into King's Bench Street. Jeremiah told him. He laughed. 'Ha! Jeremiah born yesterday, eh?'

'Well, more like born tomorrow, actually,' said Jeremiah, out of breath now. They ducked under the big railway arch at the junction of Webber Street, just as a train went past above their heads. The noise was deafening – like a thousand metal dustbins being chucked at a garage door – and the air filled with sticky steam. They stopped by a rickety fence with a couple of faded old advertisement placards on it.

'Nar ven, you 'op frew vat ver 'ole in va fence, will yer,' said Ed Viney, pushing Jeremiah bodily against a gap in the fence, which was filled by some planks with wires pulled across them.

'No, you're doing it again,' said Jeremiah. 'Could you say that again, a little more slowly?'

Ed Viney started to repeat himself, but he was instantly drowned out by a huge siren, like a massive ship's horn. It made Jeremiah jump. 'What the hell was that?' he asked when it finished a few seconds later.

'Vass va lunchtime 'ooter at va faktree, vat is. I fort you said yer was from rarnd 'ere, fort you said yer was a Eliphant Boy.'

'No, I never said I was an Elephant Boy,' said Jeremiah, 'but I am from round here. Do you have to be both?'

But Ed Viney had had enough of polite conversation. He grabbed Jeremiah by both shoulders and roughly started to shove him through the gap in the wall. 'Nar, you jess be a good 'un 'n 'op frew vat ver 'ole in vat fence, will yer.' He pushed and kicked and bustled Jeremiah through the gap, tearing Sir Rodger's precious trousers at the thigh. If he was meant to be a fellow member of the Elephant Boy gang then he had a strange way of showing allegiance. He climbed in after Jeremiah.

They were in a scrappy and bedraggled yard with a few old bedheads and broken barrels in it; some torn clothes were strewn across the large oily puddles which had accrued despite the recent lack of rain. A broken shed smelling of tar was leaning precariously against the brick wall of the railway arch. There's a wine bar there nowadays, thought Jeremiah, and over there, a graphic-design studio.

The moment they were both through the gap in the wall, Ed Viney turned on Jeremiah and quickly rammed him up against the back of the wall, pushing his neck with an iron grip. His breath stank and his teeth looked like a row of miniature rotten apple cores. 'Nar ven, you fort yer was all safe and sarnd wiv anuvver Eliphant Boy, eh? Well, fink again! We're ve Forty Feeves, my frenn, and we can slit yer.'

'Oh, not this again,' said Jeremiah, as best he could with Ed Viney's hand around his neck. 'Look, I'm not in a gang, OK?'

'What are you then?' a young girl's voice cut through. 'Let 'im go, Eddie. Billy? Smasher? Grab 'im.'

Ed Viney backed off while two other guys were suddenly there from nowhere, grabbing Jeremiah and holding him back against the wall. Billy and Smasher must have been about fifteen, both shabbily dressed and filthy. Unlike Ed Viney, they had unkempt curly hair and dirt on their necks and under their fingernails. A girl came out from the side of the collapsed shed. She was dressed in several layers of old clothing, wearing leather shoes with holes in, and her hair was piled up messily on her head. She smiled at Jeremiah; her teeth were ghastly too, like the bottom of a student's coffee cup that has been used as an ashtray for two terms. As she walked closer, it became apparent how short she was. But she made up for it in charisma; she was very much in control of these boys.

''Ello, mucker. Kitty Angel a vottra serveece,' she said, walking around Jeremiah and observing him like a specimen. 'So you not one of the Elephants, you say?'

''N 'e sez 'e's from rarnd 'ere, so 'e's not one of va Forty Feeves niver,' said Ed Viney.

'Well, we already know that!' said Kitty, turning on him.

'Oh. So how's vat ven?' asked Ed.

''Coz *we're* the Forty Thieves, plank-head!' She turned back to look at Jeremiah more closely, edging in until she was eye to eye with him. ''N stop sniggerin', Billy, Smasher.' Billy and Smasher stopped laughing immediately. Kitty looked at Jeremiah quite hard for a few seconds, and then, without warning, poked him in the eye with her finger.

'Ow! Look! Just stop poking and hitting and kicking me!' Jeremiah was losing his patience with all the physical abuse. 'If you talk to me nicely, I might be able to help you with whatever it is you want, but not if you just keep beating me up! All right?!' They all found this hilarious. Then they shut up the moment Kitty started speaking again.

'We can slit yer, if I says the words,' she said slowly. Ed Viney produced a nasty-looking blade from somewhere inside his jacket. 'And the words is…' She paused for effect, like the voiceover in a TV talent show on a knockout round, 'The words is… slit 'im. But I'm not gonna. Not just now.' Ed Viney put his blade away.

'Well, that's very big of you,' said Jeremiah, who was finding a sort of crazed bravery in himself that he'd never known before, 'and it's very nice of you to rescue me from the Grouts and everything, but can I please go now?'

'Thass good. Let you go. Ha! We gotta get recompensated, innit…' she said. Billy and Smasher grunted their agreement. 'What's in 'is pockets?'

Suddenly all three of the boys were pushing and pulling to get inside Jeremiah's pockets. Ed Viney won, ramming his hands right down to the wrist into both of the long pockets of Sir Rodger's tweed trousers.

'What's 'e got in there?' asked Kitty.

'Nuffin,' said Ed Viney, still rummaging. 'Sweet wrapping, and ooh, wass viss?' He pulled away with Jeremiah's mobile phone in his hand. 'Sorta bit o' shiny glarss fing.' He turned it in his hand.

'What's that then?' asked Kitty. 'Give us it 'ere.' She took it off Ed Viney.

'That's my mobile,' said Jeremiah. And then an idea occurred to him. 'Woah! Watch out! Don't look in that black glass whatever you do!' he shouted. 'The dead will come and get you!'

'What d'you mean?' asked Kitty, perhaps a little scared, thought Jeremiah.

'It's a black glass! Haven't you heard of them? If you look in that, you see the dead and they come for you!'

'I 'ave 'eard of that,' said Kitty, 'like a gypsy thing, innit? Like magic.'

Smasher and Billy released their grip a little. He'd got them.

'That's right,' said Jeremiah. 'It's magic, and all the bad things you ever did, the dead will know and come and get you if you look in that thing. Don't even touch it!'

Smasher and Billy were already backing off towards the shed. 'Billy! Smasher! Come back 'ere!' Kitty shouted at them, but they scarpered. She turned back to Jeremiah. 'So is it real, then?' For a moment she reminded him of Ruby, before she got wise to his teasing. He gave Kitty the full benefit of his thousand-yard stare, practised often on his little stepsister. Kitty looked rattled. ''Ere, you 'ave it!' She made to toss it back to Ed Viney, but he wasn't having it.

'Doan givvit ta me! I doan wanna see ver dead! No fank you!' He backed off, and Jeremiah grabbed the phone from Kitty.

'Best give it back to me, I know how to control it,' he said. She gave it up easily. He held up the phone as if he were having some kind of FaceTime relationship with the dead. 'Hello? Are you there? Would you like to come and meet Kitty? Kitty Angel, wasn't it?' He looked across to her for confirmation, but she was retreating now and trying to avoid his gaze. 'Yes, she's right here,' he said, turning the phone round to face her. She was peeking out from behind the shed now. Jeremiah started to back out through the gap in the fence, still pointing the phone at them as if it were a gun.

'Oi! After 'im, Eddie! Don't let 'im get away!' she shouted across the yard to Ed Viney, who was cowering behind a broken bed frame.

'Wha', me? I'm not gettin' inter a whole ghosty fing!'

'Go on! Yer cowardy custard!'

On the other side of the fence, Jeremiah ran as fast as he could. He turned a corner into Rushworth Street. Behind him he could hear them arguing, but not for long. Ed Viney must be out of the yard and running down the road after him now, because Jeremiah could hear his leather shoes tapping on the pavement. At the corner of Rushworth he turned into Pocock Street for a few yards, then Great Suffolk Street and almost bumped into a horse and cart. 'Yagboons!' The man driving the cart had a call like a mournful seagull. The horse was skinny and tired. In the back of the cart was a pile of old clothes and a few broken pans and some baskets which had unravelled. Jeremiah could hear his pursuer's steps coming nearer, and for a moment he had the idea to leap up into the cart and hide under all the rags. But only on telly, he thought, would something like that work. Ed Viney was a bit smarter than Mr Grout, and Yagboons might be a friend of Ed's anyway, so he just kept running.

There were so many streets around here, small and winding and similar-looking. For a moment Jeremiah became disoriented. Which way was west and Blackfriars Road? He heard another train in the distance going from in front of him on the left, to behind him on the right. That meant the river would most likely be in front to the left; north. He turned left and kept running. Eventually he hit Surrey Row and then came out onto the wrong end of Blackfriars Road – probably better to stick to the main road where Forty Thieves and Elephant Boys would be less likely to jump you.

SEVENTEEN

Despite the strangeness of the circumstances, the house at Blackfriars Road still felt like home. Or the nearest thing. He only stopped running when he got to the dustbin alley around the back of the house, which he ducked into after a quick check to see whether Ed Viney was still on his tail. For a few seconds he just stood there, out of breath, before sidling along the narrow passage to his back gate and into the yard. He went down the concrete steps to the double barn door of the basement. Come on, come on! Phyllis Independence Stokes! he thought. Be in! He knocked, but he could see through the round window that there was nobody there.

If it was nowadays, he'd be able to get into the house somehow. There'd be a key under the stone Buddha on the step, apart from anything else, so he wouldn't need to think about climbing through windows, or picking locks on doors. He went back up the three steps and looked around the yard. The shed. Their shed. Sticking out from behind the shed was the end of a ladder. He hauled it out and found that it was a very long ladder. Brilliant. He heaved it across the yard, knocking over a few flowerpots, and leaned it against the back wall. It was just tall enough to reach the window; his bedroom window nowadays. And up he went. It was only when he was about three quarters of the way up that he realised climbing a tall ladder is not such a straightforward or pleasant thing to do. It's not such a safe thing either, really. It's something you see people doing every day, but never stop to think what it would be like. What sort of training do window cleaners get, for instance?

Three rungs before the top of the ladder, he froze. Don't look down, he told himself, but of course he did. And that seemed to make him unable to move. Except for his knees, which started to tremble. Stop shaking, he ordered his knees, you're making it worse. But they wouldn't listen. Letting go with one of his hands to try to push the window up required substantial mental discipline. His skin started to prickle all over, and blood seemed to leave his extremities. He would have to go up the last three rungs in order to look in through the window.

Summoning courage, and hanging onto the window ledge, he forced his feet upwards and his knees outwards so as not to bang those last rungs. He did not look like a ninja, that was for sure. He peered through the window into the room beyond. His room. He had one of those lucid moments of self-observation that always come when least needed, at awkward, stupid times. Here I am, he thought – precarious, frightened, peering into my own bedroom window – looking less like Spider-Man and more like a spatchcock chicken.

Inside he could see two beds with iron head- and footboards, a table and a washstand with a jug and bowl. Sitting on one of the beds, with her back to him, was Daisy Wallace.

'Hello?' he called out, but his voice came out in a high register, as if it had never broken, as if he was still ten years old. Physical fear had made any diaphragm or groinal support turn to marshmallow. 'Hello! Daisy?' He sounded like a little mouse, hanging from a thread. With what he considered phenomenal bravery,[18] he let go of the ledge with one hand and knocked on the window. His knock was too soft. His stomach churned, but he had another go, this time knocking more vigorously.

This time Daisy heard it and came over to the window. When she saw who it was, she lit up and, unlocking the window, slid the sash up. 'Oh my! It's you! Mr Jeremiah!'

Jeremiah tried to sound as if he was completely on top of the situation. 'Yeah, hi, it's me. Daisy, isn't it?' Wrong moment to try and be cool, really, but there we are.

'Have you come to rescue me?' she asked.

'What?' he answered.

'Are you sure you'll be able to carry me safely all the way down to the bottom?' she asked, looking down, and then at Jeremiah's trembling knees.

'You must be joking!' he said, then, 'Sorry, I meant, can I come in?'

'Certainly,' said Daisy, standing back from the window to let him climb in. But it wasn't as simple as that. He grabbed the inside of the window frame and hung there like a cartoon, grunting, until she took pity and helped drag him into the room, where he fell, spluttering, at her feet.

'Oof, ahh, thank you, Daisy,' he said, picking himself up and looking back out of the window to check that he hadn't been seen. 'It's just, I may be being followed by some very dodgy people, so it's probably best if I...' He leaned out of the window and gave the ladder a big push. It tipped and

---

18 Some people may not get this – but fear of heights is a thing. It does not afflict everyone and is less likely to get the young, who tend to have very little idea of how dangerous everything actually is. As people get older and falling over goes from being regrettable to life-threatening, things like fear of heights become more acute. But nevertheless, some young people do suffer from fear of heights – more intelligent young people, Jeremiah used to tell himself.

clattered to the ground below, breaking more flowerpots and flattening a couple of bushes. He pulled the window closed. 'Now, I have to get down to the basement, because I think that's how I can get out of here.' He smiled at her, for the first time, and she smiled back.

'And you will be taking me with you, Mr Jeremiah. I knew you would come to save me, because you are a good man.'

'Well, I'm not sure… I am trying to help, but I'm not sure I can, even if I wanted to. Which I do, it's just…' He looked around the room. It was strange to be in his own bedroom one hundred or so years ago. Same floorboards, same door, same wall panels – the ones Stepdad Pete had made him glue back in because they were always sliding off. 'I seem to do you more harm than good, to tell the truth, and I think it's better if I just disappeared again. And my best chance of doing that is if I go back to the basement in this house, so if that's OK with you, I'll just…' He tried the door handle. The door was locked. 'Ah. It's locked,' he said.

'Yes, Miss Quentinbloom was angry with me, for the thing we talked of, so she has locked me in. Someone must have told her.'

Oh God. He was definitely causing her more harm than good. 'Look, I'm really sorry, I didn't mean to, but I think that was probably me. Well, it *was* me. Who told her. I'll make it up to you, I promise, but right now, we're stuck.'

'But you will have a plan. That is why you threw away the ladder.' Her belief in him was embarrassing.

'Thank you, Daisy Wallace, for your confidence in me,' he said, 'but, sorry, no plan.'

'You are a wizard and a gentleman and will think of something,' she said, as if that was an end to the matter.

'I wish you'd stop saying that, because I really don't have a clue—'

They were interrupted by a surreptitious knock at the door, and a whispered voice from outside. 'Daisy? Daisy, are you in there?'

Daisy went close to the door and whispered through it, 'Lucy Bonnet? Is that you?'

'Just to warn you, she's on the warpath! Prowling up the stairs now!'

Clementina Quentinbloom's large voice came bouncing up from below. 'Lucy Bonnet! What are you doing up there outside the dorm? Daisy is to have no visitors.'

'Sorry, Miss Quentinbloom, ma'am, just washing the stairs again.' They heard the clanking of Lucy's bucket.

Daisy looked at Jeremiah with a level of trust that was almost threatening. 'Come along, Mr Jeremiah, if you have an idea, the time to exercise it is now,' she said with what seemed like indignation.

He looked desperately around the room for something, anything. The little washstand, the beds, the door, the floorboards, the wall panels. The wall panels that he recognised. And there it was, she was right, he did have an idea. A little tingly feeling came over him. 'Help me move the bed,' he said, as he shunted one of the beds away from the wall. He felt as if he was looking through a time lens at the moment he'd been working with Stepdad Pete on the restoration of this room. He knelt down and fiddled with the wall panel, knowing exactly where to look. It was a bit loose and rattled in its frame but was jammed and needed levering away from the wall. He tried with his fingernails, but it was wedged in. He looked back up at Daisy, who, without being asked, had produced a comb from the washstand, which she thrust at him.

'Try this,' she said. Jeremiah took the comb and rammed it behind the edge of the panel. The comb cut a nick in the soft wood, but it did get a purchase and he was able to prise off the panel, which came away without much further resistance. Behind it was a diagonal timber, and then the panel of the outer wall. He gave that a small push and it came away too. He pulled that panel sideways back into the room and gazed with satisfaction at the small hole in the wall he'd managed to create. He looked back proudly to where Daisy had been, but she was already squeezing herself through the hole.

'Wait! Where are you going?' Jeremiah whispered at her.

'To the basement like you said,' she whispered back, before disappearing out into the corridor.

EIGHTEEN

'Lucy Bonnet!' They could hear Clementina's voice coming from the landing. 'Why is the ladder all over the begonias?'

'Don' know, ma'am.' Lucy Bonnet was at the end of the corridor with her bucket. She was surprised to see Daisy. 'How d'you get out 'ere,' she whispered, 'and where on earth did you just come from, sir?' She grinned at them both. 'Go on! I'll distract 'er. Go on!' She marched round the corner and they heard her bucket clang and roll across the floor. 'Oops,' she said.

'Lucy Bonnet! You clumsy girl!' Clementina was brought away from the landing by the entire contents of a mucky bucketload of water sloshing over the floor.

'Sorry, ma'am.'

'Now use the dry mop and clear up all the spillage!'

'Yes, ma'am.' Lucy ducked back and gave them the all-clear.

Daisy raced ahead of Jeremiah. 'Come on, this way!' she whispered and shot off around the corner to the top of the stairs.

'I know. I do know the way to the basement!' he answered, following her.

Clementina was standing with her back to them, supervising Lucy, who was making as much of a business out of the spilt bucket as she could. 'Goodness, what's got into you today, my girl? Can you not just squeeze out the mop into the bucket? Here, give it to me!' Clementina got down on all fours and gave Lucy Bonnet a lecture on how to wipe a floor.

'Sorry, ma'am, could you show me that again? So's like I don't make a mess of it next time?'

Daisy and Jeremiah crept down the stairs at speed. When they got to the bottom, they both made a move to open the door to the basement stairs. 'Here, this leads to the basement, Mr Jeremiah,' said Daisy.

'Look, I know the way. I live here too, you know,' he said, but she was already flying down ahead of him. He carefully clicked the door closed behind them and ran down the basement stairs.

The basement was exactly how Phyllis Stokes had left it. Neatly stacked chairs and the table shifted to one side. There was the bench where Jeremiah had managed to get half a night's sleep, but apart from that, the meeting room of the Society for Theosophical Research and Anthro-Psychology, Women's Branch, remained unchanged.

'This is the basement,' said Daisy, making sure the door was securely closed behind them.

'Look, Daisy, I know where everything is in this house because, I know this sounds incredible, but I live here.' Daisy was now listening attentively. She didn't even raise an eyebrow when he explained that he had come from the future – her future, that is.

'I don't know how I did it, but it was from this basement. Somehow I must've travelled in time, and… it sounds so stupid, doesn't it…' Daisy didn't find it stupid.

'You have come here from the future to save me,' she said, with certainty.

'Actually, I reckon Phyllis Stokes is your best bet, in terms of being saved and everything. You could just hide in here until she comes back for her next meeting. There's a whole pile of blankets in this drawer here,' Jeremiah opened the drawer from where Phyllis Stokes had given him a blanket, 'and you could curl up behind the stack of chairs.'

Daisy didn't think this was a satisfactory idea. 'And what would you be doing in that case, Mr Jeremiah?'

'Well, I've got to figure out how I got here, I suppose, and then, somehow, reverse the process. So I can go back home. I mean forward.'

'Would I be permitted to keep my baby in your time?' she asked. He began to explain how things have changed over the last hundred years, but she stopped him. 'Then I shall come with you,' she said, as if it was a done deal.

'Not so simple. I don't even know how I did it myself, so I don't think that's very likely.'

'I'm scared,' said Daisy, in a matter-of-fact voice. 'I wonder what the future will be like.'

'Yuh, well, I'm beginning to doubt it ever existed. Did I just dream it?'

'May you hold my hand? I feel I should not be so afraid then,' said Daisy, without sentimentality.

'I'm scared too, if I'm honest,' said Jeremiah. His voice cracked a little while he said it. Holding Daisy's hand seemed like a good option. He wasn't sure who was helping who.

They sat for a moment, hand in hand, gazing out ahead of them. 'What is it like in the future?' asked Daisy.

'Well, it's a lot faster and more stressful,' Jeremiah began, and then had second thoughts. 'Actually, this is pretty stressful.'[19]

---

19 When did 'stress' come in as the catch-all phrase to describe everything bad? When the doctors don't really know what's wrong with you, they put it down to stress. If you're late handing in a test paper, you can always blame stress. Caught shoplifting? Stress. Rude and bad-tempered? No, just stressed. In them good old

‘What is this room like in the future?’ she asked.

Perhaps to relieve his anxiety, Jeremiah gave her a fairly extensive history of the house; how it had been a women’s refuge in the sixties and seventies, then old Mr Varma who’d bought it, Mum moving in with Stepdad Pete, then Stepdad Pete taking over the whole house, followed by his obsessive attempts to restore it to its former glory. Daisy listened to it all, scrutinising every detail of the room.

‘Stepdad Pete would be so jealous of me being here and seeing all this,’ he went on. ‘You see the alcove where the chest of drawers is? Well, at some point, probably in the eighties, that got completely covered over with plasterboard. And all the dado rails? – he loves dado rails, Pete – well, they all got taken off at some point. He’s trying to find matching ones at the moment.’

They sat staring at the room. ‘And what colour will the walls be in the future?’ Daisy asked. ‘I hope it’s a jolly colour, it’s too dark in here.’

‘Well, they were a dirty yellow, rather like this, which was not very nice, so was the door and the skirting and everything. But Stepdad Pete’s redone it in a sort of apple-greeny-white colour. He knows the names of all these classic colours. And he did the ceiling in some kind of rose pink, but at the moment it’s still got these terrible seventies spotlight fittings, there and there…’ Jeremiah could picture the room exactly as he remembered it.

‘Yes, I see it,’ said Daisy, tightening her grip on his hand.

‘Well, I suppose you’d have to use your imagination with the seventies spotlight fittings. They’re pretty disgusting.

---

days, people used to eat stress for breakfast and then get on with their morning. How a person dealt with stress was how one judged their character – a stress-resistant person would have been considered an asset. Mind you, they did all die a lot younger then and people thought bullying was funny, so…

Big design mistake. They're on a metal track…' The words were echoing a bit in Jeremiah's head. It was rather like when he was getting over his sinus infection and it had left him with slight ringing in his ears for weeks.

'Yes, I see it exactly as you describe it,' said Daisy, 'and I see the strange cup!'

'Cup?'

'Yes, the big cup with writing on it.' She read the words slowly: 'Mister… Messy…'

'That's my Mr Messy mug! What's that doing here?' The ringing in Jeremiah's ears had turned into a hissing and then a fizzing. He was in the room with Daisy, but now was noticing things that didn't belong here, in a sort of double exposure. The noise had become more insistent like an approaching train. Daisy gripped his hand tighter still.

'Oh, bloody 'eck!' she screamed out. 'What the ff… flamin' 'ell is going on?' Her shout seemed to swallow up all the rushing sounds and, in an instant, there was silence, the two of them sitting hand in hand, in a daze, in Blackfriars Road in 2019.

NINETEEN

What's the first rule of time travel? Physicists argue over this one. But surely the one thing scientists and sci-fi aficionados would agree on is that you shouldn't go randomly messing with the past. Changing what happened. Making nonsense of history. These were Jeremiah's first thoughts as he sat there, with Daisy's hand still tightly hanging on to his.

'Wow! We've done it. Could you let go of my hand now, please? My knuckles have gone white,' he said, blinking.

'*You* have done it!' she said, her eyes shining. 'You have rescued me and my baby!' Oh God, he'd forgotten about the baby. Were there time-travel rules about having a baby in the wrong time?

Having pulled his hand free from Daisy's grip, he dared to stand up and look around the basement. He touched the upholstered armchair that he'd been working on, yes, it was real. He picked up the Mr Messy mug; still got coffee in the bottom, but completely cold now, so normal time had passed. And there was his inhaler, where he'd left it. He picked it up, took a puff, for reassurance really, and put it in his pocket. He felt relief trickling through his body, but also doubt and fear. How had he done this? Or had he had no volition in it, was it just random? Daisy sat with a huge smile on her face. 'So now try and tell me you are not a wizard and a gentleman!' she said.

'You can't stay here,' he said, 'you'll have to go back somehow. This can't be right.'

'Jem, is that you?' Suddenly the door swung open, and Ruby was there, talking without drawing breath. 'Jem! Where've you been? You're in *deep* trouble! You didn't come back all last night! My dad was so angry, he was ringing around all the hospitals and police stations in case— Hello, I love your ankle boots, where'd you get them? Can you get me some?' She'd noticed Daisy.

'Hi, Ruby,' said Jeremiah.

'And your dress, that's amazing.'

'Daisy, this is my stepsister Ruby. Ruby, this is Daisy Wallace. We just had the weirdest thing happen…' He thought about it for a second and decided not to go straight into telling Ruby. She wasn't listening to him anyway.

'And what are you wearing, Jem? Nice retro suit. Where'd you get it, Retro Shop? If you grew a big beard you could be like a hipster, except you can't grow a proper beard yet, can you… are you pregnant, Daisy?'

'Yes, Miss Ruby, I am,' said Daisy.

'Ooh, Jem! What have you been doing?' said Ruby. She had no filter.

'No, Jeremiah is not the father, Miss Ruby,' said Daisy, smiling.

'Well, that's a relief! But he is your boyfriend, right? I get it, just good friends. So how did you two meet?'

'In a Retro Shop,' said Daisy, sounding confident and convincing, as if she'd been around and knew what a Retro Shop was.

'That's right,' said Jeremiah, 'we met in a Retro Shop.'

'Well, I think you've made Jem look actually quite good, Daisy,' said Ruby, 'which is a first.'

'Thank you, Miss Ruby,' said Daisy, 'I do my best with him.' Taking it a bit far, thought Jeremiah.

They heard Stepdad Pete's voice coming down from the top of the stairs. 'Is that Jem? Jem! Thank God you're OK! We've been so worried,' he said, coming breathlessly into the room, 'it's not like you to go running off without telling anyone where you are— Oh hello.' He'd noticed Daisy.

'Hello, Stepdad Pete,' said Daisy, as if she already knew him.

Jeremiah introduced them. 'Hello, Daisy, pleased to meet you,' said Stepdad Pete.

'They met in a Retro Shop,' said Ruby, filling the words with innuendo.

'I see,' said Stepdad Pete, not seeing.

'Don't worry, Stepdad Pete,' said Daisy, 'the baby is not Jeremiah's.'

'Right,' said Stepdad Pete, nonplussed now.

Jeremiah let out a groan. This was definitely not how he would have wanted his return to go. He would have preferred a gathering of the elders and everyone listening attentively to his amazing story.

'And Jem says he's not her boyfriend, but they're just good friends,' said Ruby.

'Jeremiah is my gentleman rescuer,' said Daisy, as if a gentleman rescuer was a regular thing.

'Well, glad to hear it,' said Stepdad Pete, still mostly in the dark. 'Jem, that nice Nandy Banerjee girl was round here earlier for your maths session, but you weren't here, so she went away again. You mustn't take advantage of her good nature, you know. She's very clever – you're lucky to have her.'

'Oh, sorry,' said Jeremiah, 'I'll give her a call later.' He didn't know why Nandy had offered to come round and help him with his maths twice a week. He suspected she might fancy him a bit, but that might just be him being conceited. Nandy wanted to go to City of London School after GCSEs, for which she'd need a scholarship. But no one doubted she would get it – she was a maths genius. Her ambition was to be a maths professor at Cambridge. Perhaps she was using Jeremiah to practise her teaching skills.

'So long as you're both safe and sound now, that's all that matters,' said Stepdad Pete, smiling at Daisy.

'Jeremiah has made me safe,' said Daisy, 'and sound too. He has told me all about you bringing out the former glory of the house.'

'Has he now?'

'Would you like a piece of angel cake?' Ruby moved across and stood near Daisy. 'I made it myself.'

'Well, I didn't think Jeremiah made it!' said Daisy and the three of them laughed. It seemed to Jeremiah that it was a three-way conversation now, to which he had not been invited. 'Yes please, thank you, Miss Ruby,' said Daisy.

This was going horribly wrong. Jeremiah tried to step in. 'Stop,' he said, 'before we go any further!'

'Oh yes, of course you're right, Jem. Sorry, Daisy, very rude of me,' said Stepdad Pete. 'Do come upstairs. Would you like a cup of tea?'

'And angel cake,' said Ruby.

'No!' shouted Jeremiah.

'Yes, thank you, Stepdad Pete,' said Daisy, sweetly. They set off towards the door.

'And Jem? Bring up that empty mug, would you?' said Stepdad Pete, leading Daisy up the stairs.

Jeremiah heard them chatting as they continued up into the kitchen. 'And you must tell me all about your dado rails,' Daisy was saying.

'Oh, you know about dado rails?' Pete replied.

Jeremiah looked around the room. His experience must have been caused by something in the basement itself, he thought, but what?

He found the empty biscuit tin, abandoned on the floor where he'd left it. The two pictures had fallen face down beside it. He picked up the smaller one – the one with the woman's portrait on it – but immediately had second thoughts. What if looking at it again took him straight back? He put it back down again without turning it over. But even without looking at it, he found he remembered the face. It came to him in a rush that she was the woman in the dream he'd had the other night. Had he conjured her up in his opium-induced sleep? He felt a chill creep over his skin as he realised that the opium had released not a fantasy, but a buried memory, a real one, of an event that happened. It came back to him now; suddenly alone, nine years old, standing in Tooley Street. What about Mum's taxi? Our taxi? After Mum had crossed the road, followed by the woman, he had just left the taxi there and ran, as fast as he could, through the back streets. At first he was lost, as Mum had always driven him there, but when he turned into Weston Street and saw the half-built Shard peeking out behind Guy's Hospital, his panic subsided enough to get himself home, panting and upset, to find Mum already there, waiting for him as if nothing much had happened. Yes, she had taken him in her arms and hugged him. 'Sorry, my darlin' boy,' she said a couple of times, but it had left him bewildered and afraid. When he asked her later, who was that woman, she'd said something vague like: 'Oh, just someone from where I used to live.' 'What, you mean like your old family?' he had asked. 'Yes, something like that. My old family. There are some people who I'd rather didn't know where we are. Sorry, my darlin', you do come from a rather odd family.' It must have been shortly after that, he figured now, that she had gone. Perhaps her leaving had buried all memory of the incident under a pile of emotional topsoil.

'Jem? You coming?' Pete called down to him. He followed the others up. At the top of the stairs was the hall, and then, to the side, was the kitchen area which had a small dining table in it. Stepdad Pete had decided against converting back to a period kitchen for the meantime. What with looking after the two kids on his own, he'd had to compromise historical accuracy in a couple of places – the box room where they were allowed to watch telly, and the front kitchen where the fridge was and where, typically, most of the twenty-first-century family activity took place. Perhaps he would change it, he thought, if ever the house were to become a place to visit, its own museum.

'Well, at first we could only find three-mil replacement beading, or simple quarter and a half inch dowelling, no good at all.' Stepdad Pete was filling the kettle, talking over his shoulder to Daisy, who was looking around in wonder at all the modern kitchen devices. Ruby had the angel cake on the table and was cutting it into crude slices and putting it onto small plates. 'Until I discovered an old shop, a local one, who still supplied four mil, so I measured up. The whole house, that is…'

Jeremiah stood in the doorway, wondering how he could put a stop to this. An extraordinary thing had happened, and he would have liked a moment perhaps of acknowledgement. Daisy had stolen his thunder, chatting away with Stepdad Pete as if she'd been here always. 'And then you will paint them in French Grey? Or would you consider using Sage Green?' she said, taking a plate of cake from Ruby.

'You certainly know your stuff! That's right, either of those would be accurate, period colours,' said Stepdad Pete. 'Where did you find her, Jem? She's a real treasure, this one.'

'Oh, she works for an institute, a historical institute,' mumbled Jeremiah. But no one was listening.

'You see the thing is, Daisy my dear, we don't use lead-based paints any longer, quite rightly, so we have to find equivalents of those old classic colours.'

'This is a picture of Jem sitting naked in a bucket when he was a baby.' Ruby had taken out the family photos and was giving Daisy a little show and tell. 'And here's one where he's in a complete sulk because we used his Anvil T-shirt to hold fireworks and it got singed…'

'Yes, he does look very cross there,' said Daisy, giving Ruby her attention.

'So, Daisy, my love,' Pete was sitting down pouring the tea now, 'where are you living yourself right now?'

'I am sadly without a home at present,' said Daisy, 'thank you for asking, Stepdad Pete.'

'Yeah, she meant she just got down from uni, didn't you, Daisy?' said Jeremiah, peripherally.

'No,' said Daisy, firmly, 'it was impossible to stay where I was, due to the regime.'

Pete and Ruby looked puzzled. 'What are you talking about? What regime?' Jeremiah said, rather too forcefully.

'A regime where they treated girls like me very, very badly, and that's all I want to say,' said Daisy.

'But you will tell me later, right?' said Ruby.

'I would rather not.'

'Wow, *that* bad.'

There followed a brief and loaded silence, which was broken by Stepdad Pete. 'Well, goes without saying, my love, you're more than welcome to stay here. Until you get yourself sorted out.'

'Yesss!' said Ruby, putting out her palm for a high-five from Daisy, which was not returned.

'Thank you, Stepdad Pete, I accept,' said Daisy, with formality.

'What? No no no! This can't happen!' said Jeremiah and left to go up to his room.

He heard Stepdad Pete shout after him as he stomped up the stairs, 'Don't be such a grumble, Jeremiah. When times are tough for someone, you have to step in!'

TWENTY

However good your memory is, even if it is a super-memory, it doesn't necessarily mean you will remember everything the same as everyone else. In fact, eyewitness accounts are notoriously unreliable, no matter how confident the witness. As the late Queen said in 2021 of Harry and Meghan's statements to Oprah Winfrey, 'Recollections vary.' The reason for this, given in research, is that human memory is 'malleable'. It's sometimes known as the 'Rashomon effect', after the eponymous Japanese film which shows the same events four times, as told from the different points of view of the participants, each with a different outcome. So, when it came to Jeremiah's mother's leaving note, he remembered it rather differently from her. It's probably something to do with the emotional investment in a particular memory, which bends people's recollections to make sense of what they are feeling. And Jeremiah hadn't looked at the note for a few years because it made him feel sad. Or at least that's how he remembered it.

He got back up to his room, closing the door on the sound of laughter from below. He looked around the room, his room. Daisy's room. He took out his mobile and plugged it into the charger on the chair and was overwhelmed by a feeling of loneliness. Such a shame the battery had run out, otherwise he could've taken some photos and come back with some proof other than a pregnant girl in ankle boots who everyone thinks is really nice. He opened the wardrobe, crouched down and, reaching into the back, behind his shoes, he dragged out a battered old Nike box. His 'Mum' box. He hadn't looked in here for ages. Sighing, he pulled the lid off and started to sift through the familiar objects: a small and shiny antique coffee cup, important to Mum for some reason; her thumbed copy of the 2002 World Cup album, with a stamp on the front cover which said: *Do Not Remove. This book is the property of Blackfriars Road Residents' Association R and M*; a brochure from the Greenwich Observatory, Mum's favourite place; a few of his childhood toys – cars, some old coins, soldiers; and Mum's note to him in its ratty blue envelope. He took out the folded card and opened it. He hadn't read this note for over three years and there were bits he'd forgotten about. The three 'luvyas', for instance, had been completely erased from his mind; he was surprised to find them there. What he remembered most was two phrases; the first said: 'I've done some stupid things and got my life into a mess', and the second: 'Trust me.' Trust me? Jeremiah hated that phrase. Only in lousy TV dramas do people say 'Trust me'. They do it a lot; they're always doing it at points where the plot needs to take an unlikely turn. This is usually just after they've said something equally stupid and unlikely, such as: 'I have to do this alone.' Jeremiah hated that his mum had put 'Trust me' in his note. It seemed like bad script writing, or in her case, bad farewell-note writing. It made him feel like he was the person on the other end of the phone line in the same lousy TV programme, when the hero says, 'I'll be right there,' and then just hangs up the phone! No 'Goodbye, thanks for calling, what was that address again?'

Jeremiah realised, looking through his Mum box, that the reason he hadn't looked in it for so long was not because it made him feel sad, but because it made him feel angry. And it didn't make it any better, re-reading it now, that she said she couldn't regret the stupid things she'd done because if she hadn't done them 'there'd be no you'. Like it was his fault. He hated that note. He'd spent the first year after she left staring at it, initially crying, then later, hardened with resentment. It left him with so many unanswered questions. Was his mum some kind of criminal on the run? Was it really for the best, or was she saying that so she could run off and do what she wanted?

He chucked the envelope back in the box with the other things and gave the box a mean kick across the floor and under the bed. He sat on the floor gazing at the walls for some time – maybe twenty minutes – then pulled himself back together again, like he always did. Always had to. Time to get on and do something. His mobile was almost fully charged, so he unplugged it and put it back in his pocket. Sir Rodger Allcott Standish's pocket, actually. One thing: he was getting used to the trousers. They weren't so bad; they seemed to mould around you. He looked out of the window at their yard below; a couple of large pots with unidentifiable dead plants in them, nothing like as good as the same bit of ground over a hundred years ago, with its vegetable patch and begonias. The sash window was the same; it clanked when you opened it by sliding upwards against a counterweight in the frame. The walls, the floorboards, the skirting boards, the panelling. A thought occurred to him. He slid the bed away from the wall and there, easy to see, was a nick in the frame of the panelling. Covered in several layers of paint, yes, but definitely a nick. A V-shaped indentation where he'd used Daisy's comb to lever off the panel. That had not been here when he'd painted these with Stepdad Pete – he would've remembered. So he had actually changed history. He'd taken a small slice out of history, or at least made a V-shaped scuff mark on it.

He crouched down on his knees to have a proper look. He could hear someone's voice coming up the stairs calling for him, and asking, 'Where is Daisy?'

'I thought she was downstairs with you,' he shouted back, and his voice seemed to echo under the bed, where he was still crouching.

'No, she's not. And I think you have a lot of explaining to do!' said the voice, much nearer now. Blood rushed to Jeremiah's head as he stood up, and his vision started swimming. There was that fizzing noise again and a sort of rushing of air. The voice spoke to him again; it seemed to be in the room now.

'You are coming with me, young man!' It was Clementina Quentinbloom, standing right in front of him.

He looked wildly around him. His Mum box was gone, so was his bed, his desk, his charger and chair. Everything reassuring that had been there just seconds before. 'Oh no, not again!' he said. 'This is really not funny any more! I wasn't even in the basement.'

'I'll show you what's not funny!' said Clementina, leaning forward and grabbing his ear. She pulled him painfully towards her, then turned. 'Lucy Bonnet? What are you doing? Listening at the door?'

'No, ma'am.' Lucy Bonnet was there, looking in amazement at Jeremiah, who she'd last seen running down to the basement, now found in a locked room two floors above.

'Stop gawping and return to your duties at once!' Clementina Quentinbloom snapped, and then pulled Jeremiah out into the corridor and round the corner to the landing. He was too surprised to say anything. Whatever the phenomenon was, it wasn't confined to the basement. Was every bit of the house a potential temporal doorway that could suddenly open and drop him with no warning into the past?

'We will see whether these friends you claim to have know anything about you,' said Clementina, shoving him roughly down the corridor, 'because as luck would have it, they are right here, in this house, visiting.'

Lucy Bonnet whispered at Jeremiah as they passed her on the landing, 'I thought you went downstairs.'

'I know!' said Jeremiah. 'So did I!'

'Don't talk to him, Lucy,' Clementina ordered, pushing Jeremiah ahead of her, down the stairs, 'and get on with whatever it is you're supposed to be doing.'

'Yes, ma'am.'

At the bottom of the stairs looking up at them stood Sir Rodger Allcott Standish. He was wearing clothes this time: trousers with colourful braces stretched over his massive belly, a silk dressing gown cum smoking jacket and the same red velvet cap that he'd worn on their first meeting. 'Jeremiah Bourne? As I live and breathe!' Phyllis came out from the front room to join him. She was in the same dark, plain clothes as before. Her hat was hanging on the hat-stand by the front door.

'Is that Jem?' she called out. 'How marvellous! How did you get on with the... phenomenon? Did you travel forwards? How decent of you to come back to see us. Did you discover anything more?' She was almost as demanding as Ruby.

Jeremiah was relieved to see them. They were the only people of his recent acquaintance who didn't want to punch, poke, pinch his ear, cuff or kick him. On realising that they knew him, Clementina released her grip and dusted herself and him down, trying to cover her earlier harsh treatment.

'It appears you were telling the truth, so no need for introductions then,' she said. 'Perhaps we should all go into the withdrawing room and not make an exhibition of ourselves in front of the girls.' As she mentioned them, a few of the girls' faces vanished from behind banisters or from doors left ajar. 'This way.' They walked across the hall and into the front room, roughly the area where Jeremiah had just been an hour before, he thought. Weird to know that in a hundred years' time or so, there would be angel cake in this very room.

TWENTY-ONE

'Did you get home?' asked Sir Rodger.

'Yeah, I did. It's not just the basement, it seems to be the whole house.'

'Jeremiah really is an interesting case, Clementina,' said Phyllis. 'He is experiencing unexplained somersaults in the time continuum.'

Sir Rodger waited until the two women were seated before sitting himself and gave Jeremiah a look indicating that he should do the same, so he did.

'It appears I owe you an apology, Mr Bourne, which will be forthcoming as soon as I have an explanation as to the whereabouts of Daisy Wallace,' said Clementina when they were all seated.

'Ah. Yes. There's been a bit of a problem with Daisy,' said Jeremiah, 'but I honestly think she's doing all right now, where she is. In fact, more than all right. Better than I am, for starters.' There was a muffled clanging from the front doorbell, and, without releasing Jeremiah from her gaze, Clementina called for Lucy Bonnet to answer the front door.

'Yes,' said Sir Rodger, 'how is she, this Miss Wallace? We meant to talk with you, Clementina, about her welfare. That was one of the reasons for our visit.'

In the hall Jeremiah could hear Lucy opening the door to someone and offering to take their hat. Then the door to the front room opened and she announced the visitor.

'Dr Henry Davenant Hythe,' she said, with a face that was determined not to give away her distaste for the man.

Into the room swung Henry Davenant Hythe, smiling from ear to ear. Not a thing which came naturally to him. Clementina was surprised to see him, as were Phyllis and Sir Rodger.

'Henry! How unusual to see you south of the river!'

'I thought you were due to give your talk at the Royal Society?'

'Oh, you know, most of them are incapable of following my line of thought anyway,' Davenant Hythe said, then, seeing Jeremiah, 'Ah, Jem Bourne! The Man of the Moment! Still playing your little "black glass" trick, eh?'

'Well, yes and no,' said Jeremiah.

'So, you're not Dr John Dee yet?'

What is it about some people, and it's men, mostly, that makes them try the gently barbed mockery approach as a way of being liked? It never works, never has done. And yet they persist, at every opportunity, to pick only the phrases that sound like sarcastic attacks or silly affronts on people they would probably prefer to have as friends. Is it public school? Is it beer? Is it testosterone that makes them treat all social contact as a sparring match of semi-witty insults? Inside, are they all frightened schoolboys, trying to kid us that they don't care, because they didn't want to have us as friends anyway?

Clementina looked puzzled. 'Jeremiah has a piece of black obsidian, Clementina, for purposes of Necromancy,' Sir Rodger explained, 'and which was likened by Phyllis to Dr John Dee's black glass in the British Museum and by myself to that of Pliny. Pliny the Elder of course, not the Younger.'

Clementina looked at even more of a loss. In fact, she'd stopped listening at the word 'obsidian'. She always found

Sir Rodger unfathomable. She preferred logical thinking which went from A to B and then perhaps to C if the coast was clear.

There was a sudden crash at the back of the house; a bang followed by a tinkling. Jeremiah's glance shot immediately over to Lucy Bonnet, who had heard it too, and looked back at him in alarm for a brief, disobedient second.

'What on earth was that?' asked Sir Rodger.

'An upstairs window perhaps?' added Phyllis, concerned.

Henry Davenant Hythe was the only one who seemed unfazed. 'Well, I heard nothing,' he drawled confidently, 'and I am blessed with perfect aural function. Possibly one of those girls dropped a plate or some such?'

'Lucy Bonnet!' snapped Clementina. 'Stop standing there like a garden gnome – you may go. And let me know if any of the girls has broken a plate. It will have to go in the book.'

'Yes, ma'am,' said Lucy, bobbing out of the room.

Clementina called after her, 'Posture! Shoulders back! Walk straight! Off you go!'

'Yes, ma'am,' said Lucy.

'My heart breaks for these poor creatures,' said Davenant Hythe, looking after Lucy, 'born with congenital diseases most of them; low intelligence, short-sightedness. No control over their own instincts. Some must wish they'd never been born.'

'Oh, bleak! Bleak! And also unfair, say I,' said Sir Rodger. 'I'm sure they do the utmost they can and are as capable as you or I of enjoying life to the full.'

Henry Davenant Hythe did not look as if he did, nor ever had, enjoyed life to the full. 'And what about this Wallace girl, eh? Daisy, was it? No sign of her, then? One might almost suspect that our young crystal-ball gazer here had absconded with her.'

'Clementina has dedicated the best part of her life to these girls, Jem,' said Phyllis, leaning across to him, 'training them in domestic service and saving them from an unfortunate life of chronic want. And that includes young Daisy.'

There was another loud bang. This time at the front of the house, and it was more of a thud, with no tinkling. Someone had thrown a rock or a brick at the front door. Or to be more accurate, someone had thrown a rock or a brick and it had hit the front door.

Henry Davenant Hythe carried on, apparently oblivious. 'I look forward to a time when these girls will be free of their biological limitations—'

Clementina called Lucy Bonnet back. 'Lucy? What was that noise at the front door just now?'

Lucy had reappeared, hovering at the door; perhaps she had never gone. 'Beg pardon, ma'am, it was a stone thrown at the front door. Well, a rock…'

Sir Rodger looked dismayed. 'A rock? Forgive my interruption, Henry, but, what did you say, Lucy? A rock? Thrown at this front door? At us?'

Out in the street there were voices. 'Come on, let's be 'avin yer!' and 'Forties Forever!'

'No, I don't think as how it was thrown at us, more in this general direction.'

Clementina admonished her 'Lucy Bonnet! Shush! Only when you're spoken to.'

'I *was* spoken to, ma'am, in fact I was actually asked,' said Lucy, gathering courage and stepping into the room to speak to Sir Rodger. 'It's them Forty Thieves again. Looks like there's a scramble kickin' off in the street.' She went to the window to peek out between the curtains, then let out a shout as if she was a West Ham supporter on a Saturday afternoon. 'Goo Orn the Elephants!'

Clementina was horrified. 'Miss Bonnet! We'll have none of your vernacular in here! And close those curtains at once.' Lucy obeyed. 'Now, if there is to be a riot, you must gather up all the girls and take them quickly to the loft room. Here is the key…' she took one of the keys off the key ring on her waist and handed it to Lucy, 'and you shall lock yourselves safely in there until I call to you that all is clear. Hurry now.'

The shouting in the street increased and there were the sounds of a fight, objects being thrown and the clattering of sticks, bottles and pans.

Henry sat back in his chair and expressed his deep pity and concern. 'It is incomprehensible to me how they survive in such an ill-educated environment, where there is no compassion, no understanding,' he sighed.

'What the heck is going on out there?' said Sir Rodger.

'Actually, I think I know what this is about,' Jeremiah chipped in. 'It's two local gangs, fighting it out: the Elephant Boys and the Forty Thieves. They're staking out their territory and we happen to be in the crossfire. It's a sort of postcode war. If you have postcodes.'

Phyllis and Sir Rodger looked impressed. 'I say, Jeremiah, how very smart of you. Did you read that in a history book in your own time?' said Phyllis. 'Does this street become notorious?'

There was another commotion, but this one came from inside the house. The sound of many of the girls arguing in the front hall, voices being raised and then shouted down. Lucy Bonnet burst into the room. Behind her stood several of the girls peering over her shoulder.

'Ma'am? The girls won't go upstairs until they know that Mrs Grout has their little ones safe.'

Clementina was having a bad day. She was not used to any insubordination at all, let alone the catalogue of disobediences that seemed to be piling up like patients in an overcrowded waiting room. 'Won't?' she hissed. 'Won't go upstairs?'

It got worse. 'Mabel Hopper and Sally Fawcett has been askin' if they can go to see if their own little ones is safe,' said Lucy, firmly.

'Will you all excuse me?' Clementina rose and ushered Lucy out into the hall.

Henry Davenant Hythe continued to hold forth, but nobody was listening. '...a rapid descent to the lowest common denominator of humanity. I feel for them, I really do...'

TWENTY-TWO

In the hall, the girls, defiant, clustered around Clementina, who was overwhelmed. 'Just one look. One little look, to see if 'e's all right, like,' and 'I'm not goin' upstairs till I've seen my little 'un.'

Clementina stood in shock among them like the centre of a maypole which they spun around. She lifted her arms and her voice to stop the chaos. 'Enough! Upstairs, all of you! All those children next door are no longer your concern. You are domestic servants now, so for goodness' sake behave with due deference.' The girls grudgingly subsided their noise, but did not budge.

Phyllis and Sir Rodger had come to the doorway and were looking on. 'Poor things,' said Phyllis, 'I do think they could at least be given photographic likenesses.'

'Yes, I do hate cruelty,' said Sir Rodger, 'we should at least be kind. The girls have already suffered enough.'

Jeremiah joined them. 'You mean, all of those kids at the Grouts' are theirs?' Now he understood why Daisy had been so keen to scarper.

Lucy Bonnet was standing by the front door looking at the fight outside through the little glass side panel. She repeated her football chant: 'Goo Orn the Elephants!' Another girl went over to her and pushed her aggressively in the shoulder. 'Forties Forever!' she shouted, right in Lucy's face. A fight kicked off. The two girls were soon in a knotted struggle, banging up against the hat-stand and knocking it over. The other girls started to cheer or boo, as the front hall was rapidly turning into a bear pit.

'Girls! Girls! Stop this at once!' cried Clementina, having no effect. Then, to Sir Rodger, in desperation, 'Sir Rodger? You are a magistrate and a man! Can you not put an end to this?'

Sir Rodger's social skills did not stretch to dealing with fighting young women. 'Come come, ladies,' he said weakly, 'probably best not to take sides in matters that are beyond our control, eh? But I do understand this thing about the bairns. I too felt a terrible wrench when my nanny…' But he was drowned out.

The commotion came to an end suddenly with the sound of the lock on the front door being opened from the outside. Everyone in the front hall froze and for a second all that could be heard was the voice of Henry Davenant Hythe still sitting in the front room, pontificating: '…if social problems could be dealt with biologically, matters could be resolved once and for all, a final solution…' He seemed oblivious to the fact that no one was in there.

The door swung open, and there stood Mr Grout. ''Ello 'ello, everyone all in one piece?' he said, putting the keys back in his pocket. 'Apologies for not ringing on the bell, Miss Quentinbloom, but I figured as you'd not hear it, see.' A bottle whizzed past his head outside and smashed on the ground at the bottom of the steps. He ducked into the house, closing the door behind him.

The Quentinbloom girls stopped fighting and stood in a row, tidying up their appearances for Mr Grout. They seemed pleased to see him. Not so Jeremiah, who hung back in the doorway so that Grout would not notice him.

'First to report – not that it should concern these girls,

but…' Mr Grout smiled at the row of expectant faces, 'all of them babbies next door is safe as houses.' There was a collective sigh of relief from the girls. 'Mrs Grout had 'em all tucked away in the back room at the first sign of trouble, she did.'

There was a general murmur from the young mothers: 'Thank you, Mr Grout,' and 'Good ol' Grouty', 'Ta very much, Grouty.' He seemed to be held in some respect. Some of them curtseyed.

He was quite convincing as a good guy now, thought Jeremiah, but he'd been pretty convincing too when he was punching and manhandling the day before. Jeremiah slipped back into the front room, where Henry Davenant Hythe was wilfully ignoring events; perhaps it was his way of coping.

'…the wildest animal behaviours, manifesting themselves untrammelled.' The lecture continued as Jeremiah went to the curtain and opened it a crack to look outside. What was going on out there was not what he was expecting to see. The so-called riot consisted of Kitty Angel and her two henchmen, Billy and Smasher, bashing sticks and bottles together and occasionally throwing something at the house, a brick, or stone. Every second or two one of them would shout 'Gerr off!' or make the noise of a struggle. No sign of any Elephant Boys and not so much forty Forty Thieves as three. Jeremiah looked back at Henry, who immediately looked away from him and continued his diatribe.

'Almost like a lower form of life…' Henry muttered. Jeremiah went back past him out into the hall, where Clementina thanked Mr Grout and ordered the girls back to their places, which they were more willing to do now that Grout had put their minds at rest. For a moment, Mr Grout caught Jeremiah's eye and smiled. A pretty good act, thought Jeremiah, or was that the act yesterday?

'Now, if 'n you'll excuse me, ladies, Sir Rodger, time to scare orf these ne'er-do-wells.' Mr Grout went back outside, waving his stick. 'Clear orf, the lot of yer! Geertcha!' and he was gone.

Clementina ushered Sir Rodger and Phyllis back into the room and invited them all to sit down again, ordering Lucy Bonnet to fetch tea.

'Psst!' Lucy hissed at Jeremiah as she passed him in the doorway. Checking behind him, he followed her out of the room and into the hallway.

'Thanks for helping earlier on,' he said, once they were out of sight of the others.

'Ssshhh!' She pulled on his sleeve and walked him urgently to the bottom of the stairs. 'Did you 'ear that window bein' smashed upstairs? Before it all kicked off out front?'

'I did actually, now you come to mention it.'

'I think someone's broken in upstairs, in the room you was in with Miss Daisy,' she whispered.

Clementina called to her from the front room. 'Lucy! Tea!'

'Just comin' up how you like it, ma'am,' she shouted, and then, to Jeremiah, 'Well, you better go 'n 'ave a look up there, hadn't yer?'

'What, me?' But he could see from her look that it was the very least that was expected of him, as a male: to put himself in danger. 'Right, OK.' He started up the stairs and looked back at her for reassurance. She shooed him onwards.

Why do people always go upstairs to the attic, alone, where they know the killer birds/murderer/ventriloquist's dummy is waiting for them up there? Because they haven't spent their whole life watching TV series and films like you and I, so they don't know they're walking into an obvious trap. But Jeremiah had seen enough old films to know that what he was doing was really stupid. So, no excuse.

At the top of the stairs he turned into the corridor towards the bedroom, pushed the door open and called out timorously, 'Hello? Anyone there?'

Inside, the room was a total mess, the bed was overturned, the washstand was kicked over and the bowl cracked. One of the floorboards had been levered up and kneeling beside it, trying to pull up another one, was Ed Viney.

''Ello, Jim-Jam, me ole cocker. Where you spring from viss tarm, ven?' he said, grinning a grin which exposed his rancid teeth.

'Ed Viney? How did you get in?'

'Should'na left ve ladder lyin' ver. Bit obvious like,' said Ed, pulling up the second floorboard.

'What the hell are you doing?' asked Jeremiah.

'Arm juss lookin' for your little black diamond, see? You hid it, 'ave yer?' Jeremiah didn't reply. 'I got 'n importan' client whass interested in acquirin' it. Bit of a "Necromancer" 'isself. So, you juss pop it in viss 'ere 'ankerchief, like a good boy, an' arl be orf.' He held out his hand with a cloth hanging over his palm and looked away so as not to be caught out looking into the black glass. Jeremiah held his ground.

'No way,' he said, 'no way am I giving you my mobile.'

'Well, arl juss 'ave to take it orf yer, ven, woan' I?' said Ed Viney, still smiling. 'Iss in yer little pockety-wockety still, is it?'

Jeremiah said nothing initially, but he knew the outline of the phone could be seen through the trousers half-way down his thigh. His eyes flicked down to it; he wasn't that good at the bluffing game. 'No, it's not,' he said, and that's when it all went crazy.

TWENTY-THREE

Ed Viney was on Jeremiah so quickly, he didn't even see him cross the room. He seemed to have octopus arms and legs, all of which were either hitting, kicking or gripping. With one hand he tried to reach down into the pocket where the phone was, so Jeremiah tried to grab his wrist and twist it, like he'd been taught once in karate, which his mum took him to at the Tooley Street Karate Club every Wednesday. But it's a bit different when your opponent is not wearing an ironed white canvas karate outfit, waiting for you to try out the latest technique so that they can roll away on the mat and slap the floor making a satisfying 'Ush!' noise. Ed Viney twisted Jeremiah's arm back and punched him hard in the neck. Then he leaped onto Jeremiah's shoulders and, gripping his waist with his knees, landed other punches on his head and throat. The two of them looked more like a blurred ball in a cartoon cat fight than a martial arts combat class.

Jeremiah lumbered around the room with Ed on his shoulders, trying to bang him up against a wall and shake him off. 'Carm orn, matey! I know iss in yer pocket! Giss it!' Ed snarled in Jeremiah's ear.

'Pworr! Your breath stinks!' Jeremiah grunted. 'You need to see a dentist!' He succeeded in swinging Ed off his back, where he landed on the floor in a bundle. But Ed was swift to recover and, still crouching in the corner, he slid his long knife out from inside the sleeve of his jacket. It glinted evilly at Jeremiah. Ed slithered along the ground, waiting for the right moment to pounce. But to tell the truth, any moment would be the right moment; Jeremiah felt completely defenceless against this fifteen-year-old veteran of street war.

Ed lunged forward for a tiny second and back to his crouching position, never taking his eyes off Jeremiah. It took Jeremiah a couple of seconds to realise he had in fact been slashed. Across his upper arm.

'Take vat, yer little runt!' hissed Ed. 'An' vers more where vat came from!' He lunged forward again and sliced Jeremiah's arm again. 'An' vat's fer all me trouble!' Jeremiah was cut, badly, in two places on his right arm. Ed lurched across and easily wrestled the phone out of Jeremiah's pocket. 'Got it!' he crowed as he wrapped it carefully in the cloth. Jeremiah was weakening and stumbling around the floor. Ed Viney put the wrapped phone in his pocket, but instead of leaving he went back to his ominous crouching position with his blade still drawn. 'I 'ad enuf o' you, yer little ponce!' He didn't need to stay and strike again, he was just being vindictive now his blood was up.

'Jeremiah? Jeremiah, listen to me.' Another voice came into Jeremiah's left ear, a soft voice. 'Hold my hand. Now.'

'What? Who's that?' There was the vague outline of a smallish person standing just behind him with an arm outstretched for Jeremiah to grab.

'Hold my hand, idiot! Hurry. Do it, now!'

Jeremiah did as he was told just as Ed Viney was leaping forward to make his final, perhaps fatal, slash. The hand pulled Jeremiah immediately away from Ed, further than was possible with just one tug. It felt as if he was flying, the hand continuing to pull him through rushing air. Then they were falling, not slowly, and only for a few seconds, before crunching into the branches of a tree. They crashed downwards, snapping twigs as they went, until finally they landed in very long grass at the bottom of a massive horse chestnut tree.

Jeremiah sat up, confused and shaken by the bashing given him by the chestnut tree. Standing over him was a boyish-looking woman with curly hair, wearing a sort of purply-blue pyjama suit with a frayed yellow scarf. She looked like something from an early episode of *Rentaghost.* She knelt down by Jeremiah and took a pair of scissors out of a leather shoulder bag. She started to cut away the sleeve of his jacket, working deftly and swiftly.

'What?' said Jeremiah. 'What just happened?' He suddenly realised how much his arm was hurting. It was hurting a lot. The sleeve was cut open now and hanging loose from the shoulder, to reveal two gashes, both about four inches long, leaking blood fast and stinging like mad. He bent his right arm up to his chest and hugged it to him with his left arm.

'Straighten your arm,' said the person, getting a bottle out of her shoulder bag, 'put it here.' She held out a sort of wide belt and tried to take Jeremiah's wrist and straighten his arm, but it hurt too much. 'Sorry I called you an idiot just now.'

'Where are we? What happened?' Jeremiah looked around in a panic. They were in a vast meadow of long grasses which bent and swayed in the wind. It was only now that he noticed the wind. He scrambled to his feet, still clutching his bleeding arm. 'Where is this? I mean… woah, that was freaky!'

'Straighten your arm,' she told him again. 'You don't have much time, you're losing blood. Put your arm in here.'

'Oh my God! And who are you?' Jeremiah staggered a few steps away from the tree.

'Don't move from this spot, stay exactly here. Stay in this spot and put your arm in here, come on! Idiot! I'm not meant to be here, you know, I'm already in so much trouble, so... And, erm, sorry I called you an idiot again.'

Jeremiah came back to where the person was standing waiting with the belt thing and the bottle. 'Now, put your arm in here.' But Jeremiah was still too shocked to obey. 'Oh, for crying out loud!' She was getting exasperated. 'Jeremiah? Listen to me – you're not listening, are you? I thought you'd be smarter than this!'

'How do you mean? How do you know my name? What just happened to me? Where are we?'

'Just shut up and do as you're told. Arm. Straight. In this. Now.' She gave up asking and grabbed Jeremiah's wrist, jerking his arm straight and laying it in the belt. 'Sorry,' she said as she yanked the arm downwards.

'Ow! Like, OW?!' She tossed her head sideways to shake her curly hair out of her face. She took the bottle, which had an old-fashioned nozzle on the top of it, and sprayed it up and down over Jeremiah's arm. He winced, expecting it to sting like saltwater or alcohol on a wound, but it didn't. It was just cool and numbing. The liquid coming out of the bottle was thickish and milky, and as soon as it landed on his skin it began to set like glue, forming a transparent casing over the whole area that had been slashed. He could see the two cuts on the arm underneath, joined together by the fast-solidifying gunk.

'What's that? That's amazing,' he said, as he felt the pain of the cuts subsiding a little.

'High-speed vitrification.' The boyish woman was packing away the belt and the bottle into her leather shoulder bag. 'Flexible glass. Didn't hurt much, did it? In a few hours you can just shatter that with a hammer, good as new.' She knocked on Jeremiah's now glazed arm and it sounded like she was knocking on a window pane. 'Well, might leave a little scar, he did cut you badly, but—'

'He took my bloody phone too.'

'Forget your devices, that's just toys. But remember this place, yuh? Look around you. Remember this place. Remember its details. Remember everything you can about it. Everything. Use your memory. It's important. Might come in useful.'

'Thank you, Air Ambulance Person, but where are we?' said Jeremiah, trying to remember details; tree, roots of tree, earth, grass to horizon. There wasn't much to identify.

'Same place as we were before, a moment ago. But a long time before, a very long time.'

'What're you talking about?'

'Blackfriars Road,' she announced, tossing her hair out of her face again.

'Come on. Seriously?'

'Yeah, but a long, long, long time before. The settlement is somewhere over there, by the river, I believe,' she said, pointing vaguely to the shrubby horizon. 'Time to go now.'

'And who the hell are you?' asked Jeremiah.

'I suppose I'm family...' she said, grabbing Jeremiah's left wrist, '...unfortunately. Come on now, I haven't got long. I'm going to be in such doggie-doo as it is. Hold my hand.' She gripped Jeremiah's hand and pulled him a few yards clear of the tree. 'Might not be one hundred per cent accurate, I'm not that good at this, but here we go,' she said.

'Where to?' asked Jeremiah, but it was already too late. The wind seemed to rise, at least it did in Jeremiah's head. There was the sound of fizzing, then hissing, which grew into a torrent. Jeremiah was becoming familiar with the experience, so he didn't resist it as much as before but was able to relax and throw himself into it.

They landed in a confined space and the woman immediately let go of Jeremiah's hand. 'Shit. Not brilliant, sorry, but it'll have to do. Be seeing ya, Number Two,' she said, as if she was in the sixties TV show *The Prisoner*, and faded away into shadow, then nothingness, leaving Jeremiah in the dark. He felt his glass arm; it was indeed reasonably flexible and relatively pain free. As his eyes grew accustomed to the space, he realised, with growing gloom, that he had been dropped off back in the Grouts' coal cupboard.

TWENTY-FOUR

'Oh no! You are joking!' he said out loud.

From the other side of the door he could hear Mrs Grout ticking off the children, and the general domestic noise of too many people crammed into too little space. 'Samuel, mind yer fingers on that blade!' and 'Dolly, wipe up that spill, how many times does I 'ave to tell yer?'

Various of the children were keeping up a constant set of demands on her: 'Ma? I done my chores, can I go 'n play on the roof?', 'When's supper, Ma?' and 'How much is this 'ankerchief worth, Ma?' To which her replies were: 'Not after last time you can't,' 'When you cleared away all that mess' and 'Where'd you get that, yer little scallywag?' respectively.

Jeremiah called out, 'Hello? It's me! Can you let me out?' He pushed on the door and found that, unlike before, it swung open. 'Oh.' So, he walked out into the Grouts' parlour and made Mrs Grout start.

'Oh, young master! Goodness! Where you spring from? Like a blinkin' ghosty.' She was on her knees by the fireplace with her hands covered in black gunge, which she was scooping out of a tin and rubbing all over the iron grating. All around her were the children of various ages, and some of them were working too, while others jumped about trying to annoy them. Two girls were polishing boots from a whole row of dirty footwear. Their hands were covered in black gunge as well. Two of the boys had a huge pile of old rope, which they were shredding with their bare fingers and putting into an even huger pile of wiry fluff. There were cuts and scratches all over their hands and forearms. An older girl and boy were coming in from the backyard, carrying a big bucket of coal between them. All of the children stopped what they were doing to look at Jeremiah.

'How d'yer get in there?' Mrs Grout said, heaving herself up into a standing position with a groan. Wiping the black grime on her apron, she put her hands on her lower back to ease the pain.

'I have honestly not the faintest idea,' said Jeremiah. 'That was one of the weirdest things that's ever happened to me, and there's been quite a lot of weirdness in the last few days. There was this woman in sort of seventies sci-fi clothes and…'

'All right, all right!' growled Mrs Grout. 'I was just askin'.' Some of the children laughed at Jeremiah. 'Shut it!' She growled at the children too. Growling seemed to be her default. She looked back at Jeremiah and nodded her head in what he assumed was an invitation to come in. He stepped tentatively into the room. The air in there was steamy and rank. 'Mr Grout tole me 'e saw yer over at Miss Quentinbloom's, so yer not one o' some gang or whatnot, then?'

'No, I'm not, thank you, Mrs Grout. It's a relief that at least someone believes me.'

'Jolly! Sam! Clear a space for young master, so I can serve 'im a brew!' Her growl had a second, louder, register. Then she turned back down to neutral: 'Wanna cuppa tea?'

'Actually, that'd be really good. Just had a bit of a shock,' Jeremiah said as he sat down at the table.

She took a mug from a shelf and wiped it with what looked like a car mechanic's rag, stuck it on the table and poured hot tea into it from a pot that must have been bubbling on the stove for several years. She took about six brown chunks of sugar and plopped them into the mug, giving it a stir with a filthy spoon.[20]

Jeremiah took the mug and brought it near his lips. He looked down into its greasy brown surface and smelt its aroma, like a builder's toolbox. 'I'll just leave it there to cool for a bit,' he said.

'Ma? I finished them boots, can I stop now, Ma?' a boy of perhaps eight years old said, tugging at her skirt to get her attention.

'Look at yer! Got polish all over yer, Samuel! Clean it up!' she growled, which, coming from a woman with black grease from the fire grate half-way up her forearms and all over her apron, was pushing it. 'And Poppy, go an' 'elp Jack 'n James with the rope shreddin'.' The girl called Poppy started whimpering; obviously rope shredding was not a popular job. 'An' stop yer whinin'.'

Another, younger girl chipped in with, 'Can I go in ve street 'n play now?' This seemed to be an idea they could all go for. There was a general hubbub of children asking if they could go out to play in the street.

'And I'll 'ear no more from you, Tess, while we're about it, or I'll send yer off with the Mudlarks and see hows yer likes it.' Despite the low, gravelly level of her speech, Mrs Grout never choked nor became hoarse.

A cheeky-looking boy whose hair had wood chippings in it came and stood right between Jeremiah and Mrs Grout. 'Can I go in va mud again, Ma? Wiv va Mudlarks?'

---

20 In fact, having a cup of tea after a shock only works if it's sweet tea, so even if you normally don't take sugar in your tea, you should if you've been shaken up. But for some reason, the sugar doesn't have this calming effect on its own. You never hear, 'Oh, you've had a shock – sit down and have a sherbet fountain.'

Mrs Grout wheezed in indignation. 'No, you cannot, Jolly! Else you'll cut yer feet on somethin' sharp 'n that'll be an end of yer! Oooffff!' She had a twinge of back pain.

'I don't know how you do it, Mrs Grout, with all these kids.' Jeremiah looked around the room at the debris on the battlefield of Mrs Grout's existence. The walls were a dingy brown that might once have been yellow, and cooking grease had layered the ceiling with an opaque varnish.

There was a picture in a frame on one wall, hanging beside a couple of the iron saucepans. In the picture was the entire Grout clan, a messy row, with Mr and Mrs Grout at the centre. To the right, standing behind Mrs Grout, was a taller woman with long hair. She stood out because her hair was not tied up like all the other women Jeremiah had met recently. He got up to get a closer look. The picture was hanging quite low on the wall, so he had to stoop. Yes, it was definitely her. The woman in the photo in the biscuit tin, the woman in Tooley Street in 2011. A fellow time traveller, then. His heart rate went up. He reached into his pocket and, keeping it in his palm so that Mrs Grout wouldn't see it, took a mini-puff on his inhaler.

There's a word Jeremiah had learned from Stepdad Pete: numinous. 'Numinous, Jem. Very lovely word. It means when something has some kind of special power that sets off vibrations inside you,' he had said one day when they were scraping paint off a wall at the top of the house. 'It might be like an amazing view or a very tall building. Like there's kind of spiritual stuff oozing out of it. It could even just be the way the sun shines on a certain door. Sets you off. Like that time we went to Battersea Park and you loved the bandstand, remember?'

The photo of the woman with long hair was having an effect on Jeremiah now. But whether it was numinous or not, he wasn't sure. Spiritual stuff was not exactly oozing off her, but there was a very unsettling vibration.

'Mrs Grout?' He turned back to her. 'This picture on your wall?'

'Oh yes, that's our photygraph that is,' she smiled; perhaps it brought back happy memories. But even smiling didn't soften her tone. 'That's us all on a day out in Hampton by the river, that is.'

'Who's the woman in the back row? The one with the long hair?'

'Oh, that's Amanda. Doctor Amanda I should say. Or Professor Amanda or somethin'. Amanda Vergilius, right clever she is. She never did like to do up 'er 'air proper. Bit Bohemian, like, as they say. But I weren't shocked; she was a decent lady she was.'

'Do you know where that Dr Amanda Vergilius is now, Mrs Grout? Where I could find her?' he asked, as casually as he could.

'Not exactly. She was staying at an 'ouse over in the village of Twickenham, but I wouldn't know if she's still there. 'Aven't seen 'er for a couple o' years. She was always good to these poor children, though. Showed an interest. The only one 'oo did, as it 'appens. Why you askin'?'

TWENTY-FIVE

Artemesia Plutarch opened a packet of Cheesy Wotsits. She knew they weren't authentic Wotsits – they were a more recent rebrand, and in any case the original Wotsit is a nineties snack, not a seventies one. But she wasn't in the mood to care. She munched disconsolately on the salty puffed corn, which dried out the saliva in her mouth; somehow the rebrands never managed to simulate the artificial flavouring of a genuine twentieth-century snack. Without thinking, she stuffed another one in her mouth before she'd finished the first one. Scoobeedoo whined; he'd thought that second one might be for him. He put his paws up on Artemesia's knee and cocked his head to one side as if to say, 'Go on, you mean bastard, you were twirling that one near my nose for at least ten seconds – how many more have you got in there?' Absent-mindedly, Artemesia let him have one, then another. They created a crumby mess on the sofa. She patted the back of Scoobeedoo's neck, unintentionally rubbing the salty oil from the snack behind the dog's ears. If she had to go back to help her bloody sister out – yet again – she was definitely going to take her dog with her next time to keep her company. This last little expedition was the scariest yet.

When she got home, there had been a notice in the lobby, by the drinks dispensers, calling an 'Immediate Special General Meeting' of the Residents' Association sub-committee. She'd run upstairs, slung her leather satchel on the bed, and then gone straight to the meeting room without feeding or watering the Scoob. Best not to draw attention by being late. But she was sweating right across her back and was sure it was obvious she'd been out somewhere.

The meeting had been gruelling. The great Dr Mandar Vergeelis herself put in a brief appearance, just long enough to receive some lashings of praise and a round of applause. She made a short speech about how much she cared, which everyone had to sit through appreciatively. She also managed, in passing, to mention all of her recent data-harvesting triumphs and then thanked everyone from the bottom of her heart, lying that she couldn't have done it without their support. Just when Artemesia thought it was finished and they could go, Mandar Vergeelis had stopped, looked slowly around the room into each of their eyes in turn. (In fact, she was defocusing on the little space in the middle just above their eyes; a technique she'd learned in public-speaking class, to make everyone think you were talking to them directly.)

'Oh, and one other thing – little theory of mine about the boy? The boy who's been jumping around? I think we'll find he's Enid's son…' There was a general 'ooh' and 'aah' and a couple of 'tuts'. She went on, '…and I think he may lead us to her.' Her eyes finished on Artemesia and stayed there for a long moment. She tried not to show how much she was squirming inside, but Vergeelis's stare seemed to burn through several outer defence layers. 'It is just a theory at the moment, and we have nothing to fix Enid with him, but, as you know, we are still working on fixing Enid. She's been AWOL for a long, long time. Too long.'

'Matter of interest; anyone know what exactly AWOL stands for?' asked Beatlejohn Basho, who was young and had not done military history as an option.

'Absent Without Leave,' said Dickensian, leaning over while polishing his glasses, and then, more quietly, 'or Abducted When Outside London.' He nodded the nod of a conspiracy theorist. 'It happens.'

'Thanks,' said Basho. 'Without leaving what?'

'Ssshh,' said Ordnari Cervantes, whose earrings were making as much noise as their talk, 'let her finish.'

Toto Chairman stifled a laugh, which made her yawn. She was ready for the cakes and tea.

'Thank you, Ordnari,' said Mandar Vergeelis. 'What I was going on to say was that although we do have a sighting of her in 2011 near London Bridge, we don't yet have a locational fix on her in 2019. We can, however, fix the boy there. Possible set-off is a photo – of me, as it happens, rather a stylish one – and we have a biscuit tin. So he's here, in this house. Which leads me to think that he's Enid's child, which would be a serious breach indeed. And might explain her disappearance. What was she thinking; that she could just give birth in any time she liked?' More disapproving tuts and sighs from the members of the committee, particularly from Conrad, who was trying to ingratiate himself with Dr Vergeelis. She went on, 'I would stress that this is still a theory, but if I am right, it could be of great interest to Epi-Genetic Mem and all of us at Morphic Resonance, and I'll be writing up a full report to present to them at the next "Way Forward" convention.'

I bet you will, thought Artemesia, and asking them for a job, no doubt.

'Sorry?' said Vergeelis. 'What was that?' Perhaps Artemesia had thought slightly too loudly.

'Nothing,' she said nervously. 'Bravo, Epi-Gen Mem, bravo, Dr Vergeelis. Way Forward! Way, Way Forward.'

Mandar Vergeelis's face remained completely unruffled, and she blinked slowly, like a crocodile lurking at the surface. Then she snapped out of it into what she thought was a warm smile. 'It could be the breakthrough we've been waiting for!' She concluded with her standard inspirational speech, honed and practised in the mirror over many years. 'And remember, all of you, it's *you* that really matter, *your* ideas, *your* hopes, *your* aspirations. And if I can leave you with just one thought: *Let It Shine!*' She left the room to further applause, which subsided into nothing the moment she was past the door.

'Yeah, and we know where yours shines out from,' Toto Chairman murmured under her breath.

Conrad raced out after Vergeelis, hoping that she would remember him next time she needed a research assistant.

Later, back in the apartment, the Scoob stopped licking the empty Wotsits packet and jumped up onto the sofa again. The dog started making a pathetic weeping noise that could be translated as: 'No proper walk for a whole week. I now regret ever liking you, or licking you, even.' Artemesia sighed. She took the lead off the hook and put her leather satchel over her shoulder. She took a couple of cardboard scoopers from the pile on the shelf and stuffed them into the bag. All in all, she thought, things were getting tighter. The horizon was getting nearer. The Breach crew were getting closer. If she did have to go on another secret trip to the 2000s, she was definitely going to bring the Scoob with her – why not? If you're going to risk a Trallypaz sentence, you might as well make it worthwhile. Perhaps she could take in the seventies while she was about it, make a round trip of it. She could harvest some really cool pointless toys; perhaps a Barbie and Ken? A Space Hopper, even? Although that might be difficult to transport back. 'Would you like that, Scoob?' The dog jumped up and down, sensing Artemesia's excitement at the thought of a few days' holiday in the seventies.

On their way out of the building, Artemesia went to stop at the first-floor communal medical-equipment stack to sneakily return the illegally taken Vitri-nozzle. But there were two large people there, with very thick necks, and matching hats and gloves, going through the ledger. They were taking photographs of the pages with an analogue camera which had a flash attachment. They looked official. From County Hall?

'Come on, Scoob,' she said, quickly turning on her heel and hurrying past them down the stairs.

One of them noticed her, turned and shouted after her, 'Hello? Wait, please. Just like to ask you a few questions. Stop. Ms?' Artemesia hated being called Ms.

TWENTY-SIX

The River Crane is a small tributary of the Thames that runs for about nine miles between Richmond and Hounslow, passing through Twickenham on its way. It's a little, hidden sanctuary for river wildlife and nowadays is mostly to be discovered at the bottom of people's gardens as a small stream – not really big enough to moor a boat on, but lovely enough to indulge in fantasies of idyllic country scenes as you blank your mind to the sound of the heavy-goods lorries thundering past nearby on the A316. About fifty minutes' drive to central London from here, depending on traffic, or a twenty-five-minute train ride.

The whole area has been served by London and South Western trains since the 1860s, and the easy commuting has meant a gradual expansion of the area into what can nowadays rightly be called a 'leafy suburb', with lots of tree-lined avenues and terrifying house prices. There are still many of the larger houses which sprang up with the railway, mostly divided up into spacious flats now. In this borough, even the terraces of what were known as 'workmen's cottages' are fairly grand, compared to those in, say, Blackfriars or Bermondsey. Gardens abound.

There is a lot of snobbishness about north of the river and south of the river in London. It's generally thought that north of the river is where the towny sophisticates live, while south of the river doesn't really count. The reality is that, like the line between right and wrong, between true and false, between past and future, the Thames is very wiggly. Posh areas such as Barnes and Kew are actually south of the river, whereas places that sound as if they belong south – Ealing or Barking, say – are actually north.

Twickenham, which sounds like the sort of place swanky townsfolk might laugh at, is actually north of the river, along with Chiswick and Fulham and Kensington, and all the other areas where such people might consider going to a dinner party, or perhaps just 'drinks'. So, no more bad-mouthing Twickenham, all right? Personally, I have mixed feelings about the place, but I think I've found a way round my editor. Just don't tell her it's a footnote, and don't put it in a smaller font size with a little asterisk meaning 'footnote'.[21]

When they came out of Twickenham station, Jeremiah and Phyllis Stokes turned left, crossing the little River Crane and turned right into Cole Park Road, the epitome of a leafy suburban street. Plane trees created a canopy above them, through which afternoon sunlight trickled. There was perhaps the hint of a light drizzle, but there was nothing in the sky that suggested proper rain. Behind them, they could hear the chugging of the train as it left the station and set off for Teddington. The streets were empty apart from a uniformed nanny pushing a magnificent iron pram with suspension springs and big, spoked wheels. Jeremiah was wearing replacement clothes given him by Sir Rodger: a pair of flannel trousers and some braces which had needed shortening as far as the clips would go, a stiff-collared shirt, an old jersey (too big), a thick jacket and brown

---

21 Ed. just told me I've got to stop 'going all postmodern' in the footnotes. Which seems ironic, since the story is about what happened post-nowadays, i.e. in the future. In the future we'll all be 'postmodern'.

leather lace-up shoes with hefty toe-caps. He'd insisted on changing in private to avoid questions about the strange glass dressing on his arm, which, luckily, the voluminous sleeves of the shirt had slipped over quite easily. Phyllis had given him quite a telling off for tearing the previous trousers and mysteriously shredding one of the sleeves of the tweed jacket: 'An outfit like that should have lasted you thirty years.' Nevertheless, she agreed, he would have had to change in any case for today's expedition to the back of beyond; a tweed suit would have made him appear too wealthy, too much like a gentleman, and the whole idea was to keep a low profile. He was to behave as if he were her servant and, she thought, it might be good for him to learn some respect and deportment.

'Now, I may only be able to detain Mr Briggs for a short while. By all reports he is a cantankerous old man. So you will need to be quick and to keep your wits about you,' she said, looking at the numbers of the houses on their right. She slowed her pace. 'There it is, number twenty-three.' She indicated a large white and brick house three further along from them. 'And those must be the guest bedrooms, there on the first floor. You can see the backs of the dressing-table mirrors in the windows.'

The house was set back from the road by about twenty feet. It was double-fronted and detached, with wide passages on either side before the fences of the neighbouring houses. 'A substantial property on three floors, comprising five bedrooms, study, three living areas, possible loft extension, pending planning permission, could do with some modernisation, must see at earliest opportunity,' is how an estate agent might describe it nowadays, although, of course, it would now be at least seven separate flats.

Phyllis stopped before opening the buff-coloured wooden gate to check with Jeremiah. 'Are you ready?'

'Yeah. I mean, indeed I am, ma'am,' he said, straightening his back and trying to look servantly.

'And for goodness' sake, sort out your collar!' She grabbed hold of his shirt collar, a twist of which had escaped from under the jacket, and gave it a yank. They arrived at the front door and Phyllis gave the bell pull a tug. They waited.

Jeremiah had spent the night before in Sir Rodger's ghostly spare room in Gordon Square. He couldn't sleep, lying under the high ceiling in the freezing-cold room on the first floor at the back of Sir Rodger's enormous house. At about two a.m., he'd got up and wedged an oak chair under the door handle, to try to feel safer. At three he'd found the chamber pot under the bed and had a wee. Poor Janet the maid, he thought, she probably has to empty these for the whole house every morning; maybe I should offer to help her tomorrow. Then he had lain there wide awake for a further hour or two, straining at his memory, trying to force it to recall something more, anything, about the woman in the photo and what exactly his mum had said about her: 'You do come from a rather odd family.' Then he must have drifted off, because at about six he was woken out of a half-sleep by the sudden clanging of a bell and the voice of Mrs Jarvis, the cook, shouting up the stairs, 'Breeeeak-faaaast!'

After what seemed a very long time standing on the front step in Twickenham, they heard the noise of some bolts and chains, and the front door of number 23 opened about five inches. A weary-looking woman's face appeared in the gap. 'Yes?' she said.

'Mrs Doreen Briggs?' asked Phyllis, sharply, yet with a pleasant smile.

'I am she. How may I assist?' said the woman, not sounding as if she felt like assisting anyone.

'May I speak with your husband, Mr Contumely Briggs? I have come about a room to rent,' said Phyllis brightly.

'All the rooms is taken,' said the woman, and started to close the door again. Phyllis interrupted her with the verbal equivalent of a foot in the door.

'Please, Mrs Briggs. We have come all the way to Twickenham from *London* on the train.' She said the word 'London' as if it had been as far as Delhi might be to us nowadays. The woman's eyebrows raised involuntarily. 'From Waterloo,' added Phyllis, as if that were an exotic bazaar on the road to Agra. The door edged open and the woman invited them in.

'All right, you can try him. But he'll say same as me,' she said.

'Thank you,' said Phyllis, with a self-satisfied upward inflection. They followed the woman through to a large, high-ceilinged front room. The floorboards were varnished to a dark shine, so there was an echo. Unlike Sir Rodger's, everything in here had its place and was dusted and clean. A glass case with a model ship in it. A wooden filing cabinet with multiple small drawers, each with its own polished brass knob. A clock that ticked. At the end of the room opposite the door was a sizeable mahogany desk with neat piles of papers on it. And sitting at the desk was a frowning man in a dark green velvet jacket. His hair was rigidly combed and his side whiskers were trimmed. He was looking through ledgers. He sneezed as they came in, and, taking out a handkerchief, blew his nose unpleasantly, inspecting the hanky afterwards before putting it back in his trouser pocket. He didn't look up at them.

TWENTY-SEVEN

Phyllis stood facing the desk, with Jeremiah standing behind her and to one side, as he had been instructed. The ghostly woman stayed back by the door. 'Contumely?' she said, tonelessly. 'Woman about a room. I told her they're all taken.'

'Well, why bring her in here, then?' he said, looking up briefly to raise his eyes to the ceiling.

'Good day, Mr Briggs!' said Phyllis, like an evangelist bringing good news.

'Is it?' said Mr Contumely Briggs, returning to his paperwork.

Phyllis carried on, undaunted. 'A friend of mine, Dr Amanda Vergilius, told me that you might have a room to let?'

'Who?' he said. 'Never heard of her.' He sniffed and then, picking up a little tin from the table, he took a pinch of snuff and deposited it in the crook of his thumb. He put his long nose over the base of his thumb, and, blocking one of his nostrils, gave an almighty pull on the other one, hoovering all the snuff up into it. He blinked and exhaled. The tobacco mixture didn't seem to have made him any more cheerful.

'Amanda Vergilius?' said his wife from the door. 'Yes, you have heard of her, Contumely, if you'll beg my pardon, sir, for disagreeing with you.'

He harrumphed. 'Really? Is that so?' Jeremiah sensed that Mrs Briggs rather enjoyed disagreeing with her husband, and perhaps also enjoyed asking to be forgiven afterwards. They seemed a pretty dysfunctional couple.

'She was the odd lady with the long red hair who used to be in number four,' said Mrs Briggs.

'Oh, her. Mad as a frog. *Woman* scientist?' He looked at Phyllis and then Jeremiah as if for support. 'Whoever heard of such a ridiculous thing!' He gave a humourless grin, as if he had just been quite funny and was hoping Jeremiah, as a fellow male, would get the joke.

'Ah yes, number four,' said Phyllis, bluffing, 'that was her room number, of course. I knew that. She often told me that.'

Mrs Briggs dared to take a couple of steps forward into the room. 'We haven't seen her for a couple of years or more, have we, Contumely?' she said.

Contumely Briggs sneezed again, loudly, and Mrs Briggs stepped back again to her place by the door. He dragged the handkerchief from his trouser pocket and trumpeted into it, again checking it before slipping it back into his pocket. Jeremiah caught sight of it too, this time, and wished he hadn't.

'So, she no longer lodges here?' said Phyllis, ignoring the sneeze and pressing on as positively as she could. 'So her room, number four, might be available.'

'Didn't say that,' said Contumely Briggs, giving Phyllis a steel-eye stare.

'Might I see the room?' said Phyllis, pressing forward with their plan.

Mrs Briggs spoke up from behind them. 'She paid a lot of money in advance, so, really the room's still taken. We thought it was odd at the time...' She petered out after a scathing look from her husband.

'So, she has definitely gone, you say?' Phyllis persevered.

'Good riddance, I say. And to you,' said Contumely Briggs, sniffing again.

'I apologise for my husband,' said his wife, softly, more to provoke him than for Phyllis and Jeremiah's benefit.

'What was that?' he snapped. It was as if the arrival of others had given them the chance to bicker, for which they needed an audience.

'Nothing, Mr Briggs, nothing at all,' Mrs Briggs spat back at him. Time to intervene, thought Jeremiah, and gave a loud cough into Phyllis's right ear, their pre-arranged signal.

'I do apologise,' said Phyllis, 'but this is my servant, Jeremiah. He is thirsty. Might he have a small glass of water in the servants' quarters?'

Mr Briggs gave an astonished harrumph, as if to say that, obviously, Jeremiah could not have a glass of water in the servants' quarters and he was offended that Phyllis had even asked. His wife took pleasure in contradicting his wish.

'Of course he may, Mrs...?'

'Stokes, Phyllis Stokes.'

'Of course he may, Mrs Stokes. Jeremiah? Follow me.'

Mr Briggs did not know how to react to this disobedience, so he sneezed again and dragged out his snuffy handkerchief.

'Thank you so much, Mrs Briggs,' said Phyllis and added, 'Jeremiah? I shall ring for you when I am ready.'

She's enjoying this, thought Jeremiah, but he mumbled a 'yes, ma'am' as he was led out of the room by Mrs Briggs.

Phyllis, left alone with Contumely Briggs, did her best to keep the conversation light. She looked out of the window behind Briggs's desk for inspiration. 'So... Mr Briggs, may I compliment you on the fine landscaping of your garden?'

'You can try, but it's not mine,' he said, reaching for the snuff box and going through the unpleasant routine again; thumb, sniff, handkerchief, pocket. 'I sold it to the neighbour. He's in the theatre, so there's lots of money there…' He rubbed his thumb and forefingers together as if he were the first person ever to have done that and was being quite clever.

'Oh really? How terribly, terribly interesting, aha ha…' said Phyllis, wondering how long she would be able to keep this going.

Mrs Doreen Briggs led Jeremiah from the room and down the steps towards the back of the house. She opened a creaking wooden door with a wooden drop latch and pointed to a jug and two glasses on a table in the middle of the room. 'Help yourself.' They were in a low-ceilinged room without much light. There was a big, square, white sink with brass taps sticking out from the wall and a dresser with plates on it and drawers below. 'I have to return to my duties, but you can stay here until you see that bell go; the one that says Receiving Room.' On the wall was a box with a glass front, about a foot square, in which were about twelve little bells with labels underneath them: Dining Room, Trade, Front Door, Receiving Room, and so on. The box was covered in a layer of dust, as was the whole room. 'We don't have servants any more,' she said, as if reading Jeremiah's thoughts. 'This used to be a grand house, you know, but now I have to do everything.' Away from Mr Briggs, she was more sympathetic.

'Thank you, Mrs Briggs, ma'am,' said Jeremiah after her, as she left the room, pulling the creaky door to.

The moment she was gone, he went over to the dresser and quickly started opening the drawers. Keys, that's what he wanted, and more specifically the key to room number 4. This Dr Amanda Vergilius, whoever she was, might be part of his 'odd family', along with the one who'd rescued him from Ed Viney. But Vergilius was the only definite, followable lead he'd had since his whole life had gone into time spasm. If anyone did, she would have an explanation for what he'd been going through, so he must find her. And, most importantly for Jeremiah, she might know where his mum was.

The first drawer was full of some dirty cloths and a stiff wire brush, the second was empty. He opened the larger drawers below and there was a big ring of keys; lots of them. About twenty, by his calculation. Some with labels on them, some not. Numbers of rooms did not seem to figure. He decided to take the whole ring and try. He lifted the creaky door on its hinge in an attempt to stop the creak, and slid out of the room. In front of him was the hall, and there was no sign of Mrs Briggs. He could hear Phyllis's voice coming from the front room. 'I see you use a five-column entry book to record all household expenditure, how fascinating!' she was saying. Jeremiah quickly tiptoed past and crept up the stairs.

At the top was a corridor with an old smoky-blue carpet, which had several doors leading off it. Luckily, these were numbered, so Jeremiah went towards the fourth door along. As he passed number 3, the floor gave an almighty groan, like a plaintive cat in the night. He froze. Then, by walking as close to the skirting as he could, he arrived at the door to number 4 without any further complaint from the house. He was prepared to try every key on the ring. Of course, some were obviously not going to fit, so he passed on them. His heart was thumping and a sweat came up under his shirt. At about the seventh attempt, he found a key that slid into the lock, and, with a small wiggle, turned it. He took a deep breath through his nose, and, looking back to check Mrs Briggs wasn't around, he was in.

A smell of mothballs hit him in the face. The room was definitely unoccupied. There was a bed, stripped, a small upright chair and a washstand table with a bowl and vanity kit on it. Light was slanting through the net curtains and being dappled by the trees outside. The empty room and strong smell of naphthalene disappointed Jeremiah. He didn't know what he'd been expecting; some papers? A Tardis? Perhaps something of his mum's? But there was nothing. He went to the window and peeked out to the path up which he and Phyllis had come, and the buff-coloured gate.

He looked at the washstand with its little oval mirror and tray of comb and brushes. The light reflected boldly in the mirror and shone on the tray and its contents. Catching the light for a moment, sticking out from one of the brushes, was a long hair. It briefly appeared and then was gone as the sun disappeared behind a cloud outside, putting the room in shade. Jeremiah bent down to look at the hair closely, in the shadow. It was a dark, browny red.

In the top pocket of his jacket, Phyllis had stuffed a handkerchief. Jeremiah took out the handkerchief and carefully picked up the hair, being sure not to touch it himself. He folded the handkerchief over the hair and put it back in his top pocket. If he ever got back home, he could run this through Family Ancestry Net and see if this Dr Amanda Vergilius was really family like his mum had said. He'd paid £39.99 for the app, so he might as well use it.

TWENTY-EIGHT

Back downstairs in the pantry, Jeremiah just had time to pour himself the glass of water he was supposed to have wanted, when Mrs Briggs came in. He looked guilty as hell. He'd managed to get the keys safely back in the drawer, but his breathing and the startled look in his eyes gave him away.

'Oh, you didn't drink your water,' said Doreen Briggs, looking at him suspiciously. He stammered wordlessly in reply. 'Why did you go upstairs?' she said, without releasing him from her gaze.

So his careful tiptoeing had not worked. 'I, erm, was just trying to… sorry,' was all he could manage. He'd have done better if he'd just smiled and said, 'Because I'm a thief on a recce.'

As if she'd read his thoughts, she replied, 'There's nothing to take here. Husband sold it all to pay off his debts. But you just thought you'd have a little snoop around, did you? Is that what you thought?' She let that hang in the air, expecting a reply. Jeremiah blinked in the terror of her headlights. He couldn't think of anything remotely convincing to say and, without considering whether it was the most sensible move, he dashed to the back door, opened it and ran out into the back garden. 'Young man! You didn't drink your water!' she yelled after him.

The moment he was in the back garden, he realised

quite what a terrible idea it had been. A large dog on a chain leaped at him, barking with the ferocity of a Harley-Davidson with no silencer. He jumped out of its way as it strained on its leash, showing teeth like a shark's. This sent him stumbling over onto the back lawn, where a gaggle of about seven geese objected strongly to his arriving among them. He got up and backed away from them, tripping on a paving stone and falling back into a small pond. His trousers and bum were now soaked. He scrambled out of the pond, still pursued by the geese, and ran along the passage at the side of the house out to the front garden. He was hoping to make it to the gate and into the street, but Phyllis was on the front step saying goodbye to Mr Contumely Briggs.

'Ah, there you are, Jeremiah, I've been ringing and ringing. Where have you been? And why are you wet?' she said.

'I had an accident with a duck pond,' he smiled, weakly.

'You silly servant!' she scolded, rather too severely, and then to Mr Briggs, 'I really think I shall have to get myself a more professional one.'

'Do you want me to give him a thrashing with my stick?' said Mr Briggs, as if it were the most generous offer.

'No. Thank you, Mr Briggs. Most kind of you. But I have my own methods of discipline,' said Phyllis.

'Are you sure?' said Contumely Briggs. 'I can easily give him the kind of hiding he will remember for a lifetime. It would be my pleasure.' I bet it would, thought Jeremiah.

Mr Briggs reached inside the front door where the umbrellas and walking sticks stood in an elephant's-foot bucket and selected a thin, knobbly stick. He whipped it through the air a couple of times and stepped towards Jeremiah. He seemed to come alive with a stick in his hand.

With perfect timing, Mrs Briggs came out into the front garden, having followed Jeremiah through the garden and the passage. She was carrying his glass of water. 'You daft boy! You never finished your glass of water! Here!' she said, giving no indication that she'd discovered him snooping. Perhaps she would have liked him to have robbed her husband.

Phyllis turned to Jeremiah and said, 'Honestly! Complaining of thirst all the way down here! One more misbehaviour of this kind and you'll find yourself in the Workhouse, do you understand? You drink it all, now. All of it, if you please.'

Jeremiah took the glass and glugged it all down. 'Yes, ma'am,' he mumbled, resentfully, and handed the empty glass back to Mrs Briggs.

'Well, Mr Briggs, it's been educational,' said Phyllis, grabbing Jeremiah by the collar. 'Thank you so much for the extraordinary insight into the workings of the Elvedon steam tractor, but we really must be going now. Come along, Jeremiah.' She pulled Jeremiah towards the front gate. Mr Briggs followed them up the path, still brandishing the stick menacingly and swishing it through the air.

'Apologies, Mrs Stokes, my husband does tend to get a bit carried away,' said Doreen Briggs. Her husband turned on her.

'Mrs Briggs? Inside! Now!' he shouted at her, and then sneezed. In the moment while he took out his handkerchief to blow his nose, the two women seemed to reach an unspoken agreement. Doreen Briggs said goodbye and disappeared inside the house and Phyllis managed to pull Jeremiah out into the street, where she walked as quickly as she could away from the house. By the time Mr Briggs's handkerchief was back in his pocket, they had gone.

Once they were out of earshot and eyeshot, Phyllis let go of Jeremiah's collar. She was fuming. 'That is the last time I play one of your games, or "scams", as you call them, Jeremiah Bourne!'

'You didn't have to lay it on so thick, you know,' he said. The wetness of his trousers was making a dull scraping sound as he walked.

'After all the efforts I have made on your behalf,' she said, indignantly, 'leaving me with the most boring and obnoxious man I have ever met! I hope it was worth it.'

A man with a cart was driving past in the opposite direction. 'Afternoon!' he called across to them. Phyllis returned the greeting.

'Who was that?' asked Jeremiah.

'I have no idea, but we are in the country here. So, did you find anything?'

Jeremiah told her about finding the hair and tried to explain the principles of DNA identification. 'Do you know what fingerprints are? No two people can have exactly the same one. Well, DNA is similar to a fingerprint, but running throughout every part of one's body.'

'Yes, yes, we do have forensic fingerprinting, we're not in the Dark Ages, you know,' she said defensively as they reached the end of Cole Park Road and turned left over the Crane. 'It was discovered by a team of Bengali gentlemen and introduced over here ten years ago.'

From below the bridge they heard the shout of the platform announcer: 'The next train will be for Waterloo. Stopping at Mortlake, Barnes, Putney, Clapham Junction, Battersea, Vauxhall and London Waterloo.'

'Come along, Jeremiah, or we shall miss the train,' said Phyllis, hurrying to the ticket barrier in the station. 'Ticket?' she said, impatiently, waiting for Jeremiah to produce their tickets.

From his wet trouser pocket, Jeremiah took out the tickets, which were damp but not soggy, and the inspector clipped them with a punch-hole. The long red hair was thankfully still safe and dry in the handkerchief in the top pocket of his jacket.

Once at the bottom of the stairs, they could see the train in the distance, puffing its way ever so slowly towards the platform. There was no cappuccino latte bar, no digital arrival screen, no transparent plastic waste bin, but apart from that, the platform was virtually the same as it is nowadays. The iron pillars and tin roof, the layers of thick over-painting, the colour scheme of cream and green. Opposite, on the other side of the rails, was an overgrown embankment, being enjoyed by all manner of insects, birds, snails and, no doubt, rats. Phyllis sat on a platform bench but objected when Jeremiah tried to sit too.

'Jeremiah! You are still a servant until we get out of here, so when the train comes, I shall expect you to open the door for me and help me up into the carriage. Goodness, I hope you have learned at least something of use from our expedition today!'

Jeremiah did as he was told and they found a compartment to themselves. No walk-through, open-plan commuter trains in those days. Phyllis was out of sorts; the encounter with Contumely Briggs had stretched her patience. 'Imagine being married to the ghastly so-and-so! I pity his poor wife. If my dear Mr Stokes were still with us, he would have given that Contumely Briggs a stiff talking-to with regard to what it means to be a husband!'

They sat down by the window, which was open, and a breeze buffeted them as the train picked up speed. The scratchy upholstery of the seat pressed like needles into the wet flannel of Jeremiah's trousers, making the journey an uncomfortable one.

Phyllis sat muttering and tutting. 'I don't know how I was persuaded to come on this wild goose chase, to retrieve… what? A hair in a hanky!'

'But this woman could be the key to what's happening to me,' said Jeremiah. 'I'm sorry if you had such a bad time, and thanks and everything, but it's really important.'

'Jeremiah, your theory about this Vergilius woman seems to be based on very little, other than wishful thinking,' shouted Phyllis over the din of the train in motion. 'How can you be sure that the woman who followed your mother and the lady whose rented accommodation we have just invaded are one and the same?'

'Well, OK, I can't be a hundred per cent, but my memory hardly ever lets me down; it's the one bit of me I know I can rely on. My mum told me that.'

The afternoon light was slicing across their faces in time with the train as they passed a row of sycamore trees in Barnes. And then the weather changed and the light drained from the sky.

'My own feeling is that you are embarking on an unwise course of action, Jem, which may only upset you. A mother should never abandon her children, but once she has done so, it is best to leave well alone.'

Jeremiah was defensive. 'Oh yeah?' he shouted back. 'My mum didn't abandon me, actually, she had her reasons.' The train gave a massive toot, and a blanket of sooty steam wafted through the open window. Jeremiah got up and slid the window closed, but even now, the chugging and banging of the train's ironwork was all around them, underneath them. 'And what about those girls at Clementina's? Aren't you just forcing them all to abandon their children?'

'Jeremiah,' said Phyllis, staying irritatingly calm, 'those girls have no hope of bringing up those children. No husbands, no economic security, no family, even, most of them. Clementina is helping them all to a better future, the mothers and the children.'

'What, like Daisy Wallace, you mean?' he said, raising his voice again. 'She's having a much better future now. In the future. Away from all you lot.'

A proper row had presented itself to them, but Phyllis was not taking the bait. 'I am merely trying to help you, and if my counsel is no longer required then I shall button my lip and say no more.' She turned away from him and looked out of the window at the meadows as they approached Putney.

'Oh, this is really childish,' he said, after she'd continued to look away for two stops. 'We're just going to sit in silence now, are we, for the rest of the journey?' She turned and gave him a withering look, then turned back to the window. The train left Battersea station and the landscape became more citified. Factory buildings and rows of workers' cottages, winding streets, a coalman on a wagon being pulled along by a sorry horse.

They sat like that, not speaking to each other, until the train came to an exhausted stop at Waterloo. 'You're like my stepsister Ruby, you are,' said Jeremiah as he got down and helped Phyllis onto the platform, 'and she's eleven.' Phyllis kept her nose in the air and walked past him as if he were a stranger.

She was waiting for him at the ticket barrier, where he produced the damp tickets again and then she set off towards the steps. Two or three men in dark blue jackets and caps stood in her way shouting, 'Luggage, ma'am? Carry your luggage?' and 'Need a porter, ma'am?', but she steered through them to the large exit gateway at the top of the grand Waterloo stairs. Jeremiah followed her, desperate to get her to turn round and acknowledge him.

'You don't understand what's been, like, happening to me! I was in the middle of being, like, slashed to death by this bloke Ed Viney, when suddenly this woman appears from nowhere and takes me to this, like, wilderness place and put this glass thing on my arm, and suddenly I'm, like, cured...'

Phyllis turned back to him at the top of the steps. The grey light was reflecting off the river behind them, silhouetting her. She fixed Jeremiah with her eye. '"*Like*" cured? "*Like*" cured, Jem? Well, were you cured? Or were you "like" cured? Which is it?' she said.

'Aha, you spoke to me,' said Jeremiah.

Phyllis drew in her breath. 'Only to be clear on the correct use of the simile. You must stop saying "like", it is intolerable. Must everything be approximate? It either happened or it didn't. Now, I shall take my leave, and speak to you only when you have learned some civility. And some English grammar. Good day!' She walked down the steps and was gone in the evening throng.

TWENTY-NINE

Artemesia Plutarch had reacted swiftly when she saw the two official personages at the communal medical-equipment stack. Picking up the Scoob, she leaped down the rest of the stairs three at a time to the ground-floor lobby, where an old woman in a dressing gown was slowly filling her empty bottle from the gin dispenser, which was positioned right in front of the indoor plant area – a row of bushy ficus trees in large pink pots. Gin was big in London again. Local distilleries proliferated. Not since the 'Gin Craze' of the early eighteenth century had so much of it been put away by so many Londoners.

'Hi, Mrs Glamper. Didn't fancy the Residents' Association Special General Meeting, then?' asked Artemesia.

'You're joking,' said Mrs Glamper. 'Waste of bloody time.'

'Could you, erm, let me past, please? I'm in a bit of a hurry.' Mrs Glamper ignored this request and carried on filling her gin bottle. There were no prohibitions on the amount of local gin a person could drink, so it'd be true to say that Mrs Glamper was mostly pickled. Artemesia barged past her, still carrying the Scoob, and knelt down behind the plant pots. These ficus trees had done extremely well in the corner of the lobby here, and had grown outwards as well as upwards into the stairwell. Artemesia was breathing heavily now but couldn't be seen from the stairs, nor from the lobby. Sitting on the floor, she opened her leather satchel and quickly took out the Vitri-nozzle and the little bottle of liquid glass that she'd used on Jeremiah's arm. She could hear them coming down the stairs after her, shouting for her to stop. Their voices echoed in the stairwell. Mrs Glamper gave her a raised eyebrow.

She rolled back the cuffs of her tunic, uncorked the bottle and poured out the milky fluid over her wrists and the back of her hands. She waved her forearms in the air to get the treacly liquid to set. She dumped the nozzle, belt strap and empty bottle in one of the large pink pots and covered them as best she could with a handful or two of earth.

The two large officials reached the bottom of the stairs. One of them went to the opaque glass front door and opened it to see if Artemesia was in the street. A breeze swept in.

Mrs Glamper finished filling her gin bottle. 'She's behind the plants,' she said, as she ticked the ledger with the pencil on a string and padded back up the stairs in her slippers.

'Thanks, Mrs Glamper,' Artemesia shouted after her, 'I'll do the same for you one day.' Scoobeedoo barked at the receding dressing gown.

The two lugs approached Artemesia. On their hats were written the words 'Blackfriars Breach Brigade'. She just had time to refold the cuffs of her tunic before they pushed a path to her behind the plants.

'Are you Archibald Bluetak?' said the first one.

'Near enough,' said Artemesia. 'Can I help you?'

'You gotta come with us now,' said the second, holding out a gloved hand for Artemesia to take.

'Rightio,' said Artemesia, holding the gloved hand with her now flexi-glass covered one. 'Come on, Scoob!'

Scoobeedoo kept close to her heel, despite being shoved away by the hostile boot of Official Number One. 'So, what can I help you guys with?' said Artemesia, with an unnaturally bright smile, as they opened the front door.

'Don't play the innocent cub with us,' said Official Number Two, who was carrying the first-floor communal medical-equipment ledger tucked under an arm. 'You know exactly why we're here, and the game's up.'

'All right,' said Artemesia, 'just don't take it out on the dog, OK? Very inventive phrasing by the way – innocent cub, game's up – did you think that up all by yourself?'

The one who wasn't holding the ledger had taken out of their pocket a strip of stickers and peeled one off. The sheet had 'TP patches' printed across it. Artemesia offered the back of her hand; she knew the routine. The official slapped a Tralezepam patch on it. The flexi-glass was now completely transparent, so the patch was sticking onto an invisible, river-glass compound, with no chance of reaching her bloodstream. She was then pulled through the door, which the other goon was holding open.

Blackfriars Road was quiet. The cold air made Artemesia shiver. There was sharp afternoon light on the vertical wall hanging gardens, which covered every house on the street. Great drooping bunches of fuchsia, lobelia and some eucalyptus, dangling down low over the pavement. The push-me-pull-you rail-cart track was empty.

The peace was momentarily broken by the screechings of a flock of London parakeets passing through the plane trees overhead. For a few seconds the air was filled with their swooping and cackling, and then they were gone.[22]

---

22 Parakeets started multiplying in London in the seventies. Some people say a pair of them escaped from the set of *The African Queen*, which was filmed at Ealing Studios, others that Jimi Hendrix, of all people, bought a couple of them and then

A horse-drawn cart with rubber tyres from some old lorry was trundling past, slowly. An unshaven man was sitting up high, at the front, keeping a slack hold on the reins. Every now and then, he would call out in a mechanical way, 'Reesackle! Reesackle!' The back of his cart was open and had a large, random pile of old computers, laptops and electrical equipment on it – mobile phones, cables, monitors, hard drives and keyboards.

---

set them free in a moment of psychedelic abandon. But whichever urban myth you choose to believe – *The African Queen* was released in 1951, by the way, so the seventies connection is tenuous – by the middle of the twenty-first century they had become the most populous bird in London, ousting starlings, sparrows and even pigeons. It might seem strange to us, but by 2080, a tourist must-see will be the parakeets of Trafalgar Square. Rather like the famous 'London plane tree' which in fact arrived here from Europe in the late seventeenth century.

THIRTY

Without Phyllis, Jeremiah felt suddenly lonely. Perhaps it was not his fault, perhaps it was Contumely Briggs. Phyllis had mentioned her husband, Mr Stokes, who'd passed away. I should have asked her about him, thought Jeremiah. Stupid of me. She was probably missing him and I'm only thinking about my own stuff; I didn't ask her about hers. Just because she's strict doesn't mean she doesn't have her own feelings. Damn, I must remember to ask her about her husband if I ever get the chance again, he resolved to himself.

Taking another discreet puff on his inhaler, he set off down the Waterloo steps, eastwards towards Blackfriars. There was really no other direction to go. It was nice of Sir Rodger to let him stay in the scary cold room last night, but he couldn't turn up again at Gordon Square after the falling out with Phyllis, and anyway, he wanted to get home to nowadays and the best chance of that was Blackfriars Road.

As he walked down Roupell Street and into Hatfields, he felt vulnerable. He was a stranger on his home turf. The air was damp and insipid, a typical London afternoon. The clouds hung low, the light was pale. There was the back of the Rose and Crown pub, at the end of Paris Gardens, where he'd been messing about with Jayden and Bradley and some of the others when they got caught and reported to the Head. How come they'd all managed to scrape through to Year Twelve and he hadn't?

When he got to the house, Lucy Bonnet was scrubbing the front steps with a stiff hand-brush. She had a bucket of soapy water and was on her knees, attacking the dirt with vigour. She filled the entire entrance.

'What you doin' back 'ere? I thought you run away with our Daisy,' she said between breaths, after he'd called out her name from the bottom of the steps. She didn't stop working. 'Come back for another one, 'ave yer? Take me! I'm ready to be rescued!'

'Hi Lucy, thanks for your help earlier. Could you let me in?' he asked. 'I really need to get into the basement again. I think that's my best chance of getting home.'

She stopped scrubbing, and knelt up, taking a deep breath. 'Basement's been locked up, now, since you and Daisy fled.'

'Damn. What about the upstairs bedroom? Lucy? Can you get me in there?' She turned her back to him and carried on with her work, the scratching of the brush on the stone the only noise between them for a few seconds.

'What 'ave you done with our Daisy, then? You 'aven't done away with 'er, 'ave yer?'

'No. She's safe where she is. In fact, she's probably safer than we are,' he said. She carried on heaving the brush over the steps with the full weight of her shoulders and back. Her forearms were red from the abrasive soap. 'Lucy,' he said after a small pause in which she continued her rhythmical toil, 'do the steps really have to be that clean?'

'They do,' she said, sloshing the brush into the grey water in the bucket. 'And Miss Quentinbloom's allowance does not run to a cook nor a housemaid's girl, so I have to clean the knives, put the laundry on the line, scrape the grate and prepare the soup.' She wasn't complaining – more proud, it seemed.

'I don't think my Stepdad Pete has ever actually cleaned the steps. I must remember to tell him, if I ever get back,' he said, and watched her pushing the brush to and fro for a few seconds. 'You know, if I ever do get home and then come back here, I could bring you some mega chemical-type cleaner that you could just foam over it and it would save you all that scrubbing.'

'Don't need your charity, sir. I can manage the domestic arrangements perfect without your interference, thank you very much,' she said, splashing a new brushful of water over the top step.

'Sorry. It'd be really bad for the environment anyway, so, probably not such a good idea,' said Jeremiah.

Then, tossing the brush in the bucket with a plop, she pulled herself stiffly to a standing position. 'All right. You'll 'ave to go behind my back so I don't see yer, mind.' She looked nonchalantly up the road away from Jeremiah. 'And you'll 'ave to jump up. Not one dirty foot on my nice clean steps!'

Jeremiah took one step back and leaped up all the steps to the top, past Lucy and into the hall. She turned round and whispered, 'Floor's creaky in the middle there. And the third stair makes a noise, so be careful and step over that one.'

'I know,' whispered Jeremiah in response. 'I know which floorboards creak – I live here. Well, I will do.'

Suddenly, from above them, a woman's voice pierced the quiet. 'You will not continue to use this house!' It was coming from Clementina's room.

A man's voice, also raised, shouted back at her, 'Don't be ridiculous, woman! I am the only one to be active on your behalf!' Jeremiah froze on the stairs. The door to Daisy's room was beyond Clementina's door.

The argument escalated. 'Active? I fear you have been quite "active" enough, sir!' came the woman's shout. This was the ignition for a full-scale shooting match.

'But I had your full consent!' bellowed the man.

Lucy stopped her work and had entered a foot into the hall behind Jeremiah.

'How dare you!' screamed the woman, now clearly identifiable as Clementina. 'You may not behave as some Lord of the Manor in this house! There will be no "droit de seigneur" in my establishment!'

Then they heard some kind of punch or smack and a gasp from Clementina. Whoever the man was, he was a nasty customer. They could hear Clementina sobbing. Suddenly the door was thrown open and a man came striding out. He was wearing a cape and a soft hat pulled down over his eyes, so it was not possible to see his face clearly. He leaped down the stairs two at a time past Jeremiah and Lucy Bonnet, shouting, 'Out of my way!' When he reached the front door, he grabbed a stick from the umbrella stand; it was stouter than Mr Briggs's knobbly stick, almost a cudgel. He struggled with the catch for a second or two, grumbling to himself, 'Damned thing! Open, damn you!' He swung the front door open and, as a parting measure, deliberately kicked over Lucy's bucket on his way out. Grey water splashed out over the steps and trickled down onto the pavement.

'I'll go and see to Miss Q,' said Lucy, 'and go on! You get after 'im!', assuming for the second time in as many days that it was Jeremiah's natural role to enter a fight. But this time Jeremiah did not need time to consider whether it was a good idea or not.

He was through the front door and down the now filthy front steps in two seconds flat. Dolly and Tess, two of the Grout children, were playing hopscotch on the pavement outside. The man careered into them, swinging his stick. 'Out of my way, damn you!' he shouted. A large dog was barking at him. He swiped it with his stick and sent it whimpering away. Tess and Dolly started to cry.

'Oi, mister! Leave those kids alone!' shouted Jeremiah, in pursuit. 'And the dog!' But the man was fast, already yards ahead.

Mrs Grout came up from her basement to see what all the noise was about.

'Tess! Dolly! Back inside! Master Bourne! After 'im!' she growled.

'I am!' Jeremiah shouted back at her, as he set off up the street. His leather-soled shoes were not as easy to run in as a pair of trainers would have been. Up ahead of him, the man stumbled over a wooden cage of chickens, which was standing on the street while its owner chatted to another man in a butcher's apron. The man kicked the cage over, letting noisy chickens run out onto the street. The two other men tried to grab hold of him, but he was too fast, swinging his stick at them and running across to the other side of the road with Jeremiah in pursuit. Into Pocock Street, Sawyer Street, Pepper Street, Marshalsea Road and into Redcross Way.

As they made their way eastwards, the light in the sky dimmed and the air around them became foggy. A little bit at first, but by the time they were at the bottom of Union Street, visibility was becoming difficult. Jeremiah could just see the man's cape flapping in the gloom ahead, but he could still clearly hear the man's leather shoes clacking on the pavement. For a while it seemed that the only sound was that of both of their shoes. The man had slowed to a very brisk walk now. He turned sharp left, so Jeremiah did too. The man certainly seemed to know his way around the area; at each junction there was no hesitation.

Newcomen Street and into Snowsfields. The foul smell of leather tanning came back; they were running parallel to Leathermarket Street now, and the rank stink hit Jeremiah in the face like a hot wet dishcloth. It's trendy restaurants all around here nowadays, he thought, I wonder what the customers would think if they had to take a whiff of this before tucking into their tomato bruschettas.

At the top of Bermondsey Street, the man turned into one of the long tunnels which run under the rail lines of London Bridge station. The fog had accumulated here; it was like wading through floating yellow mud. Jeremiah had to rely entirely on the sound of the man's footsteps ahead. The footsteps stopped. So Jeremiah stopped. They started again, so did Jeremiah. Then they stopped again. So this guy, whoever he was, knew he was being followed. Jeremiah bent down and quickly undid his laces. He slipped off his shoes and carried them with him when the man started walking. The ground was freezing and damp and Jeremiah's socks were instantly wet. But at least he could walk silently. The man stopped again, and this time Jeremiah carried on, stealthily. But now he heard another sound behind him: a third pair of shoes clomping away on the pavement. The man ahead stopped again, and a second later so did whoever it was behind Jeremiah. So Jeremiah was being followed too. The three of them carried on like this until they got to the top end of the tunnel, when some of the fog evaporated in the breezy swirls of air coming off the river and blowing down Tooley Street.

Jeremiah recognised the building where he used to come for karate club when he was younger. The one his mum had left him outside on his own, when Dr Amanda Vergilius followed them. There was a large painted concrete archway with the words 'Temperance Society 1907' embossed on it. There's a launderette and a mini-supermarket there now, next to a McDonald's, but when he was about nine it was the Community Centre where his mum dropped him off for after-school club. Wow, the archway above the entrance was exactly the same black-and-white tiling and brickwork as it is nowadays, he thought. Same ironwork over the front door lintel, same words, same concrete crest too. But now, he'd momentarily lost the man.

He tried turning into Hay's Lane, and there was the man again, about ten yards ahead, his cape still flapping. The streets here were narrower. Jeremiah didn't know where he was now. This was further than his normal patch.

It was beginning to get dark. The buildings were cramped together here; it was more like a series of backyards joined by cobbled paths. The man turned a corner and immediately disappeared down some rickety stairs into a basement. Jeremiah could hear the shoes of whoever it was following him as they neared the corner behind him. Nothing for it, he thought, and ducked down the stairs where the caped man had gone. He crouched there, trying to get his breath back as quietly as he could. Above him he heard the shoes run past the opening to the stairs. He'd thrown off his own stalker. He was now crouched in the dark at the bottom of the stairs, clinging onto his shoes. He thought he'd stay there for a while to collect himself and control the racing of his heart, maybe take a puff on his inhaler, but a yellowy light from the basement window came on, illuminating him. He crouched further down into the shadows under the ledge of the window, and then dared to peek in.

Inside, a long wooden workbench stretched away from the window. On it were rows of glass jars with handwritten labels, test tubes of all shapes and sizes and a Bunsen burner under a large round glass bowl suspended on a triangular frame. The man had his back to Jeremiah and was taking off his cape and hat and passing them to an austere-looking woman with her hair in a tight bun. She handed him a white lab coat, which he put on. He then moved to the Bunsen burner and turned it on, using a long match from a box of matches he got from a shelf at knee level under the bench top. The whole scene was suffused with a sickly yellow light from a long light fitting which hung over the man like a snooker table's. He then disappeared from view, momentarily, only to reappear suddenly at the window and snap the curtains shut. It was Henry Davenant Hythe.

THIRTY-ONE

It was like a James Bond film. The mad scientist in his laboratory, the bubbling and hissing of chemicals in their beakers and flasks. It was as if any minute now the top was going to come off the whole house, the floor was going to split open and reveal a huge launch pad, and Henry Davenant Hythe, played by a heavily accented actor, would suddenly appear behind Jeremiah and say, 'Havink fun... Mr Bourne?'

What actually happened was similar, although possibly not so cinematic. The back door opened, with the sound of a little jingling bell suspended above it, and the woman with the bun came out into the small basement forecourt, where Jeremiah was hiding under the metal staircase. She looked straight at him and said, 'Vy don't you come in, Mr Bourne? You look very uncomfordable down zer.' Right accent, wrong movie. 'Dr Hyze vud like to speak to you. And you may put your shoes back on if you pliz.' She left the door open for him.

'Thanks, but my socks are all wet now, so...' said Jeremiah. But she was gone. He considered what to do for a moment, but then curiosity got the better of him. He walked into the lab and was immediately hit with the sulphurous smell of chemistry. He'd been thrown out of chemistry classes at school – asked not to return – for mucking about with the wall poster of the Periodic Table with Jayden Morris. Stupid really, as he could have done well in chemistry – it's all about memorising the Periodic Table and he'd done that easily in the first week. It was dumb to draw a cartoon-strip on it of Mr Pinkney, the chemistry teacher, he could see that now.

Davenant Hythe stood hunched over a bulbous glass flask which was sitting in a tripod, and writing in a hardback book. He turned briefly as Jeremiah came in, to acknowledge his presence. Jeremiah stood there feeling stupid, not knowing what to do. He bent down to put his shoes on. His socks squelched when he tried to squeeze them inside the stiff leather. Giving up, he put the shoes neatly to one side and stood in his socks.

'Thank you, Frau Hemling,' said Davenant Hythe, without looking up at the woman with the bun. 'Now bring me three fresh test tubes and a two-ounce phial of Phlogesterone.'

'Very vell,' said the woman, walking out of the room silently, apart from the cracking of her knees.

Again, without looking up, Davenant Hythe addressed Jeremiah. 'I'm glad you decided to drop by, Mr Bourne. I think you may be able to help me.'

'Why did you hit Clementina Quentinbloom?' said Jeremiah.

'Come come!' said Davenant Hythe, finishing one column of figures and closing the book. 'I've never been afraid to be firm when it comes to the greater good. So, welcome to my laboratory, where a better future is being designed for all.' He smiled at Jeremiah and invited him to sit on one of the high lab stools by the bench. Jeremiah stayed standing, while Davenant Hythe sat down on the high stool, hooking his feet up. Frau Hemling returned and quietly placed the items that he'd asked for on the bench beside him: a little rack of test tubes and a jar with 'Phg21/25' written on it.

'You must be tired after your exertions, Jem. Frau Hemling? Fetch Mr Bourne a glass of fruit-syrup squash,' he said, without looking at her. The woman nodded and padded silently out of the room again.

'Thanks, but I'm good, actually,' said Jeremiah, still not sitting down.

Davenant Hythe laughed a dry laugh, which consisted of two short stabs in his throat with his head thrown back, then a swift return to looking straight at Jeremiah. 'Yes, Jeremiah Bourne, you're very good. And that is my problem. Where is Daisy Wallace? Where have you put her?'

'What's it to you?' said Jeremiah.

'More to the point, what is she to you, young man? Please don't tell me there is some romantic attachment.'

'Erm... well, I like her, but... I don't think so, no,' said Jeremiah. He was trying to tell the truth, but the situation was intimidating, so it felt like a lie. 'Anyway, why is she so important to you?'

'Daisy Wallace is my prototype. Without her my work is nothing. All of the others have failed, in various ways. But science is nothing if it cannot learn from its failures. And I will not fail with Daisy and her child.'

'I don't know what you're talking about,' said Jeremiah, 'but it sounds deeply wrong and unpleasant.'

Davenant Hythe gave his magpie laugh again and stood. 'Very good, very good!' He smiled and beckoned Jeremiah to the back of the lab. 'Come! Take a look at these!' He picked up a lamp and walked through a small arch.

Jeremiah followed him around a corner to an alcove with a low ceiling. There was just enough room for the two of them to stand in there, shoulder to shoulder. On the wall were large photographic headshots of people from the front, the back and the side – like police mugshots – with calibrations down the side and along the bottom.

'Unfortunately – and despite my scientific interventions – the children you see in these photographs have inherited some of their mothers' more distressing attributes.' He was standing so close now that Jeremiah could feel the hot damp of his breath, which was febrile and shallow despite his attempts to appear calm and in control.

It was difficult to see at first in the half-light, but gradually Jeremiah could make out the faces in the photographs. It was the Grout children. 'That's Tess! That's Dolly, who you clobbered just now with your stick!' he blurted out. 'Why have they got measurements all down the side of their faces?'

'All inadequate in one way or another,' said Davenant Hythe, with a sigh, 'so sad. This one: short-sighted. This one: brow too low. And that one over there—'

'Samuel. That one's Samuel,' said Jeremiah. 'They have names, you know.'

'I'm sure they do,' Davenant Hythe said, dismissively, and continued, 'that one: too Semitic. All of them still showing, in one way or another, the characteristics and bone structure of the lower orders…' He shuffled round in the cramped space to point out a picture that he had been standing in front of. '…as in this photograph here.'

Revealed behind him was a large photograph of an almost Neanderthal man with a beard and shaggy hair. There was a label at the bottom of it which read: 'The Criminal Type.'

'What?' said Jeremiah. 'There is no criminal type! That's total rubbish.'

'Shall we move out of here? The air can be stifling.' They picked their way back out of the alcove. 'It is pitiful, I agree. And so far, I have not managed to eradicate any of their inherited traits. But with Daisy Wallace I have advanced my method and, with my interventions, she will give birth to a child who is completely free of any of the mother's disadvantages, racial and structural – short-sightedness, uncontrollable impulses, skin colour.'

'What interventions are you talking about, exactly?'

'I myself have none of these imperfections,' said Davenant Hythe, as if it were a matter of accepted fact, no boast, 'and so in this culminating experiment it has been necessary to invest some of myself. Put myself forward, as it were.'

'Can I say,' Jeremiah put in, 'that's disgusting, and, like, just wrong on every level.' But Davenant Hythe was not listening; he returned to the lab still holding forth as if he were giving a lecture. His stubby moustache was glistening with sweat.

'Think of the many lives I shall be saving! Out there? In those streets that you have just followed me through? Thousands of hopeless girls weighed down with the burden of motherhood, when they can hardly feed themselves. Some of them have two, three, four children of inferior stock before they have even reached maturity themselves. Think of the advantages my formula will be bestowing on them!' He turned to look Jeremiah in the eye with the self-assured grin of a politician given the chance to talk about himself on *Question Time.* 'It's Nobel Prize-winning stuff, Jeremiah!'

'It's insane, that's what it is,' said Jeremiah. 'You can't be God. Look, believe me, this whole idea is going to go badly wrong.'

Davenant Hythe put the lamp back on the desk, but stayed standing close to it, so that the light from it shone up his face from under his jaw, leaving spiky shadows up his cheeks, like a trash horror movie poster. 'So, you would have me leave these poor creatures to a life of suffering and misery, would you? Children who collect animal droppings from the street to sell to the leather tanneries, children who have to scavenge among the rubbish for a pittance?' For a moment, Jeremiah thought Davenant Hythe might cry. There seemed to be a lump in his throat. 'I am merely trying to help these girls. To save them before their lives are ruined. I am a charity, in effect.' He almost sounded convincing; he'd certainly convinced himself.

'What, you mean like a special charity for abusing young girls?'

'No, no, don't worry. No abuse takes place!' said Davenant Hythe with his over-confident grin again. 'Frau Hemling is most gentle with them. Aren't you, Frau Hemling?' he shouted over his shoulder towards where she had disappeared. 'She's a dab hand with the chloroform and everything is done clinically. No touching.'

'And do Phyllis and Sir Rodger know what you're up to?'

This exasperated him and he rolled his eyes to the ceiling. 'Oh, who cares what they think? They're old fools; vegetarian, rope-sandalled romantics. Rodger may be a Magistrate of the Realm but he is soft. A woolly, over-sentimental nincompoop.'

'I thought he was supposed to be your best friend?' said Jeremiah, and then had thoughts about Jayden, who was supposed to be his best friend, but was now in sixth-form college in Camberwell, going out with Alex, who was supposed to be going out with Jeremiah. Maybe best friends weren't what he thought they were. Davenant Hythe gave one of his nut-cracking laughs again.

From nowhere, Frau Hemling was standing at Jeremiah's shoulder. 'A glass of fruit cordial for ze yunk man,' she said, plonking a glass of pale orange liquid on the bench beside him. It sat there next to the jars which contained other more colourful liquids. She gave what she must have thought was a reassuring smile, revealing the remnants of a row of teeth surrounded by mossy-green gums.

'What's in it?' asked Jeremiah, which set off Davenant Hythe laughing again. This time the laugh lasted longer than three seconds. It was like a stalling car juddering to a halt.

'You honestly think I'd try to slip you some knockout drops, heh?' He patted Jeremiah's elbow as if they were old mates. 'No. I don't want to knock you out, Jeremiah old chap, I need you fully conscious. I need you to tell me where you have hidden Daisy Wallace.' His expression was suddenly serious.

'So you can carry out some experiment on her, like she was some specimen?'

'Specimen is a little strong, but example, yes. I only have her best interests at heart. Now, where is she?'

Jeremiah considered for a moment. Truth was probably best. 'Actually, I've taken her to the future.'

'Ah yes, your little black glass. Fancy yourself as a latter-day John Dee, don't you, I seem to remember.'

'No, I don't. Anyway, I don't have the glass any more, someone nicked it off me.'

'Ah yes, good,' said Davenant Hythe, sitting back down on his high stool, 'then at least some of my plans are coming to fruition.' He looked over Jeremiah's shoulder and raised his voice. 'Tell me, Mr Viney, did you get the glass?'

'Yer. Goddit awright,' came a voice from behind Jeremiah. He spun round to see Ed Viney standing just inside the door to the street with a cheeky smile on his face. 'An ah already slit viss geezer good 'n proper, ah did, so ah can't see as 'ow's 'e's made it art alive.'

'So, it was you following me!' said Jeremiah.

'Mighta bin,' said Ed Viney.

Davenant Hythe gently intervened. 'I apologise deeply, in advance, for saying what I'm about to say, Mr Bourne, but… restrain him, Mr Viney! Tie him to the stool!'

THIRTY-TWO

'You have got to be joking!' said Jeremiah, but Ed Viney leaped forwards and grabbed him by the arm. Jeremiah wasn't going to give in to being manhandled that easily. A struggle ensued, which brought both of them crashing to the floor.

''Old still, yer little stoat!' yelled Ed Viney as they flailed around, grunting.

'God, how tawdry this is!' said Henry Davenant Hythe, stepping back. 'Frau Hemling? Would you assist?' Frau Hemling obliged by grasping Jeremiah's other arm in a tight grip, which he managed to free himself from by kicking out with both his arms and his legs. He waved his free arm at Ed Viney and caught him across the side of the head. There was the sound of smashing glass from inside Jeremiah's sleeve. All three of them stopped in surprise for a fleeting moment and then resumed the fight. As the two of them eventually overcame him, small grey splinters of glass sprayed from out of the sleeve of his jacket. The shattered vitrification bandage fell in pieces over the laboratory floor.

Davenant Hythe bent to pick up a shard of the opaque glass and examined it, while Ed Viney and Frau Hemling tied Jeremiah firmly to the stool, using a leather belt and a length of rope that Frau Hemling had fetched from a hook on the wall. 'Hmm,' said Davenant Hythe, turning the tiny sliver of glass between his finger and thumb and looking at it closely through a magnifying glass, 'very fine, medical-grade glass. Made from river-sand, I'd say. Where'd you get this, Bourne?'

'It comes from a long, long time ago. Like a thousand years or more?' Jeremiah said, furious at being strapped down.'I just happened to pick it up last time I was there.' Inside his sleeve the skin was sensitive, rubbing up against his shirt, just as when any bandage is taken off. He couldn't tell whether the cuts were healed or not.

Davenant Hythe put down the little piece of glass and took out a wooden box which he opened to reveal a set of syringes lying in protective green felt. He removed one and applied the needle into one of the glass jars on the shelf in front of him, pulling the plunger back to fill its glass phial. 'Now, Jeremiah, it pains me to abuse the advances of medical science in this way,' he said, taking out the syringe and examining it against the light, then flicking it with his forefinger to get rid of any bubbles, 'but unless you agree to bring Daisy Wallace back here from wherever it is you're hiding her, I will not be afraid to use the contents of this hypodermic syringe,' he squirted a test plume of liquid through the air, 'which would make you very uncomfortable indeed for quite some time.' He moved his stool closer to where Jeremiah was sitting, tied down and being held on either side by Ed Viney and Frau Hemling. 'So come on, Jeremiah Bourne, where is she?'

'I told you, she's in the future,' said Jeremiah through gritted teeth. He couldn't think of a better answer right now. He was genuinely scared. His assessment of Davenant Hythe was that he probably would carry out his threat if pushed – he certainly seemed deranged enough.

'And you expect me to believe that? With no empirical proof? Foolish, naïve, stupid young man!'

Truth hadn't got him very far. Time to lie. 'Yeah, but...

I'm not "young", am I?' said Jeremiah, wildly improvising. 'I'm actually a lot older than you think, Dr Hythe. In fact, I'm sixty-three years old!'

That stopped Hythe in his tracks for a moment. 'I beg your pardon? Explain,' he said, keeping his eyes fixed on Jeremiah, and the ready syringe dangerously close to his neck.

'In the future, you see, we've, erm... discovered how to stay young-looking.'

'Oh really? How?'

'Well, it's something to do with, erm... cucumber juice actually, but—'

'Bourne! Please don't mock me!'

'Well, cucumber juice that's been stored in, erm, medical-grade glass, made from very fine river-sand. You were right. If you want proof, just look at the cuts on my arm, where Ed Viney slashed at me a day ago. They're all back to normal, like nothing happened.'

Davenant Hythe nodded at Frau Hemling, who roughly undid the belt strapped around Jeremiah's elbows, and, holding his arm, pulled his jacket sleeve off. Then she opened the cuff of his shirt and rolled it back. It was as he said, the cuts had almost entirely healed – there were two clean, whitish lines where Ed Viney had slashed deep into his arm.

'There. See?' said Jeremiah triumphantly, trying to hide his own amazement and relief.

Ed Viney's eyes had come out on cartoon stalks. ''Ow d'you do vat?' he said, then to Davenant Hythe, 'Ah slit 'im good 'n proper, Dr Hive, sir. Ah swears it.'

Henry Davenant Hythe still seemed suspicious. 'And what is your point? Old or young?'

'Well, the point is,' Jeremiah was thinking fast, but his mind went blank, 'the point is,' a small hiatus here felt like a very long pause, 'the point is, I too am a scientist,' he said, 'a sixty-three-year-old scientist.'

'Oh really?' said Davenant Hythe, close enough now that Jeremiah could feel his hot, damp breath on his cheek again.

'Yes,' said Jeremiah, wishing he'd done his chemistry revision, 'and I was sent here from the Hythe Institute... of... of High Achievers, to... to—'

'The Hythe Institute? What's that?' said Davenant Hythe. Jeremiah had his attention now.

'Oh, it's just one of the Royal Societies that got named after you,' said Jeremiah, warming to his theme. Something Stepdad Pete once told him flashed across his mind. 'No amount of flattery is too much. People will believe anything about themselves, so long as it's flattering.'

'So, my work succeeds?' said Davenant Hythe, seeming more like a child now.

'Succeeds? Ha! It's more than succeeded! It's huge, sir, it's...' Jeremiah tried to think of the appropriate measure, 'it's made a whole new department! You know, in universities and all that...'

'Which universities?' said Davenant Hythe, quickly. 'Not the minor ones?'

'God no!' said Jeremiah. 'Like, Oxford and Cambridge, obviously, and all the other big ones.'

'Edinburgh?' said Davenant Hythe.

'Yeah, probably. I don't know all of them. But the point is, your work started a whole new -ology. Like, Hythology? In 1995, I think it was—'

'A mere eighty-five years from now!' Henry was trying to maintain a veil of self-control, but it was barely concealing his vain excitement. 'And so, why were you sent here?'

'What?'

'You said you were sent here.'

'Oh, well, obviously to compliment you on your work, and to correct a couple of bits of it. You know, like point you in the right direction? Like all that "criminal type" and "lower orders" rubbish? You should drop all that and concentrate more on the, erm... science.'

Davenant Hythe came back at him immediately. 'But it's all science! That's the point!'

'Exactly,' said Jeremiah, 'it's just that it's not those bits of your work that, you know, take off in the future. So, drop those bits and you should be fine. Basically, carry on! Now, could you let me out of this chair?'

Suddenly Henry let out an agonised scream. 'But how can I carry on without Daisy Wallace? She is the apex of my achievements!'

'No. Yeah. That's fair enough, actually. I see that,' said Jeremiah, pleased with his acting skills, 'so, just give me the black glass and I'll go back there and see what I can do.'

Davenant Hythe shook his head. 'I did offer to examine the glass scientifically, Mr Bourne, when we first met, but you didn't dare.'

'Would you let some complete stranger snoop through your laboratory and research? I mean, just because you're an internationally famous figure who will go down in history for all time doesn't mean you can just take things whenever you choose from lesser men, like me. With respect, Dr Hythe, sir.'

Davenant Hythe took a deep breath and leaned the syringe carefully up against the open wooden box. 'Mr Viney?' he said. 'Hand him the black glass.'

'But ah ain' bin recompensated yet,' said Ed Viney.

'Oh for heavens' sake! Frau Hemling? Pay this imbecile something.'

Frau Hemling took a small purse from a pocket in her apron and handed Ed Viney a couple of coins from it.

'Thankin' yer 'onour,' said Ed Viney, taking the money and giving a small salute.

'Now, untie Mr Bourne here and give him the damned glass,' sighed Davenant Hythe, then added, 'taking care not to look into it yourself, of course!'

'Aha,' said Jeremiah, 'so you do believe in it a bit!' He flexed his arms and legs as they became free.

'I am an empiricist, not a believer,' said Davenant Hythe. Bloody maniac more like, thought Jeremiah.

When Jeremiah was untied and standing again, he put his arm back in his jacket sleeve. Ed Viney took the phone, still wrapped in its filthy handkerchief, from his pocket and handed it to Jeremiah. Jeremiah took it, praying that it still had some battery left. It did. The screen lit up, and Jeremiah went quickly to Settings.

'Iss all lit up!' said Ed Viney.

'Mein Gott!' said Frau Hemling.

When Jeremiah found the Robot Bugle ring tone and pressed Play, all three of them jumped back a foot.

'What was that?' said Henry, alarmed. 'What's going on?'

'It's the signal,' said Jeremiah, thinking he might take up story-telling for primary school children. He tried another couple of ring tones on them: Moonlight Boogie and Smooth LA. 'It's calling me. It's the linear, erm, sonic... paradoxes. They all have to be in alignment.'

'What does that mean?' asked Henry, not quite believing.

'It means I have to be in the open air, above ground, for it to work. And we must hurry.'

'Why?'

'Because they may have moved Daisy Wallace to another zone, for all I know, Dr Hythe, sir. So I have to get back now, or we may lose her.'

'Very well, quickly then. Let us go outside,' said Davenant Hythe.

Jeremiah was basking in the power he seemed to have, just by acting a lie convincingly enough. Probably a bad thing to learn how to do, but, hey, it was all for the right reasons. He walked to the door, followed by the others.

'No, not all of you,' he said, 'this is something I must do alone,' and then for the hell of it, he added, 'trust me.' This was fun; to be able to use all the clichés from naff TV shows on people who had never seen naff TV shows.

'Sir?' said Frau Hemling. 'You forgot your shoes.' She passed them to him.

'No time to put them on, but thanks, I'll take them with me. I have to go immediately.' He took the shoes and went up the metal staircase in his wet socks, holding his mobile ahead of him as if it were a weapon.

Henry Davenant Hythe shouted after him, 'You must return with Daisy Wallace as soon as possible!'

'I will!' he shouted back, and then for good measure, 'It's been a privilege meeting you, Dr Hythe, sir. Wait till I tell my friends at the Institute!'

THIRTY-THREE

Across the cobbles in his socks, back into the alley, checking behind him to see if they were following. He put his mobile deep in his trouser pocket and ran, not wanting to stop long enough to put the shoes on.

As he turned the corner back into Hay's Lane, the shoes were suddenly snatched from his hand, which brought Jeremiah to a halt. A small child ran off with them, laughing. Then he became aware that there were other children; he'd walked into their patch. 'Oi! Mister! Give us vat jacket!' said a grubby boy, who must have been about seven. 'Give us some money!' shouted another, a long-haired one.

'I haven't got any on me,' he said. There was one street lamp, giving off a dull circle of light, like a torch under a duvet. He could make out the shapes of at least eight children. None of them had shoes on, all were filthy. The youngest must have been about four. They had snot on their faces and the haystack look of their hair would take a stylist a whole morning to achieve.

The long-haired one came close up to Jeremiah. 'Come on, mister, I said give us some money,' he said. He was probably about ten and shorter than Jeremiah by a good foot, but emanated a dark malignity. He also emanated an absolutely revolting smell.

'Look, I honestly don't have any money,' apologised Jeremiah. Their existences are miserable, he thought,

Henry Davenant Hythe was right. Well, right about the problem, not the solution.

The grubby seven-year-old grabbed on to the bottom of Jeremiah's jacket. 'Well, give us vat jacket, ven.' Another of them wrapped her arms around his leg. He was surrounded now. He tried to keep walking, pulling them along the street with him.

A girl of perhaps twelve, who looked like a zombie, stood in his way. 'Wanna buy some watercress, darlin'?' she said, menacingly.

'Watercress?' he said.

'Yeah, it's right 'ere under me skirts.' They all laughed again.

A small boy suddenly jumped on his back, shouting, 'Oi, mister, give us a piggy-back ride!' He stank as well. Jeremiah ploughed on, dragging three of them with him as they hung onto his legs, trying to reach into his pockets. He plunged his hands into his pockets and pushed onwards like a rhino. By the time he rounded the corner, he'd managed to shake off all but the small boy on his back. ''E got no money! 'E's a pauper!' the others jeered after him.

Jeremiah carried the boy the few steps to the end of Hay's Lane and then slid him off his back, down onto the corner of Tooley Street. 'You better get back to your mates now,' he said. The boy ran off, scared. 'Fanks, mister,' he shouted over his shoulder.

Back on his home turf now, he slowed down to regain his breath, as there was still a way to go; Blackfriars Road was a good ten minutes' walk from here. His feet were numb, as if he were walking on a couple of frozen bricks.

He set off up Tooley Street. The 'Temperance Society 1907' building was there, with its black-and-white tiling and brickwork over the archway, the same ironwork over the front door as when he used to do karate here. The same concrete crest, too. He remembered the Community Centre used to have a little noticeboard in a glass case on the outside and a hatch in the entrance hall to show your membership card. And they didn't have so many parking restrictions then, which is how come his mum was able to bring him here in her taxi and park it outside, just there. He heard the hissing of a steam train going into London Bridge station, but it seemed nearer than that. A breeze came up and buffeted him in the face, as if a heavy goods vehicle had just gone past too close. The hissing noise didn't stop – it continued and swirled between his ears like tinnitus. He looked back to the building and there was the glass case with its information noticeboard, just as he remembered it, there was the hatch to show your membership card. He felt queasy, as if he'd just got off a roller coaster and had to find his legs. He grabbed the wall to steady himself. The street was full of traffic; a bus was waiting at the Tooley Street traffic lights.

The noise was still ringing and fizzing in his ears, but now it was the normal underswell of London traffic. He heard the repeating 'oi oi oi' noise of a siren in the distance and for the first time ever it filled him with relief; it was a wonderful sound, a sound he felt at home with. But he wasn't home, not nowadays, not 2019. There was the Community Centre in the Temperance Building, yes, and there was the karate noticeboard, but no launderette next door, no mini-supermarket, no McDonald's. He must have arrived some time before they were all built. It was as if he'd remembered himself into his own past.

Oh my God! he thought. I just remembered it and it happened! Not in Blackfriars Road, not the house, not the basement, not the bedroom, just me! Like I've got some kind of superpower! Wow! If it hadn't been so scary, he would have been able to savour the exhilaration. He looked up the road, alarmed, and there was his mum's taxi, with the side lights on, parked outside in its usual place! The engine was running. The cab was empty. That meant his mum must be inside the building, just about to pick him up! Whatever the fundamental rules of time travel are – or were – they seemed to be disintegrating. You're not meant to meet yourself, surely? And there's probably something quite important about never meeting your mum either. He thought about that day they'd been followed by the Vergilius woman, but this couldn't be that time, because that was in daylight, midsummer, and this was early evening, September.

What am I supposed to do? he thought. Go in and meet myself and my mum? No, that doesn't sound right. Didn't work out too well for Harry Potter in *The Philosopher's Stone*, did it? Just walk away. Walk away from it now. He started slowly to force his legs up the street, away from the Community Centre. The cold wet socks squelched on the pavement. But he couldn't. He couldn't resist the temptation. He turned back and walked towards the entrance hall of the building. He stopped there for a moment. Obviously, he didn't have a membership card, but from there he could see the whole of the entry lobby and hear the echoey clash of sounds, as fitness and karate classes competed for ear space; Lady Gaga's 'Bad Romance' fighting off forty kids shouting the violent 'Ush!' cries that accompany a karate workout.

People in tracksuits with sports bags were checking in and out, ambling past Jeremiah and shoving him in the shoulder. He felt frozen to the spot, dreading and yet longing for the end of the class and the emergence of the karate kids – and his mum. He went up to the membership hatch to see if he could persuade them to let him in, so that maybe he could just peek through the glass pane on the door, and he could see them but not be seen. But what if they did see him, peering through at them? Walk away! He felt a strong urge to get out of there, but he was rooted to the spot.

In desperation, he tried to think of another way out. He tried to recall exactly where the counter of the McDonald's is nowadays. And looking across the lobby area, he imagined where all the plastic dining tables are. The chaos of noises continued, unabated. And the whole of that wall over there got turned into the front window, and where the door to the classes is, is where the McDonald's loos are nowadays. The sound blended into one echoey cacophony, like in a swimming pool on school morning.

'Whass your order, bro?' said a voice from the other side of the hatch.

'What?' He looked behind him to find a queue of stressed people. In front of him a young guy in a paper hat and uniform was waiting for Jeremiah to speak. 'What?' he said, again.

'Can I help you, bro?' The noise was deafening, or was it just in his head?

'I did it again!' Jeremiah shouted at the guy. He was standing in the brightly lit and crowded McDonald's. 'All I have to do is remember it! It's me! I just remembered it, and it actually happened!'

'Well, don't hold back, then. If you just remembered it, tell us what it is,' said the young guy, 'then I can get it for you and then you could pay me and then you could eat it. Right?'

'Why did I do that, actually? Damn!' said Jeremiah. 'Damn! I could've seen my mum, but I chickened out.'

'Nuggets?' said the guy behind the counter. 'In a meal deal? Or just with fries?'

'Get on with it!' said a man in the queue behind Jeremiah. 'It's supposed to be *fast* food.'

'Yeah, not some existential discussion,' said a grumpy-looking woman with expensive clothes.

'Yeah, like "to gherkin or not to gherkin",' joked a younger, studenty-looking guy, picking up the thread, which wound up the first man who'd complained.

'And we don't need some lecture from you neither,' said the first guy to the studenty guy.

Jeremiah said sorry to each one of them individually and ran out of the building towards the new London Bridge pedestrian underpass. It was great to be back.

THIRTY-FOUR

The cycle rickshaw ride to County Hall from Blackfriars Road was difficult and uncomfortable for Artemesia Plutarch. For a start, the two members of the Blackfriars Breach Brigade were very large people and Artemesia was wedged between them on the bench seat like a sandwich, mostly bread. And as their thick thighs pedalled, they squished against her knees. But her main difficulty was Scoobeedoo. Pretending to be unconscious from the Trallypaz patch might work on the guards, but she couldn't fool the Scoob. The little dog kept jumping up from her lap and licking her face and barking as if to say, 'Whachoo playing at? Come on! Don't tell me you can't feel this? Slobber, slobber, slobber.' She wished she could brush the dog aside or snap at him to shut up, but she had to sit there wedged between the two meatloafs, with her chin slumped onto her chest as if the Trallypaz patch had taken full effect.

'Yes, can I help you?' A hostile whine came over the intercom at the Belvedere Road barrier, around the back of County Hall.

'Delivering a breach, mate,' said the slightly larger of the two of Artemesia's captors.

'Oh really, is that so? Strictly speaking, you can't deliver "a breach"! A breach is an action. A breach*er* is the person who performs that action.'

'What?'

'I said a breach is not a person, it's an action…' the whiner shouted back over the intercom, but it was hard to make out what they were saying because the Scoob started barking loudly, trying to get Artemesia to play something with him.

'All right,' said the guard, 'we're delivering a friggin' breach*er* then. Open up the friggin' barri*er*.'

Scoobeedoo nosed down further onto Artemesia's lap and managed to get his head inside the leather satchel. There's gotta be a ball in here, he thought, she won't be able to resist that! She loves throwing a ball, loves it! Ah, here's something… He found a hard, roundish object and pulled it out of the satchel triumphantly.

The barrier started to go up slowly. The guard mumbled 'arsehole' under his breath as the rickshaw edged forward towards the steps of County Hall.

'I heard that!' came the whine over the intercom. The barrier started to come back down again before the rickshaw was fully through. The arm stopped just short of the canopy roof of the rickshaw, making it impossible to proceed.

'Right,' said the first guard. He got out of the rickshaw and walked across to the small red booth on the other side of the road, ready for a fight with whoever the petty official was, sitting in there on the other end of the intercom, enjoying their few moments of control over the lives of others.

Matthew Christopher McTennant had been this objectionable since he was a child. It wasn't something that had come about through thwarted dreams and ambitions – he was born like that. At the age of seven, when his parents had served him a plate of minced lamb covered with mashed potatoes, he'd complained, 'This is not a shepherd's pie, it is a shepherd's pudding. There is no pastry top, nor base.' Becoming an entrance-gate operator was his dream job.

Through the little slits of her pretend-closed eyes, Artemesia could see the Scoob tossing the hard object he'd found in the satchel onto the ground outside the rickshaw, as if it were a ball, ready to play. But it wasn't a ball. It was a round tin of Green Monster Gunge, circa 1978. One of Artemesia's favourites. The lid rolled off it on impact with the ground, and green gunge spilled out.

That's the kind of thing I meant! thought Scoobeedoo. She's gonna love this! This'll wake her up! Watch this! The dog leaped down from Artemesia's lap onto the road and rolled in the gunge.

Over by the red booth, Breach Boy One had taken hold of Matthew Christopher McTennant's lapel and dragged him out of the safety of his little box and was shunting his body up against the side of his miniature fortress. They were both shouting. 'Are you going to let us through the barrier or am I going to flatten your face?' and, 'All I was saying was that, technically speaking, a person cannot be "a breach"; a breach is defined in the byelaws as—' He didn't get much further

Time to act, thought Artemesia. 'Scoobee?' she said, suddenly snapping out of her mock sleep. 'Be like Spike!'

It worked, see?! I knew this'd get her! thought Scoobeedoo, and he stood up on his hind legs, covered in Green Monster Gunge, puffed out his chest and growled menacingly at the second guard still sitting in the rickshaw. Spike is the aggressive bulldog in the kennel outside the house where Tom and Jerry live, in the cartoons of the same name.

'Get him!' said Artemesia. A dog, covered in green gunge, advancing at you on its hind legs and growling aggressively like Spike from *Tom and Jerry* could be an alarming sight if you didn't know it was only the Scoob trying to get some comedy attention. The guard pulled away along the bench seat, unsure what was going on. The first guard was walking across the road back towards them now. Guard number two grabbed Artemesia's wrist and tried to pull her out of the other side of the rickshaw. Artemesia rammed her arm up against the main canopy strut, smashing the flexi-glass casing and leaving the guard with a handful of glass splinters, while Artemesia slid her arm away and jumped down next to Scoobeedoo.

'Come on, boy!' she yelled at the Scoob and legged it as fast as she could back up Belvedere Road toward the upper walkway at Waterloo station. No one had bothered to rename it, despite objections from the French government and ABBA fans. Oh great! thought Scoobeedoo. We get to go for a run too! This is the best day! He shook his body and spattered Artemesia with Green Monster Gunge.

Artemesia leaped up the stairs two at a time. This is where not having a large, bouncer-type frame put her at an advantage. The two Breach Brigade bodies were soon way behind as they struggled up the stairs behind her.

At the end of the walkway, Artemesia picked up the Scoob and swung over the fence that led to the HyGen-trains departing from Waterloo. Then, with the dog down on the ground again, they ran together as far as was possible, right to the end of the platform. The platforms here curve around at least forty degrees from the gate, so down this end they were completely concealed from the entrance barriers by the iron pillars holding up the glass roof, their original ironwork and riveting still in place after nearly three hundred years.

'HyGen-train now departing from platform twenty-one, calling at Vauxhall, Battersea, Clapham Junction, Putney,

Mortlake, Richmond, Twickenham…'[23]

'That'll do nicely for us,' said Artemesia, 'I should be able to recall something from one of those. Let's do Twickenham, that was big in the seventies. Come on, Scoob. You ready to start a new life? Looks like we won't be able to come back here for a hundred years or so.'

Taking a quick look down to the bottom of the platform to make sure they were not still being followed, Artemesia grabbed the old-style handle on the train door and, letting Scoobeedoo jump up before her, stepped onto the HyGen-train. With a light hissing sound, it pulled forward out of the station as Artemesia prepared herself to pull backwards, into a more comfortable time.

---

23 The trouble with using a hydrogen fuel cell as a source of energy powerful enough to run a vehicle was that it took an impractical amount of energy to produce it. Once this problem was solved, in the late twenty-first century, by using vitrified cow-poo batteries, hydrogen power took off. But only for things where surface tension is low, like railways and rubble chutes. My editor seems strangely keen on railways and asked me to put in a scene set in the model railway shop on Lower Marsh in Waterloo. Ed. was upset to learn that the iconic shop closed in 2020. It was a train-spotters' paradise, where you could get books such as *Branch Line Stations South, Volume 2* and *Modern Locomotives Illustrated* and *Studies in Steam*. New layer to Ed., I discovered.

THIRTY-FIVE

'I hope this is not a sign of what the future holds for us,' said Stepdad Pete, serving the heated-up remains of lunch, 'out all night twice in one week, without letting us know where you are or ringing or anything.'

'Sorry, Pete, I really am, things got a bit difficult. I thought I found someone who knew Mum. You know – before,' said Jeremiah, suddenly realising how hungry he was. He shovelled the oven-roasted vegetables in his mouth; sweet potatoes, cauliflower, carrots, onions, garlic. Pete liked roasted vegetables. He had left Jeremiah's favourite, chilli oil, on the table, so they all got doused with that.

'I miss her too, Jem. But you could at least have texted. Sorry all the potatoes have gone – the girls wolfed them down and we didn't know when you'd be back,' said Pete. 'She can put it away, that Daisy! Still, she is eating for two, so…'

In a very short time, Daisy had ensconced herself in the Blackfriars Road household. She had interpreted Stepdad Pete's offer of 'somewhere to stay until you sort yourself out' to mean at least until the baby could walk.

Earlier that day, Jeremiah had found his room stacked with packets of nappies: hundreds of them. A whole wall-full. 'They were two for one, so Dad got loads and loads,' said Ruby.

'Bit early, I know,' said Stepdad Pete, 'but we'll soon get rid of all this lot once the baby comes.' He seemed to be almost as pleased as Ruby at Daisy's arrival.

'Aren't they meant to be bad for the environment?' asked Jeremiah.

'Disposable diaper napkins that you do not have to boil and scrub,' Daisy had chipped in, 'what's not to like?'

'Sorry, did you just say, "what's not to like?"?' asked Jeremiah.

'Boiling pooey nappies! Urrgh!' said Ruby. 'That's what they used to have to do, Jem, in the old days.'

'Not even my mum had to do that!' said Stepdad Pete. 'She's quick to pick things up, this Daisy.'

She certainly is, thought Jeremiah.

Ruby was very excited about the prospect of Daisy staying with them. 'It's my best thing ever that she's going to have her baby here,' she said. 'I love Daisy.'

'Your stepsister is so cool, she's amaze-balls,' said Daisy, without a hint of embarrassment.

'What's going on?' said Jeremiah. 'Daisy? Since when did you turn into a walking urban dictionary?'

'Don't be so awkward-balloon, Jem, dude,' said Daisy, 'or would you prefer that I went back to calling you Mr Jeremiah, sir?'

'And we got lots of baby-grows too, it's going to be brilliant, and we're going to get like a cot and a baby buggy – look here on the website: do you think this one looks too big, 'coz it's got a rain hood?' said Ruby, without drawing breath, 'And she gave me her ankle boots, look! Like Mary Poppins!' Ruby was wearing Daisy's creased old ankle boots, which were a couple of sizes too big for her. 'They're a bit big, but I stuffed cotton wool in the toes 'coz she didn't need them any more…'

'So I see,' said Jeremiah, 'and where did you get the new outfit from, Daisy?' Daisy was wearing a pair of Lycra shorts and a shiny plastic jacket.

‘Pete and Ruby took me to a screen called Nasty Gal, next-day delivery,’ she said. ‘It was peng.’

‘This is a total disaster,’ said Jeremiah.

He had tried, initially, explaining to Stepdad Pete about the time thing; as in, going back in it, and where Daisy was actually from, but it hadn’t sounded at all convincing.

‘And I thought I was the one obsessed with the past of this house!’ Pete had laughed incredulously. ‘Jem, you don’t have to take it that seriously, you know.’

Ruby butted in, ‘But she does know like, a lot, a lot, a lot about history and stuff, ’coz she used to work in some historical house, making sure everything was realistic. And she cleaned our kitchen better than we’ve ever done it, with just white vinegar and a cloth! Amazing!’

‘She certainly knows her historical interiors,’ said Stepdad Pete, ‘and listen to this, I was looking at the printouts I got from the Land Registry Office, checking the deeds of this house back to 1857, and it turns out there were these two old ladies who lived here until 1975, when one of them died, in her nineties. Her name was Clementina Questingbloom, or something. She and her partner, the other old lady, Lucinda Bonnet, used to run some sort of women’s refuge here, for local girls and their babies. Started out originally as a sort of girls’ training school and ended up more like a hippy commune-type thing, after the war. Anyway, one of those fascinating obscure little facts, or so I thought, but it turned out Daisy had heard of them!’

‘No,’ said Jeremiah, flatly, ‘what are the chances of that?’

‘She’s so clever,’ said Ruby.

‘So, we’re sort of like “in the tradition” of the house,’ said Stepdad Pete, ‘with Daisy staying to have her baby. And she’s going to need a bit more space when the baby comes, Jem – lot of equipment involved with a baby – so I thought, come the day, I could make up a spare bed for you in the basement.’

'Yes, Daisy's going to have your bedroom,' said Ruby, 'isn't that incredible?'

'Yes, it is. Literally unbelievable,' said Jeremiah.

In the first minutes after he got back, Jeremiah had been surprised at how glad he was to see Ruby. He'd impulsively given her a hug.

'Dad? Jeremiah's being all nice to me!' Ruby had shouted up the stairs.

'Well, that's unusual,' said Stepdad Pete from the landing, 'enjoy it while you can.'

'Ruby, you didn't cancel that DNA kit you ordered on my account, did you?' Jeremiah had asked. She hadn't, so he gave her another hug. He took the handkerchief with the hair in it out from his top pocket and placed it carefully in a drawer.

The huggy feelings were beginning to wear off a little now.

Later that evening, after all the roast vegetables were eaten and Stepdad Pete was upstairs saying goodnight to Ruby, Jeremiah and Daisy were left alone in the kitchen.

'Daisy? I've worked out how I do it,' he said, unplugging his mobile from the downstairs charger, 'and I reckon, with a bit of practice, I could go back there and then come back here again, whenever I choose.'

'Awesome,' said Daisy, turning her back on him to put the food waste in the bin and the paper in the recycling.

'It hasn't got anything to do with the house; it's to do with remembering stuff, even stuff that didn't happen to you. Sort of like the way birds remember how to make nests, even though no one teaches them?'[24]

---

24 The first time you make something, you don't expect to get your best result. Even if you've been taught how to build a house, for instance, you will improve after the experience of actually building one. Birds are not like that; they build

'I'm not coming with yer,' said Daisy, turning back to face him, 'I wanna stay here.'

'Yeah, I don't blame you. It was rubbish back then. But I've had this idea of how we could make it a bit better. I know I said you're not supposed to change the past, but I think we could make a little adjustment...'

'We?'

'I reckon we could stop Henry Davenant Hythe.'

Daisy shivered at the mention of the name. 'I'm not going back there. I told yer,' she said.

'You wouldn't have to, but I do need your help.'

'I'm not doing anything that'll harm the baby.'

'This won't have anything to do with the baby, I promise. We just use this,' said Jeremiah. 'Here, look.' He swiped through to the camera on his phone, took a photo of her and showed it to her. She wasn't impressed. She tutted and shook her head. She took the mobile off him and moved round so that she was better lit, turned the phone to landscape, took a much better picture and handed the phone back. Obviously Ruby had been teaching her.

'So, will you help me?' he asked.

'Whatever,' she said, emphatically.

'Do you mean yes? "Whatever" means a kind of reluctant maybe.'

'Oh,' she said, 'then, not whatever. I meant, as long as I don't have to go back there, yes, coolaboolie.'

'Coola what?'

'I'll do it!'

---

their best nest first time. Tests have been done to see if perhaps they've been helped by their experiences of being in a nest when young, or generally hanging around in trees a lot. Test birds were brought up in an entirely twig-free environment, and then let loose when nest-building season came round. They all built their exact best nest – no experience required. Just add forest and wings.

THIRTY-SIX

It is generally accepted that if you want to get good at anything, music, sport, whatever, you have to practise. In fact, if you want to be the best at it, you have to go on practising, even when you're at the top of your game. Some lessons also help, obviously. It would have been good if Jeremiah could have had some time-jump coaching, like he had in maths from Nandy Banerjee, but failing that, practice would have to do. Having managed it in Tooley Street all by himself, he thought he'd have a go at directing his own Time Traffic and pay a visit to Phyllis and Sir Rodger.

He came out of the Tube at Russell Square, crossed Woburn Place at the traffic lights and then walked past SOAS, the School of African and Oriental Studies, up towards Gordon Square. There was a chill in the air, and the white clouds hung low, leaving a kind of cool brightness. He was learning to appreciate the warmth and ease of the flannel trousers and thick jacket given him by Sir Rodger and he was getting used to braces. Not stiff detachable collars, though; they were ridiculous, he'd decided, and so he was wearing an ordinary checked shirt he'd borrowed from Stepdad Pete. It was too big for him, but it worked.

The traffic was heavy, and students from all the nearby colleges – UCL, Birkbeck and SOAS – filled the streets and the sandwich restaurants. It was 2019. Everyone out and about seemed to have an appointment to go to and he couldn't help but catch some of the excitement of people from all over the world, mingling, talking, sharing jokes and knowledge. There was tangible energy emanating from this eclectic bunch, unlike any of the local schools Jeremiah had been to.

It was quieter in Gordon Square. He walked through the gardens to the other side of the square to where he could remember Sir Rodger's house was. Number 49. The stone steps up to the front door were exactly the same as they had been a hundred years ago. The door was painted black nowadays, not blue. He tried to recall the exact shade of blue it had been; a dark, purply indigo. The number 49 itself was different; it hadn't been in brass, as it was now – it had been painted on, in curly white writing. There had been a black metal pulley where the doorbell was now. He took a deep breath, bracing himself for the possibility of a time-jump. A small motorcycle went past behind him, and for a moment he thought its shrill engine noise might be the hissing, rushing sound that he was expecting. Hoping for. But nothing happened. He tried recalling all the details of the house again, one by one.[25]

A middle-aged man in a baggy grey suit came up the steps behind Jeremiah, getting an enormous bunch of keys out of his pocket. 'Can I help you?' he barked, pushing past Jeremiah and fitting a key into the door.

---

25 OK, I've got a new editor now, who is really up for footnotes, which is good, but I've kind of lost confidence in them. Had a Zoom meeting with him and he's really into as much sci-fi, space-age whizzery as possible. He wondered whether this bit would be better if Jem had something like a 'sonic screwdriver' and could walk through walls and stuff. I'd like my old editor back now, please. I know I moaned, but she was more understanding. And there was that railway nerd thing.

'Sorry. I was just trying to remember. I've been here before, you see,' said Jeremiah, flustered at the man's hostility.

'Oh really?' said the man, eyeing Jeremiah up and down as if he were a specimen of some sort. 'In connection with what, was that?'

'I was visiting some friends, before it was... erm...' Jeremiah felt nailed to the spot.

'Well, it's been the Architecture and Design Association since 1924, so...' said the man, suspiciously.

'Yes, of course. I knew that,' said Jeremiah.

'That's what it says on the brass plaque on the wall here?' The man stopped and waited for further explanation from Jeremiah.

'Yes. Sorry. That wasn't here before,' he replied, a pathetic whisper now.

'Before what?' said the man and waited again. Jeremiah just stared at him and mildly shook his head. The man continued to scrutinise him.

'I'll just go then, shall I?' said Jeremiah, stepping back down onto the pavement. 'Goodbye.' The man shrugged, opened the door and went inside the building.

Jeremiah was disappointed. As he walked away, he consoled himself with a few clichéd pep-talk phrases: 'you have to pick yourself up and try again', 'get back on the horse', and 'the race is only won in the last ten yards'. Then, as he wandered back past Tavistock Square, more catchphrases started crowding his brain: 'Can We Fix It? Yes We Can!' Although that last one sent him off on a slightly different tack and other phrases – mostly from telly programmes – came up, randomly – 'Beam Me Up, Scotty!' and 'Oh My God, They Killed Kenny!', and then, simply, 'D'oh'.

By now he'd walked aimlessly past Russell Square, so he decided to keep walking and get the bus home instead. 'I have a cunning plan,' came involuntarily into his mind. He didn't, but he wished he did. The only thing he could think of was to return to Blackfriars Road and try practising there.

The bus was one of the new hydrogen buses, supposedly environmentally friendly, video-cam secure, with an automated voice which stuttered out the stops with upward inflections in all the wrong places: 'This? – is a – One – Four? – Eight? – bus to – Dulwich Library,' which makes the destination sound as if it were a place in a pre-school TV programme.

There were a lot of people on board, so he clambered up to the upper deck and found a seat. Jeremiah looked out of the window as they approached Blackfriars Bridge. There was the old river below. That hadn't changed much, still a huge, moving wedge of sludgy brown. 'Next stop Blackfriars – Bridge? – alight here for – Blackfriars – station? – Corn Exchange!' said as if the Corn Exchange were a fun game on a TV programme for pre-schoolers, 'and – Blackfriars – pier?' the computer voice plodded on. Jeremiah wondered if the drivers needed counselling after listening to this all day.

Up ahead of them on the south side of the river, he spotted the gigantic insignia of the 'London Chatham and Dover Railway 1864', glistening in its red, blue and gold paint high up at the side of the road. Jeremiah looked down to his left at the eight old red pillars rising redundantly out of the river.

The hydrogen engine squeaked as the bus stopped, or was it the hydraulic brakes? Or perhaps the automatic doors opening? A noise of steam escaping from a pressure cooker and gathering itself into an insistent whistle. Could this be it? Had the LCDR insignia triggered him? Jeremiah threw himself down the stairs of the bus, colliding with a large old man with plastic shopping bags and a walking stick.

'Sorry!' he yelled, as he lunged at the closing doors. If it was happening again, he didn't want to fall from a moving vehicle.

The noise continued in his head even after he rolled out onto the pavement below. It was happening: he could feel it. He kept trying to focus on the railway insignia, but was immediately shouted at to get out of the way. 'Waaatch it!' a voice screamed from behind him. He turned to see a horse, pulling a cart straight towards him, a few feet away. The driver was yanking on the reins, trying to brake in time. He had tumbled straight into the path of the traffic on the busy bridge. He rolled out of the way and bumped into a poor-looking woman with no teeth. 'You awight, young mashter?' she smiled at him.

'Git art the way!' yelled the cart driver. 'Whachoo fink yer doin'?' The cart had stopped and the driver was on the road trying to soothe the horse, which was now jumpy.

A tall man in a frock coat and top hat grabbed hold of Jeremiah's jacket collar. 'What in heaven do you think you're doing, sonny-me-lad?' he said.

'I did it!' shouted Jeremiah. 'I did it! I actually did it! Me! All by myself!'

The top-hatted man dragged Jeremiah to the side of the bridge. 'Now look here!' he said, following it up with a smack across Jeremiah's shoulder. Jeremiah slid to the floor to escape the man's grip on his collar, managed to slip free, and ran.

'Sorry about the horse!' he shouted at the cart driver as he ran back north of the river. Now for Gordon Square.

THIRTY-SEVEN

Stone steps: check. Dark blue front door: check. Curly-whirly, white number 49 on it: check. Black metal bell-handle: check and pull. There was a jangling sound from deep inside the house. Jeremiah stood and waited on the doorstep, still exhilarated from the excitement on Blackfriars Bridge. He was trying to rationalise it. There had been a single moment where, just for a split second, it felt as if he had all of his memory banks open and available to him – like a computer screen with all of the icons up – and he could pick whichever one he wanted and mentally click on it. And just for that split second, time was going slowly enough for him to click, easily, on the right one. If you've ever wondered why it's so hard to swat a fly, it's because from the fly's point of view your hand is sailing down gently towards it in slow motion, and all it has to do is lazily flit out of the way. For flies, time does not fly, it ambles.

'Uh. 'S'you. 'Lo, sir.' Janet opened the door and peered out at Jeremiah. 'Sir Rodger's in the library.' She stood to one side to let him in, expecting him to walk straight past her.

'No, wait, Janet,' he said, inside the hall. 'Do you mind me asking? Before you got this job, were you one of Clementina Quentinbloom's girls?'

'Huh,' she said, closing the front door behind them.

'And is one of the Grout children yours?' The faintest flicker of light swept across her face and was gone. 'Thought so,' he said. 'Which one? Dolly? Tess? Samuel?'

She looked at the floor. 'James,' she said, so quietly that Jeremiah had to ask again. 'James,' she repeated, more loudly, ''cept his real name is Tonks. They called 'im James.'

'I'm really sorry. You must miss him.' Jeremiah reached in his pocket and got out a tissue; she did look as if she might cry. 'Here,' he said, offering it to her, then quickly taking it back. 'Oops, not supposed to bring things like that back to this century, so...'

But she didn't cry; she looked up defiantly at him and said, ''E's in the library, as you please, sir.'

'Maybe I could get them to send you a photo of your boy, or something? News of how he's getting on?'

'No, sir, don't do that. I got the memory, like. That's enough.'

'Janet,' he asked, 'did you ever know a woman called Dr Amanda Vergilius?' But he was too late, Sir Rodger had heard his arrival and came bounding out into the hall.

'Is that Master Jeremiah Bourne?' he boomed. He was wearing a pair of yellow trousers with black checks on them, rather like Rupert Bear, a dark waistcoat, and his signature red velvet cap. His nudist days seemed to be behind him; Cook threatening to leave had done the trick. No innovative social reform was worth actually learning to boil his own eggs. 'Don't stand around! Sit ye down!' he said, striding into the front room and beckoning Jeremiah after him. 'Thank you, Janet,' he said as he threw himself into a creaky armchair, 'and Janet? Cheer up! It might never happen!'

'Sir Rodger,' said Jeremiah, when Janet had left the room, closing the door behind her, 'to be honest, I think it already has happened for Janet. You see, one of those

Grout children is hers, and I think she'd be a lot happier if she was with the kid. Not to mention the kid missing his mum. He's called James, well, Tonks. Kids miss their mums, you know.'

'D'you know, I think you're right? I still miss Nanny dreadfully. It was a terrible wrench. Terrible. As Phyllis may have told you, our own mother and father were explorers. Which is the reason we saw so very little of them! Which was possibly a blessing, because they cared so very little for us that we were spared the constant reminder of their indifference.' Sir Rodger looked suddenly crestfallen; his eyes started to plate over with tears and he sniffed. Perhaps it was he who would need Jeremiah's tissue. But he was quick to revive. 'But now, you must tell me exactly how it has all unfolded, dispatch the dispatch, Jem!'

They were suddenly interrupted by the loud squawk of a parrot. 'Put some trousers on! Put some trousers on! Kweurk!' The bird hopped from foot to foot on its perch.

'Be quiet, Dryden!' thundered Sir Rodger. 'I *have* some trousers on! Thanks to you and certain members of my staff who are stuffy and old-fashioned in the extreme!'

'Kweurk!' squawked Dryden, and then more quietly, menacingly almost, 'Put some trousers on! Put some trousers on!'

'Dryden! Enough! One more peek from you, and it's hood time, my feathery friend!' Sir Rodger leaned forward and grabbed the silk hood for Dryden's cage, as a warning. 'I do apologise for my parrot.'

After Jeremiah had finished recounting everything that had happened to him in the last forty-eight hours, Sir Rodger fell silent for a moment, then stood, went to the window and looked thoughtfully at the street outside. His look was pensive, but his brain had emptied like a sieve. The usual inner panic. Eventually he turned to Jeremiah and said, 'These Are Interesting Times,' with a meaningful look on his face.

'Yeah,' said Jeremiah, who'd been hoping for a bit more, 'but what do you reckon about Henry Davenant Hythe's laboratory?'

'It's a mnemonic,' said Sir Rodger. 'It's as if you've been using a mnemonic to recall the past. Do you know what a mnemonic is? Do you know how to spell it? I'll tell you! With a silent "M". Nemonic. It's a reminder, a pointer to help you remember, for instance, a number.'

'In my case it's not so much a number as objects and buildings and stuff. But I wanted to say, I think we should do something to stop Henry Davenant Hythe.'

'Ah, but if it *were* a number, it would break down as follows: "R" is the eighteenth letter of the alphabet, so "Are" equals eighteen. Then, interest is calculated as a percentage of one hundred, so "Interest" equals one hundred, and then of course, as you must know, the "Ting" was the ancient Icelandic Parliament...'

'Funnily enough, I didn't know that...'

'...and the *Times* newspaper costs tuppence, so "Times" equals two. Leaving us with a grand total of eighteen million, one hundred thousand, nine hundred and thirty-two. These – Are – Interest – Ting – Times.' Sir Rodger sat down again with satisfaction.

Dryden the parrot perked up and yelled at the top of his parroty voice, 'Eighteen million one hundred and ninety-two! Put some trousers on!'

'Right! That is it!' said Sir Rodger, leaping out of his chair and grabbing Dryden's hood. He started sliding it over the parrot's cage.

Dryden bent low and stuck his head near the bottom of the cage as the hood came down. 'Monica, Nemonica, remember your Nemonica!' he said, in a last desperate bid for attention, before the hood closed over him and he was left in the dark.

Sir Rodger sat back down again and put on his thoughtful face. 'If what you say about Dr Henry Davenant Hythe is true, then he is no longer a friend of mine. This experimentation with human souls is unacceptable!'[26] There was a pause, and then Sir Rodger was up again and racing to the door. 'You're right, he must be stopped! Come on!'

'Where are we going?' said Jeremiah, also getting up.

'To the attic!' Sir Rodger swung the door open to reveal a surprised Janet, caught in the act of listening at the door. 'Ah, Janet! There you are again!' said Sir Rodger, trying to look as if he'd been expecting her.

'Sorry, Sir Rodger, sir,' she said, covering, 'I was just... dusting the architraves, like.'

'Of course you were, Janet. Now, Janet, why don't you take the day off and come to Blackfriars Road with us? Mm? You could pay a visit on the Grouts.'

Janet looked shocked at the suggestion. 'And who would clean the scullery, Sir Rodger?'

'I'm sure it would do your spirits a world of good and a certain young person at the Grouts would be delighted to see you. And don't worry, I can cover the cost of the carriage home.'

The suggestion had thrown Janet, and she didn't know how to react. 'No. Fankin' you, sir,' she stammered, 'too much to do 'ere.' But the surprise of being invited had

---

26 It's hard to work out what modern politicians mean when they say something is unacceptable, which they seem to do with increasing frequency nowadays. Is this a sign that more and more things have recently become unacceptably bad, and that they are going to do something about it? Not likely. Perhaps it is more an excuse for inaction – if something has been deemed 'unacceptable' then it would indicate that a politician will not accept it, as in blocking his ears with his fingers and going 'La la la la, can't accept that, didn't hear it!'

tipped her off balance and she was puzzled by her own refusal.

'Well, think on it! Think on it, dear Janet! Now, come on, Jeremiah, it's at the very top of the house,' said Sir Rodger, mounting the stairs two at a time. 'Well, it would be. It's an attic!' He gave a massive laugh which lasted until he got to the first landing. Jeremiah followed.

THIRTY-EIGHT

Sir Rodger's attic was crammed to the rafters with bizarre and eccentric old equipment. There were things made out of bathtubs, which had wheels and leather straps; hinged wooden boxes on camping tables, which contained full shaving sets; dozens of different kinds of hatboxes and hats, some recognisable as such, some less so.

From up here, perhaps because there was no insulation, one could hear the clacking of horses' hooves and the rolling of carriage wheels on the street below, amplified by the cavernous roof. It was chilly too.

Sir Rodger had to stoop and bumped his head on the rafters. 'I love the smell up here!' he said, inhaling deeply. 'Haven't been up here for aeons. I wish I had your skills, Jeremiah, I could whisk myself back to happier times!' His eyes were starting to fill with tears again.

'Are we looking for something specific?' asked Jeremiah. But Sir Rodger was distracted by the objects he came across.

'My old watercolour box!' he said, picking up a small, messy metal box. 'Oh look! Most of them are worn out.' He showed Jeremiah the palette, with all of the little trays of hardened paint looking dilapidated and charcoal-coloured. His eye was then quickly drawn to a large book, stacked sideways on the floor. 'And goodness me! I'd forgotten all about this!' He pulled the book out and opened it up. It was an atlas with wide, flapping pages, which he lovingly riffled through. 'Completely out of date, of course.' It was as if he'd entered a different world. 'Now, tell me,' he said, 'why have we come up here?'

The sight of all these items from his past had thrown him off track. 'To stop Henry Davenant Hythe?' prompted Jeremiah.

'Ah yes! Of course! He must be stopped!' He turned and rummaged in a pile of wooden picture frames and boxes. 'Found 'em!' he shouted and turned back to Jeremiah, clutching two carved mahogany birds with squashed old feathers on their crests, joined together by a hardwood chain. 'These should do the trick.'

'What the hell is that?' said Jeremiah.

'Language, Jem!' said Sir Rodger, as he pulled on the beaks of the birds, which were jointed and opened out on hinges. 'These are wrist and foot restrainers from the island of Van'u'ala in the South Seas. Our father was governor there for a short while. Before the tribals tried to eat him.'

'That's a bit racist, actually?' said Jeremiah.

'Well, they ate the fellow before him.' He gathered up the contraption and squeezed past Jeremiah towards the door. 'These will come in handy if Davenant Hythe starts to get uppity. Jolly good, let's go back down.'

Jeremiah clambered after him. On his way out, Sir Rodger stooped down behind a large, broken model of the solar system and emerged clutching a brass telescope. 'Oh look, my old telescope! Might as well take that too.'

'Why?' asked Jeremiah.

They emerged from the attic and made their way down the narrow staircase to the landing at the top of the four flights of wider stairs which led down into the body of the house. 'Did you know that Halley's Comet is passing this week?' Sir Rodger said over his shoulder as they carried on down. 'Last chance to see it for another seventy-six years!

By which time I shall be underground. How about you? 1986? Are you going to be around then?'

'No,' said Jeremiah, 'I'm not going to be born until 2002.'

'Well, then, let's catch it while we can!'

Janet was standing at the bottom of the stairs wearing a coat and hat. She cleared her throat and announced, 'I've changed me mind, Sir Rodger. If 'n I may, I'm comin' with.'

'Splendid! Splendid!' said Sir Rodger. 'We shall be leaving you in Blackfriars Road for some hours while we attend to business in the Leathermarket area. Here, take this.' He handed her the telescope. 'Perhaps the Grout children would like to take it onto the roof and see if they can spot the comet.' The idea of the Grout children on the roof at Blackfriars Road seemed like a very bad plan to Jeremiah. In fact, allowing Sir Rodger to be in charge at all seemed foolhardy.

When they got to Blackfriars Road, Phyllis was finishing up a meeting with the ladies of the Society of Theosophical Research and Anthro-Psychology, Women's Branch, so Sir Rodger invited them all to come to the confrontation with Henry Davenant Hythe. Which seemed to Jeremiah an incredibly bad idea, especially as he did have a cunning plan of his own.

By the time they arrived at the rendezvous off Tooley Street, just around the corner from Henry Davenant Hythe's laboratory, there were about nine of them: Phyllis, Jeremiah and Sir Rodger, still hanging onto his South Seas handcuff-manacles, plus a noisy entourage of the STRAWB ladies in hats, complaining about the air. They were near the tanneries now, and the smell from the leather-tanning works, with its dung, urine and rotting hides, was overpowering.

'It is abysmal, the stink,' said Sir Rodger loudly, seemingly unable to turn the volume down on his voice box.

'Well, that is what one has to put up with south of the river, Rodger dear,' said Phyllis, almost as loudly, 'which is where you have banished us of the Women's Branch of the society. As if a woman Theosophist is not worth the clean air that the male Theosophists are privileged to breathe.' Several of the ladies agreed, especially the one with the large chins, who began haranguing Sir Rodger with her complaints about the basement meeting room in Blackfriars Road; it was too small, it did not have enough light, it was sometimes a bit damp.

'Oh, this is so unfair!' shouted Sir Rodger. 'Our society is one of the few philosophical societies that even *has* a Women's Branch! If not the only one! I thought you'd be grateful.'

'Grateful?' choked an outraged Phyllis, the long feather of her hat bobbing madly. 'Theosophy was begun by Madame Blavatsky, and carried forward by dear old Annie Besant. Both, I think you will find, women!' More noise from the women, pushing forward to make their points. Sir Rodger looked confused, towering above them all.

Jeremiah had to step in. 'Look,' he said in a forceful whisper, 'this is not the time for that conversation, OK? We have a job to do! Now, can you please give us a bit of space, and keep the noise down? We are here. At the lab.' He pointed to the corner around which the little stairs led down to the laboratory.

The woman with the chins shushed the other women and tried to get them to back up. 'Back up, back up,' she said in a loud whisper.

'What's that? Buck up?' said the one with the ear trumpet, pushing forward.

'Reverse, dear, reverse,' said another. There was a bustle as the women tried to reposition themselves a few feet further up the pavement.

'Right, so when you've stopped bickering, I think it's best if, at first, I go in alone.' It was all very well to laugh at old films where actors are expected to keep a straight face while they say, 'I have to do this alone,' but this time, Jeremiah thought, he did have a point. If all nine of them piled down into Davenant Hythe's basement, there would be chaos.

'But what if your plan misfires, Jem?' said Phyllis, who had been in favour of an intervention from the three of them.

'Yes, shouldn't we have a signal of some sort?' said Sir Rodger, still unrestrainedly loud.

'All right! All right!' said Jeremiah, losing his patience with them. 'The signal is if I shout "Help! Phyllis! Rodger! Help!"'

'Sshhh!' Rodger and Phyllis shushed him, which was a bit rich, he thought.

'Incidentally, things do get better for girls, you know, in the future. They're doing better than boys, actually. They go to university more. They become maths professors more.'

'So that's why you took Daisy there. She wanted to be a maths professor?'

'Maybe, who knows. But she's doing OK. Right. Wish me luck.'

'OK,' said Phyllis.

'You said "OK",' said Sir Rodger to Phyllis. 'How modern.'

'So did you.'

'No I didn't, I was just repeating you.'

Jeremiah calmed himself, tried to empty his mind, like at the beginning of a karate lesson, and stepped round the corner towards the lab.

THIRTY-NINE

'Well, if it ain' me ole pyjamas! Jem-Jam! Come back fer some more, 'av yer?' Ed Viney was standing guard at the door to the laboratory. He slapped his right fist into his left palm when he saw Jeremiah. 'Want some ov viss, duz yer? Carm orn ven! Less be 'avin yer!' He poked Jeremiah's shoulder, spoiling for a fight.

'Mr Viney!' Davenant Hythe's voice came from inside the lab. 'Will you please unhand that man and show him in?'

Ed Viney backed off, with a smile that said, 'I'll get you later.' He kicked the door open with his foot and stood back to let Jeremiah in. 'Hov course, hov course! Step vis way, yer Jemiah-ship.' The little bell on a spring jingled as Jeremiah walked past and into the laboratory, where Davenant Hythe was waiting for him with a crazed look in his eyes.

'Where is Daisy Wallace? You haven't brought her, have you. You lied to me!' He came up and stood too close to Jeremiah again.

'I have got her, Dr Hythe, I promise,' said Jeremiah, trying to stay calm and confident, 'she's here.'

'Where? Where is she? I don't see her!'

'Do we have to have him around?' said Jeremiah, indicating Ed Viney. 'He's making me nervous.'

'I'm losing my patience, Mr Bourne! Just bring me Daisy Wallace!' shouted Davenant Hythe.

'All right, all right. Here goes.' Jeremiah reached into his pocket and brought out a plastic bag, which was folded and wound around his phone. 'I know I'm not supposed to bring stuff like this back from the future. It's a supermarket bag. Recyclable. I just wanted to keep it dry.' He took out his mobile phone, stuffing the plastic bag back in his pocket.

'Ah, the damned black glass again. Get on with it!'

Jeremiah knew from practising magic tricks on Ruby and Stepdad Pete that a big part of it is thc set up: where you look, how slowly and confidently you chat, how to distract with extraneous activity. He took his time turning on his phone and choosing the app he was going to use. Frau Hemling came from the back room and stood in the doorway to look. He had an audience. He tapped the screen. A picture of Daisy appeared, wearing her Nasty Gal jacket. He tapped Play and she started to speak. 'Hello, Henry. Dr Hythe, sir. Daisy Wallace 'ere. I've come back, like what you asked. To help with your important research.'

'Blimey! She looks for real!' said Ed Viney.

'She *is* for real,' said Jeremiah.

'Daisy! Come back here now! I can't finish my research without you,' pleaded Henry Davenant Hythe.

Jeremiah slid the images on his phone and tapped the second one; Daisy spoke again. 'I knew you'd say that. But I *am* here with you, Dr Davenant Hythe, sir. And can I just say, your work is so important, in the future, like? Everybody's heard of you. You're, like, really famous and everything.'

'Yes, yes. But I cannot finish that work without you here in the flesh!' Davenant Hythe whispered intimately to the screen. He was having his first FaceTime conversation and it was quite touching, thought Jeremiah. He slid the images and tapped the next one.

'I knew you'd say that an' all,' said Daisy from the screen, 'but before I come an' help you properly, just wanted to ask, is there, by any chance, some other people around? Like that Ed Viney, or Frau Hemling or anything? Because, if there is, I suggest you get 'em to leave now.'

'What?' asked Davenant Hythe. 'Why?'

Jeremiah tapped the next image. 'Right now. Like, give them the rest of the day off, like, or I'm not gonna help, OK?' Daisy paused for a few moments, then, 'I said now. You haven't got rid of 'em yet, have you?'

'I think she means it. Better do as she says,' said Jeremiah for good measure.

Davenant Hythe shouted at Ed Viney and Frau Hemling, 'You heard her! Get out! Both of you! Go!'

'Huh? Vot? Ver? Ver shud I go?' Frau Hemling stuttered.

'I don't care! Just go!' He started to manhandle Ed Viney out of the door.

'But I ain' 'ad proper recompensationing—' complained Ed, struggling a bit as Davenant Hythe swung the door, jingling the bell.

'Just bugger off!' shouted Davenant Hythe, turning back to where Frau Hemling was pulling on an overcoat. 'And you too!' She only just managed to grab her handbag as he hustled her towards the door.

'Fifdeen years, I bin verking here,' she was muttering, 'fifdeen years!'

'Right, now can we get on?' said Davenant Hythe, turning back into the room and straightening his jacket and tie. 'Happy now?' he said to the phone, which Jeremiah was still holding up at eye level.

Jeremiah swiped through the list of recordings and tapped the next one. 'Now, I'm going to come and help you with your research, Dr Hythe, sir,' said Daisy, 'so, what I need you to do is go and get that big book? You know, the big one what you write all of your calculations in?'

Davenant Hythe interrupted her. 'My ledgers. The green one or the black one?'

But Daisy just carried on. 'The big book what I seen when I was visiting.'

Davenant Hythe continued talking over her. 'But I don't know which one that was.'

Jeremiah tapped Pause. 'Both of them, I think she means,' he said, and then tapped Play again.

'…and I want you to give that book to Jeremiah, because he is going to be a partner in this experiment.' Daisy gave a small cough. 'You must share your research and that with him.'

'Oh really? Do I have to?' said Davenant Hythe, looking at Jeremiah with disdain.

'She definitely means it,' said Jeremiah, giving Davenant Hythe what he thought was a long, assertive stare back.

'Miss Wallace, you are a tease. You are being an obstructive and silly girl,' Davenant Hythe shouted at the phone in Jeremiah's hand, 'but all right. Wait there!' He disappeared into the back room.

There was the sound of raised voices and a struggle from outside in the street. As Ed Viney had emerged, cursing, from the laboratory, the street kids had set on him and he'd drawn a knife on them. The women of the Theosophical Society had, in turn, set on Ed Viney. 'I command you to leave those poor children alone!' a woman shouted and that's what Jeremiah had heard. 'Unhand that child!' Then the sound of Ed Viney screaming, 'Ow! Me bum!' as the women took out their hat pins and jabbed him in the buttocks with them. 'You lot ain' no ladies, niver!' he yelled and then scarpered, the sound of his shoes on the pavement fading into the distance as Davenant Hythe returned with the two leather-bound volumes, one in black, the other in a dark green.

'Here are my ledgers. But before I hand them over, how do I know you will keep your word?' said Davenant Hythe.

'We knew you'd say that,' said Jeremiah, getting his phone out and firing up the screen again. He tapped Play.

'...the big book what I seen when I was visiting...' said Daisy from the screen, '...and I want you to give that book to Jeremiah, because he is going to be a partner in this experiment.' Then came the little cough again. 'You must share your research and that with him...'

Realising his mistake, Jeremiah quickly tapped Pause, but it was too late. 'That isn't Daisy, it's a mere photographic representation!' said Davenant Hythe. 'God knows how you've done it, but you are trying to fob me off with a phonographic recording! Very clever, Mr Bourne, but where is Daisy Wallace?'

'She's right here, I promise,' said Jeremiah. 'Look.' He tapped the screen again to bring back the image of Daisy, but it was frozen and Daisy now had cute cartoon doggie ears, nose and whiskers. There was nothing for it but to try the direct approach. 'Give me the books, Henry,' said Jeremiah and lunged forward to try to grab the books off Davenant Hythe, who pulled forcefully away from him.

'Never!' said Davenant Hythe, kicking and kneeing Jeremiah as they grappled. 'You toad!'

The little bell on the laboratory door tinkled and, in the split second while Davenant Hythe turned to look, Jeremiah managed to wrest one of the books from his grasp – the green one. But then he stood rooted to the spot, like a freeze-frame on a video. The person who had just walked into the lab was Dr Amanda Vergilius.

FORTY

'Sorry, but the door was open, so...?' said Vergilius. Her voice was smooth and low.

Davenant Hythe and Jeremiah were stunned into momentary silence by the arrival of the intruder. But Davenant Hythe snapped out of his surprise first to demand, 'Who the devil are you?'

'Dr Amanda Vergilius?' said Jeremiah.

'I think those will be safer with me, don't you?' said Vergilius, taking two steps forward and gently laying a hand on both of the books. She was taller than either of them, and her long red hair was brushed back over her shoulders and tied up loosely, but it was unmistakably her. 'Jeremiah? Dr Hythe? Thank you. Give – them – to – me.' The books were lifted firmly but easily out of their grasps as they stood, bewildered. 'This young man was going to destroy all of your research, Dr Hythe, weren't you, young man? Isn't that right?'

Jeremiah nodded, not knowing what to say.

'Now, I'd love to stay, but, tempus fugit, as they used to say when it did...' Vergilius took one step back, not quite as far as the door, and faded from view. Not so much disappearing in a puff of smoke, as failing to be there any more.

Flummoxed, Henry took a few steps towards where she had been, swinging his hands in the air. Then, realising that both of his ledgers had vanished with her, he turned on Jeremiah. 'What happened? Where did she go?'

'Back to the future, by the look of it,' said Jeremiah.

'You cheated me! Where is my work?'

'I had no idea that was going to happen,' said Jeremiah, 'I swear.'

'Very likely! Agh! Ahhhh!' Henry had what looked to Jeremiah like a convulsion. The thought of his work falling into someone else's hands affected him viscerally. His body wound into a shape like a twisted wet towel and then he exploded in a howl. Then, his eyes, on fire by now, landed on Jeremiah. 'This is your doing!' he raged. 'You!' He leaped towards Jeremiah across the lab bench, knocking over a glass bottle that, miraculously, failed to smash into pieces when it hit the floor, but rolled instead and spilled a brown syrup around their feet.

Jeremiah dodged out of the way and grabbed the first thing that came to hand: a tall glass jar with fizzing orange liquid in it. 'Keep back! Or I'll smash this!' he said, hoping that the glass would make a suitable weapon if smashed and not just shatter into tiny pieces, like the fine, medical glass on his arm had done the last time he was here.

Davenant Hythe let out a deranged laugh. 'I'd put that down again, if I were you, stupid boy. It's an igneo-glyceride compound and it's highly inflammable!'

'Don't you mean flammable?' said Jeremiah.

Davenant Hythe had to stop for a second to think. 'What? Same thing, surely. Flammable, inflammable are the same thing. How strange, I never thought of that before. It must be an anomaly of the English language. Either way it could set the whole place on fire.'

'Sounds like a good idea to me.' Jeremiah never got to test whether he would actually have thrown the jar, because Davenant Hythe made another leap at him, tackling him to the floor and knocking the jar out of his hand. It fell, smashed, and the orange liquid ignited the brown syrup trickling across the floor in a dangerous-smelling, pale lilac flame.

The bell tinkled again, and Sir Rodger was there, posturing grandly. He stood, proudly brandishing his South Seas handcuffs. 'Henry Davenant Hythe? By the powers vested in me as a magistrate of London Town, I am arresting you for...' He collapsed immediately in a fit of coughing from inhaling the toxic smoke that was by now pouring off the combined liquids on the floor. The flames reached the curtains, which were quick to combust; larger blue and yellow flames engulfed the windows like a tidal wave.

Phyllis came into the room behind Sir Rodger. 'Jem? Are you all right? We heard shouting!' But she too succumbed to the smoke and collapsed, coughing, to the floor.

Putting a handkerchief over his mouth, Davenant Hythe made a dash for the door, but Sir Rodger managed to grab his leg and bring him down. 'Not so fast!'

'Let go of me, you numbskull!' yelled Davenant Hythe, pulling Sir Rodger and himself towards the outside basement stairs. But Sir Rodger stayed clinging on, still coughing.

Jeremiah had quickly got onto his hands and knees and crawled away from the flames and smoke, around the other end of the lab bench, and now wriggled along the floor to where Phyllis was bent double, racked by coughs. 'Are you all right, Mrs Stokes, ma'am?' he said, gasping for air himself. There was a loud bang from one of the shelves under the lab bench, followed by the noise of more splintering glass. Jeremiah quickly grabbed hold of Phyllis and lifted her onto his shoulder, carrying her out of the room and up the stairs behind Sir Rodger who was still hanging onto Davenant Hythe's leg. They arrived at the top of the stairs coughing and spluttering as another loud bang shattered the windows and flames and black smoke started to vomit out from the basement.

They stumbled a few yards together, through the smoke, still choking and wheezing, and turned the corner. 'Let go of me, you cretins!' screamed Davenant Hythe, but Sir Rodger, while gripping Davenant Hythe's leg with one hand, was attempting to wrap one of the mahogany bird beaks around his ankle with the other. Jeremiah, still carrying Phyllis on his shoulder like a fireman, barged their combined weights onto Davenant Hythe to try to stop him wriggling free. In a sort of modern dance cluster, all four of them bashed up against the iron gates at the front of the 'Temperance Society 1907' building.

Jeremiah never knew if what happened next had been a conscious decision, or merely chance or even fate. He was aware that the four of them formed a unit, a circle of contact. He was aware of the black-and-white tiles around the archway, the concrete crest above the embossed writing on the Temperance building, the ironwork above their heads. He was aware that the crackling sound of the fire had become a monotonous buzz, as it engulfed the building next door. He was aware of all this, but he still wasn't sure whether, in the heat of the moment, it had been a choice he made or an accident that they landed in a heap on the pavement in Tooley Street in 2019.

FORTY-ONE

It was a normal busy day in Tooley Street, and the traffic was piling past London Bridge station. Passers-by, mostly looking at their phones, missed the exact moment of their arrival and must have assumed that they were some kind of street-theatre act. The entrance to the London Dungeon tourist attraction is only a few yards away, and there are often actors in ghoulish costumes and horror make-up handing out brochures outside it. So a small group in historical dress, sitting on the pavement, noisily out of breath and dazed, did not faze them.

The four of them sat for a moment on the ground, panting and looking around wildly. 'Good gracious, Jem! What have you done?' exclaimed Phyllis, the first to collect herself enough to speak.

Sir Rodger was still coughing and gasping for air, so Jeremiah took out his inhaler and puffed a shot of it into his mouth. As Sir Rodger breathed it in, he recovered enough to speak. 'Where are we?' he asked, tremulously.

'Sorry, but, welcome to the future,' said Jeremiah, picking himself up and helping Phyllis to her feet.

'So, your little black glass actually seems to have worked! I would never have believed it!' said Henry Davenant Hythe, standing. The manacles were not attached to his feet nor his hands; Sir Rodger had not managed to click them shut in time. Davenant Hythe stepped out from them and dusted himself down, looking around him in wonder. 'Ha! Almost everyone has a black glass!' he laughed. 'This is extraordinary!'

'Brave New World!' shouted Jeremiah, but was completely ignored.

'But Jem! The noise! The speed!' said Phyllis, astonished at all the bustle. 'It is bracing!' She turned and almost fell over backwards when she noticed the Shard behind her, towering up like a rocket ship made of glass. 'Jeremiah! What is that?'

'That'll be the Shard,' said Jeremiah, trying to make it sound uninteresting. 'It's offices and restaurants, and stuff.'

'What a magnificent erection! What engineering! How exhilarating!' she said, breathlessly. 'It's too much to take in!'

'You must all suffer from vertigo!' added Sir Rodger, pulling himself up to his feet. Then, turning to a woman who was walking nearby with a gym bag, he asked, 'Do you suffer from vertigo, madam?'

'Sorry, I got no change,' she said, hurrying past.

'No. I'm sure you're fine as you are,' said Sir Rodger, 'no need to change.'

'Phyllis! Watch out!' Jeremiah yelled. Phyllis had wandered out into the road. A car screeched and swerved to avoid her. 'You're meant to wait until the little man turns green, and it bleeps. But even then, watch out for cyclists because they don't do traffic lights.'

'I'm bleeping already,' said Phyllis, her eyes bright with everything around her, 'I'm bleeping to my fingertips! It's bleeping magnificent, that's what it is, Jeremiah!' Despite the bright, sparkly sunlight, a light rain shower began.

'Which way is London Bridge?' asked Henry Davenant Hythe, who had been looking all around to get his bearings.

Jeremiah pointed. 'Just up there.'

'Out of my way!' shouted Davenant Hythe, pushing Sir Rodger in the chest. He darted off in the direction of Borough Market, past the old London Bridge hospital, not caring who he ran into. A woman with a baby buggy had to steer it onto the road to avoid colliding with him.

Jeremiah took off after him, shouting back to the others, 'Phyllis! Sir Rodge! Stay here! Don't move until I get back! All right?' But he wasn't going to hang around to hear their replies – Davenant Hythe was fast; he was legging it across the road, dodging cars and buses as if he had no fear of them. He looked completely crazed.

A car had to jerk to a halt to avoid smashing into him. 'Sorry! He's, erm... he's my dad. He just got out of hospital,' shouted Jeremiah to the driver.

'He's a maniac!' the driver shouted back.

'Yes, yes, he is,' said Jeremiah, 'sorry!' The rain began to come down more heavily and some people stopped their journeys to stand in doorways, while one or two put up umbrellas. A woman walked by holding a newspaper over her head. But all the while there were occasional beams of sunlight, shooting down to the wet ground between the clouds. There might be a rainbow any minute.

Jeremiah chased Davenant Hythe all the way down Borough High Street, where he turned right onto Southwark Street, danced and hopped through the traffic again, and then, pushing people out of the way as the doors were closing, jumped on a 381 bus. Jeremiah watched, frustrated, as the bus pulled away. He ran, following the bus, the hundred or so yards to the next stop at the Southwark Bridge Road junction, where the 344 turns into Southwark Street. The rain began to ease but he was drenched by now. There was a 344 picking up passengers right behind the bus Davenant Hythe was on, so Jeremiah made a dash for it, splashing along the side of the kerb. 'Sorry, excuse me,' he repeated several times as he angled his way to the front of the queue and onto the bus. The people who had grudgingly allowed him through were now swiping their Travelcards on the reader, while Jeremiah stood in the front section completely out of breath and dripping wet, desperately looking out of the windscreen so as not to lose sight of the bus ahead.

'You can't stand there. Move down the bus,' said the driver. A couple of other passengers agreed. It looked like the driver wasn't even going to set off until Jeremiah stood behind the line. He moved on down a couple of feet while the bus swung out into the traffic, and then stepped forward to speak to the driver.

'Look, could you just follow the bus ahead? Like, don't stop at any of the stops? It's a matter of life and death.' The driver didn't acknowledge him.

'Come on, mate, you heard him, get down the back of the bus,' shouted one of the other passengers. There was general agreement.

'OK, everyone? Listen up!' Jeremiah announced in the loudest voice he could manage. 'In the bus ahead is... erm... my girlfriend. Yes, and, I've just realised I do love her and I want to propose to her in front of everyone, but I must catch up with her before she goes to a new job in Australia. So, could we just not stop at any of the stops until we catch up with that bus?'

Apart from one old couple at the back who did at least smile, the idea of being in the final scene of a Richard Curtis film did not seem to have appealed to the passengers. But at that moment, the bus ahead stopped and disgorged Henry Davenant Hythe onto the pavement. He tumbled out of the door as if someone had kicked him and strode off down Burrell Street by the sofa shop.

'There he is!' said Jeremiah, who was now standing right up against the front window, as the long windscreen wiper swung to and fro. 'OK, stop the bus! Stop the bus! I'll get off here!' The driver was happy to be rid of him, and opened the front doors, allowing Jeremiah to jump down into the street and run after Davenant Hythe.

'Oi, what happened to your girlfriend?' shouted one of the passengers as the 344 pulled away.

Jeremiah lost Davenant Hythe at the bottom of Burrell Street where it opens into the top end of Blackfriars Road. He looked up towards the bridge and down towards Southwark Tube and the Cut. Nothing. He started to walk aimlessly southwards. Suddenly, from behind him, Davenant Hythe leaped at his shoulders and wrapped an arm around his neck, winding him. He staggered to throw him off, but Davenant Hythe's elbow had him in a firm grip.

'I know where we are, time-boy!' he whispered, snakily, in Jeremiah's ear. 'This is the Blackfriars Road. The setting may be different, but the layout is the same.' Still holding Jeremiah's neck and arm, Davenant Hythe pulled back and stood right behind him. 'You told me my name would be on every building. You're a liar. Now take me to Daisy Wallace, or I will stick this blade into the side of your neck.' With his elbow still around Jeremiah's neck, he revealed that he was holding the handle of a knife. He pushed a button on it, and a nasty, short blade sprang out.

'Flick knives are illegal in this country nowadays,' Jeremiah managed to choke, 'just saying.'

'And one other thing, sonny; reach slowly into your pocket and give me the black glass.' Jeremiah obliged and handed him his mobile, which Davenant Hythe slipped into his pocket. 'Now, off we go!' He marched Jeremiah down the street, keeping one hand tightly on his arm and the other, with the knife, in it, pressed against his back at shoulder level. 'If one ignores the enormous glass constructions and stampede of high-speed vehicles, the old place hasn't changed that much, has it?'

Walking in that manner was slow, and so it took them four or five minutes to get to the house, including a cumbersome crossing of the main road at the Union Street lights, in which they almost had a major collision with a cyclist who was speeding the wrong way up one of the four cycle lanes. 'Idiots!' shouted the cyclist aggressively at them in passing, and Jeremiah had to stop Davenant Hythe from trying to kick down the next passing cyclist in revenge.

Finally, they arrived at the front door. 'I need you to ring on the bell and bring her to the steps,' said Davenant Hythe, shoving Jeremiah forward, while he hung back and crouched to the side of one of the pillars that would have held up the front gate if they'd had one.

Jeremiah did as he was told and rang on the bell. It was a high-pitched electric Big Ben chime; Stepdad Pete hadn't got round to changing it yet. There was no answer. After a pause, he rang again. He leaned down and shouted through the letter box, 'Hi. It's me, Jem. Bit of a problem out here!'

The door opened and Daisy was there. 'Hullo? Jem?' she said, and when Jeremiah said nothing, 'What?' Jeremiah flicked his eyes sideways to warn her. She saw the signal and looked behind him to where Davenant Hythe was. Immediately, she backed towards the door. 'Don't let him near me!' she said. 'What you wanna bring him here for?'

'Sorry, Daisy,' said Jeremiah, 'we've got to stop him somehow. He's got a knife, by the way.'

Daisy took another step back inside, but Davenant Hythe was faster, jumped up the wet steps and grabbed her arm. 'Daisy Wallace! At last, my dear! Now, don't be frightened.

I'm taking you, and your little one of course, back to where we can complete our grand project!'

'Talk to the butt, 'coz the hand ain't listening,' she said, pulling back from him.

'I beg your pardon?' asked Davenant Hythe.

'She means no,' said Jeremiah.

'Don't you want to be part of the great experiment?' he said, pleading with her a little.

'Like, I could care?' she said, trying to close the door on them both.

But Davenant Hythe started pulling her with him. 'Come along, my dear, you don't understand. It's for the benefit of all mankind!' he said, trying to appear gentle and understanding, while in fact coming across as patronising and imperious. He reached into his pocket for Jeremiah's phone. Daisy pulled and kicked and screamed to get away from him, but he succeeded in easing her down the steps with him. He brought out the phone and gazed into it. 'How does one work this thing?' he shouted at Jeremiah, over the racket that Daisy was creating. A few people in the street looked to where the noise was coming from.

'Let go of me!' she yelled. 'I'm pregnant!' Then, to Jeremiah, 'Come on, Jem, you dildo, don't just stand there!'

Jeremiah leaped round Daisy to grab Davenant Hythe, whose obsession seemed to give him the strength of several men. They stayed on the spot in a knotted angry struggle for a few seconds, each trying to shout louder than the other. Jeremiah tried to pull Daisy from Davenant Hythe's grip, but he kept a tight hold of both of them.

This time Jeremiah was certain it was a conscious choice. 'Use your memory: it might come in useful.' He remembered the words of the strange person who had rescued him from the fight with Ed Viney, who'd said she was sort of his family. 'Forget your toys,' she had said, 'look around you. Remember this place. Remember its details.' Right, here goes; big chestnut tree branches... he said to himself; big muddy field to the horizon over there... tangled bushes... sort of long wavy grass blowing in the wind. The wheels of a lorry driving past on Blackfriars Road made that swishing sound that happens on streets after a short, heavy fall of rain. The noise continued from right to left, like a splitter in a pair of stereo earphones. And, and... what else? Jeremiah tried to remember any other details; oh yes, a twisted root sticking up out of the ground at the base of the tree, there... the swishing noise of the lorry carried on after the lorry had passed, turning into the sound of wind in rushes. Jeremiah kept a tight hold on Davenant Hythe and tried to prevent him from holding onto Daisy. But Davenant Hythe caught her by the wrist, tugging her at the last moment, as the three of them tumbled together and landed, in a collapsed heap, on the ground beneath the large horse chestnut tree. It worked.

FORTY-TWO

It worked! I did that! I *am* a wizard! This is amazing! thought Jeremiah, helping Daisy up. 'Sorry, Daisy. I didn't mean to bring you too. Are you all right?'

Daisy was fine, physically, and pushed away his offer to help her up. But she was not well pleased. 'Where have you brung me now?'

'It's Blackfriars still. Just a really long time ago.'

Henry Davenant Hythe was not pleased either. 'But I have your black glass! *I* have the black glass!' he shouted, pacing around wildly. 'How can this be?'

'I don't like it 'ere, Jem,' said Daisy, 'take me back. I mean back to Ruby and Stepdad Pete's...'

'I know what you meant, Daisy. Hold my hand,' said Jeremiah, taking her hand and walking a little closer to the horse chestnut tree. He looked up into the branches that he had fallen into the last time he was here and made a quick calculation of distance. He had arrived here that time from the upstairs bedroom, so he was able to picture in his mind where the flight of stairs would be, the front hall and the front door.

Davenant Hythe, who had wandered several feet away from them, now turned. 'What is going on?' he said, looking, for a moment, frightened and vulnerable. But then he ruined it by adding, 'How dare you do this to me, you vermin! You lower forms of life!' Which made it easier for Jeremiah to do and say what he did next.

'I'm sorry to have to do this, Dr Davenant Hythe, but I'm going to have to leave you here for a while. Until you've calmed down a bit, at least. There's a settlement over there by the river, apparently, so you should be OK...' Then he added, '-ish.'

Front hall, worn-out bit of carpet there, mirror with slight blackening at the edge on the wall there, yellowing light fitting here, embossed wallpaper there. A breeze shook the leaves in the tree and they tinkled in response.

'Keep holding my hand, Daisy,' he said, as his efforts became more concentrated.

'Wooaah! I don't like this!' moaned Daisy, feeling the confusion of her senses as she started to see the items in the front hall that Jeremiah was conjuring.

Davenant Hythe took out the phone and was staring at the screen, furiously, trying to see his future beyond its black shiny surface.

Dirty brown doormat, retro light switch... what else? The breeze in the trees persisted and the leaves all stirred, making a sound like rushing water. Dark green walls. Dado rails! Jeremiah and Daisy just had time to hear Davenant Hythe shouting, 'No! Don't leave me here!' before they recognised the parameters of where they were and recognised each other standing side by side in the front hall at Blackfriars Road, panting, out of breath. The sound of the wind in the ancient chestnut tree had been replaced by the ongoing rumble of traffic outside.

'Don't ever do that to me again!' said Daisy, pulling away from Jeremiah. 'That is so maladjusted!'

'Yeah, all right, Daisy,' replied Jeremiah. Both of their hearts were racing, as if they'd just got off a big dipper ride in a funfair, except it hadn't been fun. 'I got rid of Dr HDH for you, didn't I?' Got rid of. There was a lump of guilt in the back of his mind about what he'd just done to Davenant Hythe, but he rationalised it by telling himself, 'What else could I have done?'

'Is he coming back?' asked Daisy, and Jeremiah reassured her that she was safe.

'I don't think so. It'll take him a long time to get back here,' he said.

'How long?'

'About two thousand years. Right, now I've got to go and sort out Phyllis and Sir Rodger. Take them back to nineteen-ten. You coming? No, I thought not.'

Having a superpower, or special ability, or whatever he wanted to call it, came with responsibilities, he now realised. While it was thrilling to exercise his new skill, it was sobering to think that other people's lives could be permanently affected by it. That must be why the Power and Responsibility Trophy in the *Spider-Man 2* game is an 'Ultimate Difficulty Setting'. These were the thoughts that were turning over in his mind as he walked round the back of Southwark Street, past Tate Modern, towards London Bridge. He didn't get the bus, as he needed time to think. He decided to wander along the river walkway. The sun shone on the wet pavement, from which sprung a perfect rainbow which spanned the river, just as if it were another bridge between Southwark Bridge and London Bridge. A lonely busker with a tinny speaker was singing 'You Got a Friend', which seemed appropriate. He wished he did have someone to confide in. He missed his mum again.

Back at Tooley Street there was no sign of Sir Rodger and Phyllis. He searched up and down the street, trying not to focus too much on the 'Temperance Society 1907' archway and the black-and-white tiles and bricks, in case he accidentally transported himself back. It's difficult to not think about something specific; the harder you try, the more it keeps knocking at the door of your conscious mind. He was going to have to develop some ignoring skills, he could see that now – some way to blank certain things out, temporarily – or he could end up in a perpetual swirl of time-jumps, back and forward forever.

He went into the McDonald's, which had a seating area in the window and more seats at the back and side. 'Yesss! Can I help anyone?' said a girl at the counter.

'You haven't seen a weird old couple, have you,' Jeremiah asked her, 'dressed in, like, Victorian-type clothes?'

'They're over there, mate. Been here for ages,' she said, pointing to the side seating area. Sir Rodger and Phyllis were sitting at a table littered with trays and wrappers and hamburger boxes. They were both chomping on what looked, from the detritus on the table, like their third meal and glugging noisily from a straw that stuck out of a huge cardboard cup, which they were sharing between them while deep in conversation.

'...and the speed of movement,' Sir Rodger was saying, through enthusiastic chewing, 'is so invigorating, don't you find?'

Phyllis made a rattling noise as the straw drained the last of the liquid in the cup. 'Mmm,' she nodded, 'and the women are able to walk about as they choose! Freely, safely!'

Jeremiah went over to them. 'Jeremiah Bourne! How delightful to see you!' said Sir Rodger in a voice loud enough to set off a car alarm. 'You see, sis, I told you he'd come back.'

'How did you pay for that food?' asked Jeremiah.

'A kind gentleman paid for us,' said Phyllis, 'he said it was the least he could do.'

'Apparently we'd given him a right laugh,' added Sir Rodger. 'Could you pass me the sauce, Phyll, old girl?'

'You mean the BBQ or the mayo?' asked Phyllis, searching through the debris on the table.

'The dark and spicy one in the small sachet for me, thank you,' said Sir Rodger, taking the sachet from Phyllis and expertly tearing it with his teeth, before squirting it over the top of his many-layered burger and taking another massive bite. 'Fine establishment this, Jem,' he said, munching with his cheeks full. 'May we come again to your century?'

Jeremiah sat down on one of the seats beside them. 'No. That's not a good idea, I'm afraid. And now, it's time to take you guys back.'

'But what about Henry?' asked Sir Rodger.

'I'm really sorry, but I've left him in the middle of a field in Roman times,' said Jeremiah, thinking to himself how those were words he'd never expected to hear himself saying.

'So, you're becoming quite the expert,' said Phyllis.

'So you are,' said Sir Rodger, 'perhaps you could come and give a lecture to the gentlemen of the society? They really are a most enlightened group of men.'

Phyllis's back straightened. Jeremiah felt he had to speak up on her behalf. 'What about the Women's Branch? What about STRAWB? Are they not enlightened too?'

'Hear, hear,' said Phyllis, staring hard at Sir Rodger.

'Of course they are,' said Sir Rodger, swallowing his mouthful, 'it's just that's the way it's always been done.' He stopped for a moment, then cocked his head as if a new thought had just been dropped in it. 'By Jiminy, you're right, Jem! It is absolutely crackers! Phyllis? He's right!' Phyllis sighed the long sigh of someone who had been waiting for this particular penny to drop into this particular murky pond for a quarter of a century. 'Let's amalgamate the two groups into one!'

'Allelujah!' said Phyllis, quietly.

'Ah, but I just thought, slight drawback, we won't be able to hold the meetings at my gentlemen's club.'

'To be honest, Rodge, if they don't like it, sod 'em!' said Phyllis. The neon lighting seemed to have given her a new garish courage.

'Yes! Yes! Do you know what?' beamed Sir Rodger. 'You're right, sis! If they don't like it, they can sod off! Ooh, this is intoxicating! Sod 'em! Old windbags!'

'Sod 'em, yes, why not?' said Jeremiah, standing up again. 'And now it really is time to take you guys home, so, if we could all hold hands and—'

'Can't we finish our Easy Meal Deal first?' said Sir Rodger.

Jeremiah was getting stressed. 'No! You cannot!' Sir Rodger put his hands in his pockets. 'And you can't take all those little sauce packets back to 1910 either.' Jeremiah waited. 'Come on, hand them over. And that one in your other pocket, I saw that!'

'Why not?' asked Sir Rodger, pouting and taking out the two or three sauce sachets that he'd hidden in various pockets; he plonked them back on the table.

'Because we can't have things all over the place: scientists and mobile phones in whenever it was I left Henry and plastic food cartons in 1910! There's got to be some rules!'

'Go on, just one,' said Rodger.

'No!'

'Crosspatch,' said Phyllis.

'No! I can't believe I'm even discussing this with you! Come on, we have to go, now.' Jeremiah's hand reached automatically for his inhaler and took it out, but he stopped. He didn't need it.

Reluctantly, Phyllis conceded and slid across the seat to get up. 'Come on, Rodge, we ought to do what he says.' Then, she suddenly slid back again. 'Ooh! I nearly forgot this.' She reached down below the table, by her knees, and produced a big plastic bag from Hamleys.

'What is that? Where did you get that?' said Jeremiah.

'Hamleys, the toy emporium, of course,' said Phyllis, grinning. 'My oh my, that place has changed since our day! Look at this.' She took out a plastic robot toy which made a loud shooting noise.

'How the hell did you guys get to Hamleys?' shouted Jeremiah.

'On the Underground, of course,' said Phyllis, 'and mind your language, Jem.'

'We've had a wonderful day out, thank you, Jem – it's all down to you,' said Sir Rodger, finally squeezing his large frame out from behind the table.

'No, no, no! This is all going completely out of control.' Jeremiah took the robot toy and rammed it back in the Hamleys bag. 'I'm not even going to ask how you paid for this. *If* you paid for this. You are not taking it with you and that's final.' He banged the bag back on the seat and, taking both of their hands, led them out of the restaurant.

'Spoilsport,' Phyllis mumbled quietly under her breath. Other customers had enjoyed the show.

Outside on the pavement Jeremiah gave them a lecture. How there would have to be some boundaries in time travel, how until he knew more about it, they shouldn't play with it, and anything else he could think of to vent his anger. It didn't make any difference, they weren't listening anyway – they were too buzzed on the sights and sounds and, no doubt, sugar that they had imbibed.

'Now, all hold hands, please!' Jeremiah ordered, and they drifted into obeying him. For a moment he worried that losing his rag with them might have dulled his focus, but with a few deep breaths he managed to empty his mind, like at the beginning of karate, and was able to concentrate on the brickwork, the tiles, the archway, the carving, the words 'Temperance Society 1907'; he tried to recall the faces of the street kids with their haystack hair. For some moments, nothing happened, but then everything happened at once. Less a rushing – or ringing sound, more like one big outrush of air, and they were standing on a darker Tooley Street in 1910. Sir Rodger and Phyllis were screaming and laughing as if they were on the Nemesis ride at Alton Towers.

'That was absolutely frabjous!' said Phyllis. 'Can we do it again?'

'No, we cannot. And what's with the catchphrase?' said Jeremiah. 'Where did you hear that?'

'Callooh Callay! It's a frabjous day!' said Sir Rodger, 'Lewis Carroll, *Jabberwocky*.'

'Oh,' said Jeremiah, 'I didn't know that. Sorry.'

FORTY-THREE

Small red sparks rose, crackled and then died as soon as they met the damp night air. Giant silhouettes of sycamores and chestnut trees surrounded the group sitting as close as they could to the flames, their faces illuminated in yellows and oranges, while their backs felt the September chill. There was an appreciative silence among them, as each saw what they wanted in the ever-changing patterns of the fire.

After a long while, one of them spoke. 'Why are you burning your guitar?'

'See what it sounds like,' said Charlie, grinning, as if setting fire to your own guitar was the coolest idea he'd ever had.

'That ain't no guitar, that's lazy cosmic chives,' said Hamish Bowie.

'Hang on, that sounds a bit like… erm… David Bowie?' said Artemesia Plutarch. 'I think I know that.'

''S'right,' said Hamish, scratching his smelly beard. 'Let the children prove it. Let the children *groove* it.' He gave Artemesia a meaningful look. As far as Hamish was concerned, there was not a single Bowie lyric that did not contain a hidden, profound message. If only he could remember the right words.

They fell to silence again and someone passed Artemesia the cider bottle. Scoobeedoo was asleep on her lap.

Charlie shivered a little, sat up and spoke again. 'I wonder what it would sound like if we rolled a joint.'

'And smoked it,' said Dave the Hat.

'Yeah, 'course and smoked it,' said Charlie, 'daft!' They all found that funny and laughed.

'Put another lock on the files for me!' shouted Hamish Bowie.

It hadn't been too difficult a time-leap for Artemesia, once she and Scoobeedoo arrived in Twickenham. She'd seen so many pictures of the hotel at Eel Pie Island and its famous R&B club, where bands like the Rolling Stones, the Who and Eric Clapton's Tridents had started out in the late sixties, that she felt she'd already knew the place backwards. All she needed to do was to actually go backwards now. She stood on the iconic footbridge to the island, looking across at the boatyards and wooden chalets, clutching the Scoob close to her. In fact, she'd missed the hotel by three years – it burned down in 1971, but 1974 was a good year to land in. *Bagpuss* had just started on the telly, the 'Three-Day Week' had ended and the Eurovision Song Contest had been won by a song called 'Waterloo', which seemed appropriate.

A few artisans' workshops had sprung up among the ruins of the old hotel and there was a dry dock for barges that was hardly ever used, which had been taken over by some squatters: a hippy family with three children and a small women's collective. Beyond the dry dock, facing away from the town, on the south side of the island, was what they called a community garden but which looked more like the remnants of a festival that had gone on all summer and finally collapsed. Pieces of broken furniture were slung together with bits of driftwood to make a shelter; an old minibus with no wheels was sprouting grass and fungi from every window. Beyond this enclave, further into the woods, down by the riverbank was a plastic sheet roped between two sycamore trees. This is where Charlie lived in the summer, and in the winter, well, he'd have to figure that one out when it happened.

This gang had been welcoming to Artemesia Plutarch, although Scoobeedoo had initially had a few problems with Wolfgang, the squatters' Alsatian. All OK now. Artemesia had quickly made herself useful, fixing an old generator or two, collecting wood, helping look after the children and cooking large pots of beans and rice. No one asked probing questions. She had ambitions for a café and bicycle-repair shop on the mainland. Just on the other side of the footbridge, there was an old bric-a-brac shop which had closed down.

'Here, want some of this?' Charlie said through a squeezed throat, as he gulped in a potato-sized wedge of smoke from the torpedo he'd just put together and lit.

'No, thanks,' said Artemesia. 'Messes with your memory, that stuff.'

'I got some acid if you want,' said Dave the Hat, 'if you need, like, spacing out?'

'Nah, that's worse.'

'A snack in the sky and a ham reaching down for me…' said Hamish Bowie, shaking his head.

'I don't do those kind of things. I had some bad experiences, you know, where I come from.' Scoobeedoo stirred in agreement.

They all nodded wisely, as if they understood completely what she was talking about.

'Hey, Archie?' said Charlie after a pause. 'Where *do* you come from?'

'Oh. The future,' said Artemesia, 'I come from the future.'

They all nodded again.

'Far out,' said Charlie.

'There's a banana, man, waiting in the sky,' said Hamish, 'he'd like to come and eat us—'

'But he thinks he'd lower our blinds,' said Artemesia, who understood.

FORTY-FOUR

'X plus X over seven, equals X, brackets (one plus one over seven), close brackets.' That was the equation. Jeremiah had no trouble remembering it; what he couldn't seem to get a view on was any concept of the meaning behind it. He looked again at the words and numbers in front of him, written out in Nandy Banerjee's neat hand, but nothing would bring the figures to life. Nandy waited patiently, looking at him and then at the page, then back to him again. She was smiling. She always smiled.

'I'm sorry,' he said, 'I just can't, you know, concentrate.' He pushed his chair away from the kitchen table in frustration and looked at the clock on the wall. They were only a few minutes into the session and he was already impatient for it to be over.

On the wall of Jeremiah's old classroom at school was a jolly sign, coloured in with crayons, which read: 'Maths is Fun'. That was the first thing he hated about maths – it started with a lie. Maths was not fun. It may be a lot of things: fascinating to those who are good at it, useful for grappling with infinity, good for the brain, intrinsic to all technology, but the one thing it most definitively was not was fun. That sign on the classroom wall had led to a suspicion in Jeremiah that all maths teachers were basically liars, with their politician smiles, and their repeated insistence that what they were teaching a) made logical sense, and b) was simple. It does not make logical sense in any concrete, non-abstract way, and it is certainly not simple. For instance, the instructions to Jeremiah's Year Eleven class on how to 'simplify' equations read as follows: 1) remove parentheses by multiplying factors, 2) use exponent rules to remove them in terms with exponents, 3) combine like terms by adding coefficients, 4) combine the constants. And that's how to *simplify* equations. He dreaded to think what the complicated, unsimplified equation instructions looked like.

But that is where Nandy Banerjee came in. She thought maths was more than just fun: it was beautiful, inspirational, exciting. His maths results had been improving gradually since she started coming over to Blackfriars Road to do the extra study sessions with him. Not so much mixed-ability learning as what used to be called tutoring.

'This equation was devised nearly four thousand years ago,' said Nandy, 'it's part of something called the Rhind Papyrus, because a guy called Rhind got his hands on it in Egypt in 1861 and eventually it got sold to the British Museum. But really it should be called the Ahmose Papyrus, because it was actually written by Ahmose in about 2000 BC. Which is so unfair and imperialist, but the equation still works.'

'Do you believe in time travel?' Jeremiah blurted it out. He needed to have someone he could talk to about the discombobulation of the last week.

'It is mathematically feasible,' said Nandy. 'Einstein's General Theory of Relativity states that gravitational fields are caused by distortions in the fabric of space-time. In other words, the closer to a black hole we get, the more slowly time moves. But no one's managed to make the theory a reality and actually do it. Why?'

He drew in his chair again and took a long breath. 'I have,' he said, and looked at her face for any sign of disbelief or cynicism. There was none.

'Go on,' she said. He paused, looked out of the kitchen window; it was a golden autumn day, not warm, but London was glowing amber in the afternoon sun. Then he told her the whole story and she listened, nodding occasionally. She didn't scoff, or disagree, just once or twice stopped him to ask for a bit of clarity on a certain detail – was Vergilius's name Amanda, or Ananda? Was Phyllis's a society of Psycho-Anthropology, or Anthro-Psychology?

'Wow,' she said, when he'd just about finished, 'there's a lot to think about there. Wow. I need a glass of water. No wonder you've been finding it hard to concentrate.'

'Well, it's been quite stressful here at home, too,' he said. They could hear Daisy and Ruby howling with laughter in the upstairs bedroom that used to be his. 'Lot of changes in the house, you know. That hasn't helped.'

Since he got back, all the furniture had been rearranged. 'We're not sure which is the best way round to have the room now because, look! We got a baby-changing table,' Ruby said within minutes of his arrival through the front door, 'and a cot shouldn't go directly under a window.'

A few days later, the result of the DNA test on Amanda Vergilius's hair had arrived. 'You mean you did it?' Ruby had crowded round him at his laptop. 'You sent the test off without telling me? Which is all right, I suppose, because it is yours, really. What did you use – blood? Saliva? Hair? What does it say?'

'It says twenty-three pairs of chromosomes, two hundred and ninety variations, ninety-eight per cent accuracy,' said Jeremiah, scrolling down the page. 'Ah, here we are. It says… no match. No match out of seven hundred thousand markers…'

'What does that mean?'

'It means this woman with long red hair's not in my

family like Mum said she was. I wonder what Mum meant. Or was she just lying to me?'

'I don't know who you're talking about,' said Ruby. 'What woman with red hair? Was it in a plait? Why did you have one of her hairs?'

A dark mood had descended on Jeremiah, so Ruby had done what she usually did when that happened: put her arm around him, squeezed him tightly and said, 'Never mind. You've got us.' Which had never worked on him before, but today made him feel better.

Nandy decided to finish up the maths tutorial in the downstairs kitchen. She closed Jeremiah's laptop, and said, 'I think we should leave it for today. That is some story. Sorry, I don't mean story, I mean sequence of events,' she corrected herself, lest it sounded like she didn't believe him. 'Can I have that glass of water now?'

Jeremiah was pleased to have someone to share his experience with. He ran her a glass from the tap.

'At least you should be able to get grade nine in history GCSE now. If you choose 1910 as a special subject.'

'If only I'd taken some photos, I'd have some proof,' he said, passing her the glass of water.

'Yeah, but who would believe you?' said Nandy. She was nearly two years younger than him, yet she seemed much more in charge of herself and her world than him or any of his other mates.

'I suppose I could prove it to you by taking you there,' he said.

'No, thank you!' said Nandy. 'I'm not very good at anything that requires jumping around, you see. You know what I think we should do?' she continued. 'I think we should go to the British Museum and check out this glass of Dr John Dee you mentioned and check out the Rhind Papyrus too, while we're there. I've always wanted to have a look at that. They have really good "Maths Challenges" there too, and a "Maths Trail" with African counting beads and everything, so it could be part of your GCSE revision.'

'OK,' said Jeremiah, 'that sounds more like what I could handle at the moment.'

'How's your agoraphobia?'

He reached instinctively for his inhaler in his pocket, then stopped himself. 'I forgot it. I actually forgot all about it.'

The big round reading room at the British Museum, which was impressive when it opened 150 years ago, was made even more impressive in 2000 by the addition of a magnificent glass-domed ceiling. The whole area now serves as a light-filled reception lobby, with various membership and information kiosks scattered across it, and a central staircase over the bookshop and café.

They went straight to an enrolment kiosk with a sign above it which read: 'Are you ready for the Maths Challenge Trail?' next to a cardboard cut-out of a child in an Indiana Jones-style explorer hat, looking through some binoculars. They keep trying, thought Jeremiah, to sell us this, maths is going to be fun, idea. They keep trying too hard and they keep failing. Why do they persist? People like Nandy don't need the cartoons and colourful poster proclamations and people like me are not taken in. It's a lose-lose policy.

Nandy's trainers squeaked on the shiny floor and the echo passed gently up the walls into a pleasant swirl above their heads in the atrium. There were several people ahead of them in the queue, so Jeremiah wandered over to one of the information kiosks nearby, which are built on rostra, so the staff are a couple of feet above you. He was looking up at a girl who didn't seem much older than him. She had a few piercings and asymmetrical hair.

'Can I help you?' she said. She was from Australia or New Zealand, he couldn't tell which.

'Yeah, I'm looking for something called Dr John Dee's black glass? I was told it was in here somewhere.' She asked him to repeat the name and tapped it into her keyboard. She scrolled twice. She asked him if he was sure that's what it was called. She checked again.

'No. Sorry, no Dr John Dee here. Nothing under Dee, or Dr, or John. And it's a black glass, you say?'

'Yeah. Like an ancient black glass thing that people used to think had powers. You could see the dead in it?'

'Yeah, yeah,' she scrolled again, 'well, the only thing like that we've got is the Davenant Hythe glass? That's more than a thousand years old? It's in the Historiography room. Are you all right?'

Jeremiah felt a rush of blood to his head. The huge mosaic of glass above his head started to revolve like a kaleidoscope. This wasn't a time-jump, just plain old-fashioned fainting. He leaned heavily on the desk to stop himself falling over. 'Davenant Hythe, you said? You definitely said the Davenant Hythe glass?' he managed to croak.

'Yes. It's on the ground floor? In the last cabinet in the middle through that doorway over there?' She pointed to a large open archway to their right.

Jeremiah's feet felt like full buckets of water as he pulled them towards the archway. The echoey noise of the atrium seemed far away now. Inside the Historiography room, the walls were lined with glass cases up to the ceiling, which contained artefacts from all over the world and all across time. Greek painted vases, Polynesian ceremonial weapons with dried feathers sticking out of them, helmets, manuscripts. In the centre of the room was a row of freestanding glass cabinets, some with specimens laid out on glass-covered tabletops for viewing, others taller, with collections of items inside. There was a low mumble of people, shuffling around and whispering to each other, and a group of Japanese tourists being spoken to by a guide holding a red handkerchief on a selfie stick. Down the far end of the room, in one of the taller cabinets, nestled among other archaeological items, was a small black oblong of glass sitting in a wide silver frame. The glass looked suspiciously like the top of Jeremiah's phone, covered with thousands of tiny little scratches. The silver frame around it had pagan symbols embossed in it. The whole thing was propped up on a little tripod, with a plastic disc to the side with the number 17 on it. Beside the cabinet was a panel with numbered labels and explanations of all the items.

At number 17, the caption read: 'The Davenant Hythe glass is thought to be over a thousand years old. Thought to have been used in Druidic rituals by the high priests of the Davenant Hythe cult, who may have believed in some form of early genetic engineering. It was discovered by archaeologists in 2006, when the foundations of the Shard were being dug.'

Jeremiah shook his head. 'Oh no. What have I done?' he said out loud.

'Yes. What *have* you done?' A woman's voice came from behind him, deep with a mellow resonance. He turned to see Amanda Vergilius standing right behind him, too close for comfort.

FORTY-FIVE

'Oh dear, have you gone and changed the past?' she said, fixing him with her eyes: gun-metal grey. He nodded guiltily and shifted back a step so as not to have her in his personal space. 'So, what are you going to do about that?'

'Go back and fix it?' said Jeremiah, not sure if that was the right answer.

'Go back to when? Exactly? Would you be able to locate him precisely?' she said, taking a step towards him. 'Would you take me to him?'

There was everything about her tone that told Jeremiah he should answer that with a 'no'.

She tried to soften her approach. 'So, tell me, who are you? And how are you doing it?'

'I was going to ask you the same things,' he said, calculating fast. So she didn't know as much about him as he had thought.

'Where did you train?' she asked. Jeremiah looked blankly at her. 'You did train, didn't you?' she said, raising an eyebrow. 'How are you doing it otherwise?'

'No, I just sort of picked it up as I went along. What is "it", by the way?'

'How is it you have recall if you didn't train?'

'I was hoping you might be able to help me answer that.'

'You mean it was just an accident? Tell me about your parents.' She moved in closer still, so Jeremiah shifted his weight to keep a distance between them. She smelt of soap; an old-fashioned, no-nonsense soap.

'First time it was to do with a biscuit tin. And a photo of you, actually,' he said. 'What's going on?'

'When was that?'

'Now? Like 2019? A week ago?' He didn't see why he should have to answer all these questions, when actually there was a lot he wanted to know from her, but she had a persistent, almost hypnotic authority.

'What were you doing then?'

'I was studying for my GCSEs. Again. And sanding down an old armchair,' he said, impatiently. 'Look, I haven't done anything wrong, you know.' And then he thought for a moment. 'Well, apart from the Davenant Hythe black glass thing, which was sort of the only option I could think of—'

But she cut through and carried on with the interrogation. 'Why were you living then?'

'How do you mean, "why was I living then"? I was just at home. Then. As you do.'

'As you do what?' she asked.

He tried to come back at her. 'I saw you before, you know,' he said, then he immediately thought better of revealing anything to her. 'How many other people can do this?' he asked. 'Is it just you and me?'

'How many do you know of?' she countered. She made Jeremiah feel as if he'd committed a crime, but she wasn't going to tell him what it was.

'Well, there was this woman who gave me a bandage made of glass. I think she might be one.'

Almost imperceptibly, a cloud passed across the light behind Vergilius's eyes; she did her best to hide it, but Jeremiah noticed it, and she noticed that he'd noticed it. 'Why don't you come with me and we can go somewhere

where you can get answers to all your pressing questions,' she said, trying, and failing, to smile.

'Where might that be?'

'Somewhere people will understand what you're going through. They'd be very interested to know all about you. Come.' She reached her hand to hold his, but instinctively, he pulled away before she could touch him. So she put her arm back by her side and tried to continue as if they were merely having a little natter in a waiting room somewhere. 'And where did you say your family are?' she asked.

Jeremiah made up his mind to get out. He walked as fast as he could away from her. She followed at speed. As he came to the wide entrance hall, Nandy came up to him, smiling. 'That African counting-beads thing is just for three-to-six-year-olds. Sorry. My bad,' she said. Jeremiah shook his head urgently at her and indicated behind him with his eyes that he was being followed, with a look that said 'you don't know me', and walked straight past her, leaving her baffled in the centre of the lobby.

Out into the square, where the air was windy and the sky was wide. He started to run; down the steps and through the tall gates into Great Russell Street, where all the museum shops are, and tourists were standing around slowing up the passing pedestrians. Vergilius was still behind him, trying not to chase him too obviously, which gave him a few yards on her. A bunch of Spanish students with matching shoulder bags were larking about, making a lot of noise and getting in people's way. As he emerged onto the street, a black taxi screeched up to a halt, right in front of him; the driver reached across and swung the passenger door open.

He heard the words 'Get in, mate!' and didn't stop to think. He leaped up into the taxi, pulling the door closed as it swerved into the middle of the road and sped off. They were past Museum Street by the time Vergilius got to the gates and all she could see was the back of the cab as it overtook, and disappeared behind, a slow 176 bus.

Inside the cab, the driver reached over and pulled the sliding screen open with one jerk. 'All right, my love?' It was Mum.

'Mum?' She turned and looked over her shoulder at him and grinned; one of her teeth was missing and her face looked more weather-beaten than he remembered. There were some new, deep lines on her forehead and cheeks. He had to hold onto the safety strap above the window because her driving was erratic and much too fast for central London. 'Mum! Slow down!'

'D'you want a getaway driver or not?' she shouted over her shoulder and laughed. Cackled, he would have said, if she hadn't been his mother. She turned the cab into the two-lane traffic at Kingsway, going south towards Waterloo Bridge.

'What's going on, Mum?' he shouted.

'Sorry, my love, but we don't want you falling into the wrong hands, now, do we?'

'What's that supposed to mean?'

'We don't want them knowing you exist. And we definitely don't want them knowing you've got anything to do with me! If they ever do get to you, you don't know me, all right?'

'Well, that won't be hard, Mum. I really don't know you, do I? I haven't seen you for, like, a hundred years, remember? I don't even know who you are. And who's they?' The traffic had made the taxi slow down as they approached Aldwych and Mum steered into the left-hand lane. 'Where are we going, Mum?' She didn't answer; she was concentrating on entering the stream of traffic. 'Well, if you're taking me back to Blackfriars Road, they've opened up Temple Place now, so you can get straight down to the Embankment, you don't have to go up Fleet Street. Just saying.'

'Ooh, hark at you!' The cab swung back into the right-hand lane and zipped across the lights, down the hill at Temple Place, towards the river.

'Why don't you want me to admit you're my mum? Are you disowning me or something?'

'You wouldn't want me to be sent away, would you?' she called hoarsely back at him, 'I could be put away for a very long time.'

'You've already been away for a very long time, Mum. You're still away, as far as I knew. Anyway, I don't even know what you're supposed to have done. Maybe you deserve to be put away.'

'Oh, that's harsh. That's harsh, that is. From your own son. You're right, though, I have done some naughty things. Some very naughty things.'

'Oh yeah? When?'

'Sixteen hundred and sixty-six, look it up!' she said and let out an enormous cackle. Jeremiah noticed how tangled her hair was, and how there were more bits of grey in it now. 'Gawd, I missed you, my darlin'! And I'm afraid I can't stay long this time, neither. How've you been?'

Jeremiah felt a knot of anger rise in his throat. 'I've been strange, actually. I've discovered I can, like, jump backwards in time, and it's freaking me out. Is it your fault?'

Mum blinked. 'Now that's unusual. You shouldn't be able to do that. I hadn't planned on that. There again, hadn't planned on anything. Least of all you.' She gave her cackly laugh again. 'How is dear old Pete, by the way? Is he looking after you well?' Jeremiah didn't answer but looked out of the window as they turned round and doubled back at the Blackfriars Bridge underpass.

Once they were out of the mainstream traffic, she pulled the cab into the side of the road and stopped it. Switching off the engine, she swung around in the driver's seat so that she could face Jeremiah through the little glass hatch.

'Jeremiah, Jemmy, Jem, my love. The naughty thing I done is have you. That's what they'd put me away for, darlin', having you. Out of time, out of place. Well, mostly out of time, actually. But I don't want to be put away for doing the best thing I ever did in my life, see? I don't want them sticking their noses into our business. I just want you to be safe. All right?' She started up the engine and steered the cab back into the traffic. 'So, how's school? Or is it college now?'

Jeremiah told her about his GCSE results and about his maths tutoring with Nandy. It was only then he remembered he'd left Nandy stranded at the British Museum. That wouldn't go down well with her mum. Then he remembered Henry Davenant Hythe, who he'd left stranded in some unknown past, with nothing but a phone with no battery, but who had managed somehow to make himself go down in history – his dream come true. Maybe leaving people stranded was Jeremiah's new superpower.

The cab drew up to Blackfriars Road and stopped. This time she left the engine running. She turned in her seat again. 'So, this is it, my angel. I'm not coming in, or anything. One day we'll be able to be together again, trust me.'

He really didn't like the sound of 'trust me', or the idea of trusting anyone, especially his mum. He opened the cab door and got out. He stood on the pavement and looked into the driver's window. The fare-reader above her head said £17.60, he noticed.

'All I wanted is for you to have a normal childhood,' his mum explained, 'safe from them. Safe from war and pestilence. Although, come to think of it, watch out next February, avoid crowds and always wash your hands after you been out anywhere. And wear a face mask. Trust me.' She touched her fingers to her lips and blew him a kiss, then revved the cab and drove off.

He watched the back of the cab recede towards St George's Circus, getting smaller as it went. Damn, he forgot to get the number plate. He turned and walked up the old stone steps to the front door and, realising he didn't have his key with him, rang the bell. Through the front window he could see Stepdad Pete, Daisy and Ruby, all washing up together. He was glad to be back.

FORTY-SIX

'What I don't understand is, how come they can manage to fit locks on all the medical equipment shelves in a matter of days, when they still can't manage to fix the steam-door system after almost two years? And now this...' Half-Dante Kwei was struggling with a piece of paper as large as an old broadsheet newspaper, '...how am I meant to fill all this in?'

'It's just a new way of gathering and keeping information,' said Beatlejohn Basho, who was in charge of handing out the sheets to all the members of the Residents' Association sub-committee, 'so they don't have to ask you questions all the time and your details can be kept in one place. Just put your name there on the top right where it says "Name".' He had dropped his studenty look, and nowadays wore only beige – matching shirt, tie, trousers and jacket – almost as if in honour of Conrad, who was no longer part of this sub-committee but had moved on to better things in Super-Recall and Retrieve.

'And the library shelves have all been emptied,' said Dickensian. 'Why was that necessary? Don't they trust us with books?' He had to squint closely at his broadsheet through his glasses, as the print was so small.

'There, I've done mine, can I go now?' said Faraday Tang, handing her paper in to Beatlejohn Basho. She was wearing a full-length cardigan and gloves; it was colder and darker now. The leaves from the plane trees had fallen onto the glass ceiling, become sodden in the rain, and congealed into a brown slush that was blocking what little light there was outside. The sky hung low and grey. It was January.

'And what about Toto Chairman? Why isn't she here any longer? How are her knees?' It looked as if Half-Dante Kwei hadn't changed his collarless tunic for some months, just put a blanket around his shoulders.

'Actually, I think she got barred from coming. I spoke to her the other day; her knees seemed fine,' said Ordnari Cervantes, scanning her sheet of paper. 'For whatever reason, they asked her not to attend any more.' She went quiet as she got to one section of the questionnaire. 'Why do they need to know what kind of music my parents liked?'

'I think it's so they can get a fuller picture of who you really are,' said Beatlejohn Basho, smiling, 'what your background is, where you come from, how good your memory levels are...' He was acting chairperson now that Toto Chairman had been 'relaxed out'.

'And it says here: "What kind of foods did your grandparents cook?" What's that got to do with anything?' said Dickensian, looking up from his close-up examination of the page, his normally high-pitched drone reaching a squeak.

'I think it's about identity,' said Beatlejohn Basho, as if that were a sacred thing, 'finding the authentic "you"?'

'"Do any of your family or antecedents have a history of criminal convictions?"' Ordnari Cervantes crumpled her paper in outrage. 'What is this? They'll be asking for ethnicity and religion next... oh, they are. Further down the page.' Her earrings chimed in unison.

Faraday Tang, who'd been edging towards the door to leave, slid back in and sat down. 'I just put "Not Applicable" in the criminal background section. And I'm afraid I couldn't remember what my first memory was. Does that matter?' she asked.

'Look, look, everybody! Look...' said Beatlejohn Basho with a smile that had become a permanent fixture. 'I *understand* you have concerns. And it's important that you get to tell us what they are. That your voices are heard. Of course it is.' He sat down on the arm of the old upholstered chair, like a new, cool teacher who wants to be your mate, and put his feet up on the cushion pad. 'So, I'll tell you what I'll do; if you can make up a list of all your questions, I can take them to Dr Vergeelis and perhaps she can reassure you.'

'Oh. Her again,' said Dickensian.

'Are we meant to put down what food Dr Mandar Vergeelis likes on the form?' asked Half-Dante Kwei, not quite arriving at the same point as everyone else. Then, alarmed, 'But I don't know what kind of food she likes! How am I going to find that out? This is ridiculous!'

'Why can't she come here and answer our questions herself?' asked Ordnari Cervantes.

'Yes, that would save time,' said Half-Dante Kwei. 'I mean, is it fish or beans? Is she a vegan, even?'

'Shut up, Kwei!' shouted Faraday Tang, surprising everyone. She never spoke up.

Beatlejohn Basho gave a reassuring laugh. It didn't work, even on himself. He drew a breath without losing his smile. 'OK. Look, Mandar would love to come here and answer anything you wanted to know, *love* to. This project is very, very important to her. In fact it's so important that she's having to work around the clock on it, developing new materials as the science changes. So she really doesn't have the time to come in person, but as I say, if we can just draw up a list of questions, I'll be happy to take it to her and I'm sure she'll be able to put all of your minds at rest.'

'What new materials?' said Dickensian.

'How has the science changed? In what way?' asked Ordnari Cervantes.

'Well, I'm not meant to say, but hell, I suppose it's OK, it'll come out soon enough anyway.' Beatlejohn Basho leaned forward, as if to tell them something wonderful and confidential. 'Our very own Dr Mandar Vergeelis is developing a new genetic memory programme! Based on revelations and data that she gathered on her recent harvesting expedition, she will soon be in a position not only to know who will or will not be capable of inherited memory activity, but to know it before they're even born! Think of that! And also, to develop a test, a simple test, for which of us are more likely to be able to pass this ability on to our children. Isn't that amazing?'

The members of the Blackfriars Road Residents' Association sub-committee looked around at each other suspiciously. Faraday Tang quietly left the room.

'She needs to gather as much info as poss, so she can increase the chances for all of us to make a brighter, more genetic future!'

'And if we don't pass the simple test?' asked Dickensian.

Beatlejohn Basho leaned back and laughed. It was the only thing he could think of doing.

'You mean she wants to control who we have children with, so she can create genetic super-memorisers?' said Ordnari Cervantes, also getting up to leave. Her earrings were jangling furiously with her jerky movements.

'Well, I wouldn't say control, more to improve chances, make better choices, create a superior society,' said Beatlejohn Basho, who almost looked like he believed himself. A little more practice and he'd be good at this.

'So we have to do this so that she can create a superior society?' said Ordnari Cervantes.

'Is that so wrong?' said Beatlejohn Basho.

'And what will happen to us if we don't want to fill in this form?' asked Dickensian.

Beatlejohn Basho smiled a resigned but happy smile. 'Well, it's up to you, individually, to decide whether you feel it's right – for you – or not. But I am duty bound to tell you it will go down on your record if you don't.'

'Hold on, hold on,' said Half-Dante Kwei, 'you're telling me that Dr Mandar Vergeelis, our Dr Mandar Vergeelis, is developing new kinds of genetically modified food, and we've all got to put down that we like it, on these forms, whether we actually do like it or not? That's fascism, that is.' There was a collective sigh.

It started to rain again, this time more heavily, pushing the leaves further down the slope of the glass ceiling and into the gutter, where they were forming a solid mass large enough to block the drainpipes for the whole building.

Beatlejohn Basho gave a self-satisfied smirk. 'So, if we're all done with that? Next item on the agenda... what to do about Mrs Glamper.'

ACKNOWLEDGEMENTS

Thanks to: John Mitchinson, Rina Gill, Rachael Kerr, Kate Quarry, Imogen Denny and all at Unbound. Thanks also to David Richardson, Nick Briggs, Jonny Morris and Barnaby Thompson. Also to Harvey Planer, Clare Conville, Peter Salmon, Hector Hornstein, Roberta Planer, Colin Smythe, Stephen Briggs and Marie Stopes.

A NOTE ON THE AUTHOR

Nigel Planer is a British writer and actor. An original member of the 1980s alternative comedy scene, he famously played Neil in the BBC's *The Young Ones,* winning a BRIT award for Neil's hit single 'Hole in My Shoe'.

Nigel is the voice of many Terry Pratchett audiobooks and *Discworld* games, and in 2010, he hosted the touring arena show of *Doctor Who Live.* Alongside his extensive acting work, Nigel has published eight books and written six plays. *Jeremiah Bourne in Time* is the first book in his new fantasy trilogy, The Time Shard Chronicles.

SUPPORTERS

Unbound is the world's first crowdfunding publisher, established in 2011.

We believe that wonderful things can happen when you clear a path for people who share a passion. That's why we've built a platform that brings together readers and authors to crowdfund books they believe in – and give fresh ideas that don't fit the traditional mould the chance they deserve.

This book is in your hands because readers made it possible. Everyone who pledged their support is listed below. Join them by visiting unbound.com and supporting a book today.

Geoff Adams
Pippa Ailion
The Algernon Family
Sally Allen
Mark Allison
Nicola Alloway
Richard Allsebrook
Chris Allwood
Elizabeth Alway
Keith Anderson
Bernard Angell
Kirk Annett
Mina Anwar
Stuart Appleby
Simon Arthur
Mark Ashbury
James Aylett
Bill Baker
Neil Baldwin
Jason Ballinger
Joanna Barlow
Jim Barrett
Katie Barrett
Steve Baxter
Charlotte Bayford
Bob Beaupre
Alan Beevers
George Bell
Graeme Bell
Tim Bentinck
Luc Benyon
Keith Berry
Meat Bingo
Jo Binmore

Michelle Bishop
Eloise Black
Jason & Carmel Black
Phil Blakemore
Paul Blinkhorn
Sean Boon
Helen Bostock
David Boston
Bruce Bowie
Nick Breeze
Simon Brett
Elian Bright
Tony Britten
Rich Brown-Kenna
Andy Browne
Brian Browne
Stephen Bruce
Sean Bryan
Bill Buckhurst
Robert Bundy
Neil Burgess
Joseph Burne
Marcus Butcher
Kate Calico
Matt Callanan
(@LegoAnkhMorpork)
Kate Campbell
Laird Caracan Esq.
Paul Carlyle
Deborah Carnegie
John Cary
Podcasto Catflappo
Tom Cawte
Kevin Cecil
Kyle Chambers
Tom Chapman
Dan Chard
Juan Christian
Jeremy Chudley
Claire Clark
Patrick Clark
Jenny Clarke
Andrew Clemence
Martin Clunes
Tom Cobbold
Danielle Coffey
Gaye Coleman
David Collick
Stuart Collins
Beth Compson-Bradford
Diane Cooke
Linda and Ray Cooney
Peter Corrigan
Jo Cosgriff
Lauren Coupe
Geoff Cox
Jay Cox
Jonathan Coy
Roi Croasdale
Karen Cumming
Steven D'Aprano
Mihai Dan Vica
Larry Darby
Nick Davey
E R Andrew Davis
Peter Davison
Silvana Dean
Ronan Deazley
Robert Del Maestro
Joanne Delany
John Dexter
Matthew Ditch
Mike Dixon
Tamatha Dolling
Séan G Donnellan
Brendan Donnison
Oliver Double
Linda Doughty
Peter Doyle
Dominic Driscoll
Felicite Du Jeu
Sarah Dudley
Sarah Dunant
Sheila Dunn
Dave Eagle
Greg Eagle
Sue Eastwood
Tim Edbrooke
Barnaby Edwards
Jayson Elliot
Jerry Elsmore
Ben Elton
Michele Emerson
Chris Evans

Tim Evans
Stephen Falconer
Louise Farquharson
Barry Featherston
Simon Fellingham
Jack Fenwick
Pau Ferran Roig
Robbie Fields
Paul Filipczyk
Dean Fisher & Natalie Banks
James Flannery
Charlie Fletcher
Ross Forbes
Peggy Forell
Colin Forrest-Charde
Niclas Forsen
Darren Fowkes
Beverley Fox
Mark Fox
Myra Fox
Steve Foxon
Jason Freeman
Tim Fywell
Sarah and Andy G
Sarah Gadd
Mark Gamble
Tony Gardner
Patrick Geary
Mandy Gibbs
Russell Gibson
Stuart Gibson
Rick Giglio
Richard Gillin
Su Gilroy
Emily Glonek
Isobel Glonek
Deirdre Godfray
Tero Goldenhill
Nick Goodman
Oz T Gopher
Martin F. Gorski
Jeff Grant
Mark Gray
Judy Green
Karen Green
Kat Green
David Greig
Mike Griffiths
Laura Grimshaw
Dave Guerin
Paul Guest
Shobna Gulati
Tristan Gutsche
Randy Joe Haaga
Ali Hadji-Heshmati
Grace Hailstone
Jamie Hailstone
Niki Hall
Verity Halliday
Dawn Hamilton
Stuart Hancock
Irene Hannah
Pat Harkin
Heidi Harrington
Glenn Harris
Steve Harris
Neil Harrison
Simon Haslam
Amanda Haslam-Lucas
John Hayes
Stu Haynes
Nik Hayward
Andrew Hearn
Dave Hearn
Andrew Hearse
Pamela Henderson
Paul Hendy
Adam Heppinstall
Richard Herring
Steve Hewlett, Ventriloquist
Amanda Hickling
Ben Hill
Peter Michael Hobbins
Holly Hodson
Winnie Holzman
Emma Honeywill
Hector Hornstein
Louis Hornstein
Dudley Arthur Horque
Katy Hoskyn
Joshua Howlett
Andrew Hughes
Jennifer Humpfle
Anne Hunt

Paul Hunt
Jonnie Hurn
Clair Hutchings-Budd
Martyn Ingram
Sonia Ingram
David Innes
Virginia Ironside
Martin Jackson
Christopher Jacobs
Mike James
Christine Jensen
JoeCovenantLamb
Jacob Johannsen
Laurel Johnson
Theresa Jones
Robert Jordan
Emma Joseph
Jules
Susy Kane
Gideon Karting
Dinofren Kat
Steve Kearney
Steve Kemsley
Maura Keniston
Cheryl Kennedy
Jonathan Kennedy
Jonathan Kenning
Dan Kieran
Paul King
Katerina Kloudova
Damian Knight
Daren Knight
Amelia Knott
Michael Knowles
Rafael Kwasigroch
Emily Kyne
Mit Lahiri
David Leach
Eleanor LeGuay
David Lever
Carenza Lewis
David Lewis
Florence Rose Lilley
Carrick Lindsay
Jules Lockey
Sharon Lockyer
Ashley Long
Eric Lougheed
Adam Lowes
Lucy
David Luddington
Jo Luijten
Blaire Lund
Anna Lyon
Carol Lyons
Dave Lyons
Jon MacInnes
Bruce Athol MacKinnon
Suzanne Maguire
Phil 'Ahh Kid' Maine
Dr Arshad Makhdum
Jessica Malik
Ava Mandeville
Kelly Marcel
Miriam Margolyes
Alex Marker
Jaymes Markham-Greer
SJ Marks
John Marquez
Andrew Marriott
Sean Marsh
Geoff Martin
Patricia Martin
Tony Mason
Julie Mayne
Michael McCabe
Sarah McCartney
Kyle McClean
Carol McCollough
Peter McCowie
David McGonigal
Robert McGrath
M T McGuire
Steven McKiernan
Garry McQuinn
Tony Meagher
Simon Melton
Rod Melvin
York Membery
Xavier Mestres
Ian Miller
Rachel Miller
Richard Miller
Misfortune

Grant Mitchell
Roberta Mitchell
John Mitchinson
Deena Mobbs
Rani Moorthy
Richard Morgan-Ash
Clelia Mountford
Maike Muller
Dan Mulvey
Gerard Murphy
Brian Murtagh
Thea Musselwhite
Carlo Navato
Neilio Neilio Orange Peelio
Caro Newling
Kate Newton
Al Nicholson
Marie-Jose Nieuwkoop
Rene Nilsson
Thomas Nissvik
Jo Norcup
Mark Norman
Sheila North
O & P
Rodney O'Connor
Vivienne O'Regan
Paul (orange peel) Oakley
Adrian Oates
Mark Oppe
Jemma Orme
AR Orsborn
Gracie Otto
Elad Paniker
Rosa Pardina
Sophie Parker
Steph Parker
Charlene Parkes
Joe Passero
Tom Patterson
Catherine Pearce
Rachel Pearce
Ildiko Pechmann
John Perkins
Richard Perrett
David Perry
Erica Planer
Harvey Planer
Jan & Geoffrey Planer
Josette Planer
Sylvia Planer
Rosie Polis
Justin Pollard
Neil Ponsonby
Robert Popper
Mike Portsmouth
Samantha Potter
James Pottinger
Janet Pretty
Ffion Pugh
Pearce Quigley
Nicky Quint
Victoria Rafa
Sean Raffey
Duncan Raggett
Rowan Ramona
JP Rangaswami
Ian Rankin
Angela Rayson
Becca Read
Zoe Read
Colette Reap
Sian Rees
Jonny Rex
Richard Douglas Rhodes
Christine and Neil Richardson
Andrew Riddell
Chiara Riondino
Christine Ritchie
Peter Robertson
Alun Roderick
Toby Rodgers
Kenn Roessler
Ira Rosenblatt
Robert Ross
Sharon Rossiter
Patrick "Grey Mouser" Rowley
Carol Royle
Simon Rumley
Nicholas Rusbatch
Alistair Rush
John Ryan
Peter Salmon
Julia Sandiford
Lynda Santos

Jason Savage
Linda Sayle
Amber Scott
Rosemary Scott
Tori Seager
Steve Seaman
Séan's gift for George G
Kim Seath
Keith Seaton
Alicia Seifrid
Michelle Seiler
Mark Sell
Neil Sellers
Dave Seymour-King
Fiona Sharp
Sam Sharp
Iain Sharples
Andy Simpkin
Alan Sims
Keith Sleight
Darren Small
Duncan Smith
Rebecca Smith
Stephen Smith
Colin Smythe
Karl Sparks
Paul Thomas Spencer
David Spicer
Andrew Staff
June Staff
Susan Stainer
Robert Stainsby
Claire Stammars
Hannah Stark
Michael Stockwell
Pamela Strachman
Jonathan Stroud
Susan
Michael Tarsilli
Abby Taylor
Brett Taylor
Bridget and Paul Taylor
Steven Tessmer
The Cambridge Geek
Steve Thomas
Dominic Thompson
Julia Thompson
Melissa Thompson
Ninette Thomson
Duncan Thomson and Mr Wolf
Bethen Thorpe
Alison Tompkins
Jane Towers
Simon Townsend
Donna Trett
Martin Trotter
David Tyler
Colin Udall
Clive Upton
Cara Usher
David Vachell
Fabio van den Ende
Junior van der Stel
Michelle Van Ellis
Issy van Randwyck
Lee Vel
Mark Vent
Dinofren Verity
Jatinder Verma & Claudia Mayer
Karen Vorster
Louise Romana Wade
Steve Walker
Alistair Wallace
Misty Walst
Caitlin Ward
Jan Ward
John Ward
Julie Warren
Mike Warrick
Cassie Waters
Angie Watkins-Stanlick
Andrew Weaver
Jack Weeland
Sara Wharton
Sally-Anne Wherry
Pamm & Jason Whittaker
Alexander Whittam
Gareth Williams
Gwyn Williams
Hanna Williams
Nick Williams
Noel Williams
Rae Williams
Wilkie Williams

Theresa Witziers
Peter Wood
Alan Wright
Andrew Wright
Debbie Wythe
John Young
George Zahora
Nikolaus Zierenberg
Zmira and Rodney
Matthew D. Zwick, M.D.